# Breaking Danger

# Breaking Danger

## A Ghost Ops Novel

## Lisa Marie Rice

**AVON**

*An Imprint of HarperCollinsPublishers*

BREAKING DANGER. Copyright © 2014 by Lisa Marie Rice. All rights reserved. Printed in the United States of America. No part of this book may be used or reproduced in any manner whatsoever without written permission except in the case of brief quotations embodied in critical articles and reviews. For information address HarperCollins Publishers, 195 Broadway, New York, NY 10007.

HarperCollins books may be purchased for educational, business, or sales promotional use. For information please e-mail the Special Markets Department at SPsales@harpercollins.com.

FIRST EDITION

Library of Congress Cataloging-in-Publication Data has been applied for.

ISBN 978-0-06-212187-5

14 15 16 17 18  OV/RRD  10 9 8 7 6 5 4 3 2 1

*To my fellow Brainstormers. Well, gang, here it is. The third book in the trilogy I first brainstormed with you. Here's to you all! And a big thanks to Christine Witthohn, agent extraordinaire, who helped brainstorm the books from the beginning!*

# *Acknowledgments*

Thanks to my wonderful editor, May Chen, who always believes in me.

# Breaking Danger

# *Chapter 1*

*In the air from Mount Blue in*
*Northern California to San Francisco*

*Hang in there, Sophie Daniels,* Jon Ryan thought grimly. *I'm coming for you as fast as I can. Whatever you do, whatever it takes, stay alive.* He'd only seen her in photographs and only knew of her through her friend Elle Connolly, who had also worked at Arka Pharmaceuticals. He knew only that she was beautiful and smart. A researcher, a virologist, and now a vulnerable woman surrounded by danger.

Jon Ryan looked down at the ravaged, smoking landscape. His stealth helicopter basically flew itself and for the first time he regretted that. Having to pay attention to flying would have kept his mind off what he was seeing below. Death. Destruction. Chaos.

There were so many columns of smoke, he didn't bother

flying around them but arrowed his way through. The helo's air filters could take care of the smoke.

Pity they couldn't filter out his feelings.

The helo was hermetically sealed, so he couldn't smell the smoke. But he knew what burning vehicles smelled like. And burning people.

The world was dying, right before his eyes. There was the tiniest spark of hope waiting for him on Beach Street, near Fisherman's Wharf in San Francisco. Sophie Daniels. A scientist with a vaccine against the virus that was tearing humanity apart. The Doom Bug.

Jon had never met her, but she was Elle Connolly's best friend. Elle Connolly soon-to-be Elle Ross. He knew that in his teammate Nick Ross's eyes, Elle was already his wife. Nick had loved Elle forever and had lost her, then found her again. Just before scumbags who worked for Arka Pharmaceutical's security system tried to kill her.

Arka was responsible for murdering the world, its death throes visible right below him. But the world might survive if he got to Sophie Daniels in time. If she was still alive. If he could smuggle her out of a San Francisco with an estimated 600,000 monsters roaming the streets. If they could replicate that vaccine, in a lab which was even now being prepped back at Haven on Mount Blue. If the vaccine worked.

A long shot, but the only one they had.

Was Sophie Daniels still alive?

He remembered the last email Sophie sent to her friend and colleague, Elle.

*Elle, I think Arka has bioengineered a virulently contagious virus that takes out the neocortex and activates the limbic system. If you're reading this, then you'll know that the virus has been unleashed. I hacked into the files and I discovered that there is a vaccine. It was in Dr. Lee's office in the Arka building, in a case which also contained the live virus. There was so much chaos that I was able to steal it. So I have a refrigerator case of 200 vials of vaccine and 4 doses of live virus. The electricity has gone out and I don't think the coolant in the case will last much more than 96 hours. I'm in my apartment on Beach Street and I don't dare go out. These . . . creatures are running around in the streets. All I can do is stay locked up in the apartment and hope that someone can come for me.*

*If you're reading this, Elle, send someone. This vaccine is our only hope.*

*Soph*

They'd received that message twenty-four hours ago. Elle had replied that Jon was on his way. He'd wanted to head out immediately. Go grab her and the vaccine and bring her back to safety. Their little stealth helo could make it to San Francisco and back in a few hours, easy.

That had been the plan.

But in this new world, no plans worked. He'd had to leave their main helo on the rooftop of the Arka skyscraper in the Financial District of San Francisco. He was flying an older helo that had been in maintenance. And instead of heading out immediately, he'd headed out twenty-four hours late because the rotor head had to be replaced and they had to go steal one in what had, overnight, become badlands.

Twenty-four hours was a long time in this new world. Time enough for Sophie Daniels to be caught and ripped to pieces. Time enough for the whole of fucking San Francisco to turn. Time enough for *her* to turn. Jesus.

At least her building was intact. He could see it both from the Keyhole satellite feed and their own drones that Mac and Nick had sent to hover over the Beach Street area.

To top it off, her Internet connection had broken down, but his was still functioning. Haven had an almost unbreakable connection. Its servers were in an impenetrable underground bunker about a mile away, safe and impregnable. He could talk to Haven and they could listen in and connect with anyone whose connection still worked. Sophie's didn't. Jon had done a fast check and the entire northern section of San Francisco was down.

He was flying in blind, without knowing what was at the other end. Knowing only that monsters were roaming the streets.

The creatures seemed to be able to find healthy people and go after them with unparalleled ferocity. Did they smell the healthy? God only knew. He didn't. Jon was a warrior and had been trained all his adult life in the warrior arts. But as a covert operative for the CIA and then a member of the elite and secret Ghost Ops group, he'd also received extensive training in other arts. Computer security, orienteering, a basic knowledge of mechanical engineering, and even medic training.

He was a master liar, really good at undercover ops.

But absolutely nothing in his training prepared him for this. For humanity going feral. Overnight.

Jon glanced down to the left and saw two kids up a tree. Two little kids, clinging to each other. And at the base of the tree, like a frothing mass of madness, ten, maybe fifteen, infected. According to Elle's pretty friend Sophie, with the neocortex out, the infected couldn't plan. They wouldn't be able to find a ladder to climb up to the kids, but, by God, they could pound against the trunk of the tree to loosen the kids' hold.

Jon watched as one of the children lifted his head and stared at the helo. He couldn't see Jon. The cockpit was covered with a bulletproof graphene coating that tinted the windows, making everything in the cockpit completely invisible, even to thermal and IR imagery. All the kid could see was a piece of machinery working. Maybe the last piece of working machinery in the world. And clearly someone uninfected was flying.

The kid's mouth opened in a silent scream that didn't penetrate the insulated cockpit. He let go of the branch he was holding and waved desperately, eyes and mouth wide, face turning as Jon flew by.

A second, two—

"*Goddammit!*" He slapped the instrument panel hard enough to hurt. It didn't affect the instrument panel, of course, which was made of a highly resistant epoxy resin, strong enough to survive a crash intact. All he did was hurt his hand and vent his feelings a little.

He checked his radar. The helo itself was stealth and never showed up on anyone else's radar. The new system had a hundred-mile radius, which served him well; he wouldn't crash into another aircraft. But there were no other aircraft on his radar. In the space of half a day, all aircraft had been grounded. It was possible there were no pilots left in California, maybe the United States.

"Little Bird, you copy?" A deep voice crackled in his ear. Mac McEnroe, back at base. Jon tapped the earbud.

"Copy. Sitrep." *Please*, he thought. *Give me some good news.*

"Not good, Jon." Mac's deep voice was somber. "All TV channels have lost regular programming. There's an announcement by Governor Spielberg ordering a curfew, effective immediately. Everyone is to keep off the streets. But it's prerecorded and on a loop. We haven't heard anything new in hours, except . . ."

Jon's hand tightened on the stick. "Except?"

A heavy sigh. "Our drones have showed us that all interstate highways to the north and to the east have been firebombed. All bridges leading out of state, bombed. Nothing's getting in or getting out. All aircraft grounded. You seeing anything?"

"Negative, boss." He thought for a moment. "So no one's coming to help?"

"Looks that way. Our drones show us Marine and National Guard units strung out along the firebombed highways and a presence where there are no natural boundaries. But the units are facing in. To California."

"Not to keep people out but to keep people in," Jon murmured.

"Yeah."

He gritted his teeth so hard his jaws hurt. "They're abandoning us. The fuckers."

Mac blew out a breath, then—"Get Elle's friend out, Jon. Get us that vaccine before the whole state dies."

"Roger that."

Jon switched off the entire comms system. There wasn't anything else he wanted to hear. He could see what the situation was right beneath the helo's skids on his monitor as he flew over once-prosperous towns now reduced to ashes and rubble. Some people were lying dead on the streets like feral dogs, creatures, their hands clawlike reaching out, their mouths red-stained; others were loping like wolves through the town. Occasionally, he'd see desperate uninfected faces plastered against windows, hoping for help, pleading for help.

Help wasn't coming. It looked like the country had turned its back on them.

Just like the country had turned its back on his team, Ghost Ops. Over a year ago, the Ghost Ops team had broken into a lab on the East Coast. Intel had it that the lab was brewing a weaponized form of *Yersinia pestis*. Bubonic plague. What it had actually been brewing was a cancer vaccine that was stolen. They'd been fed bad intel. It had been a trap, set to take Ghost Ops down. The Ghost Ops team had been ambushed. Jon, Mac, and Nick were able to escape, though, on their way to a court martial for treason, with the death penalty at the end of it. They'd made their way back west and set up a community of geniuses and runaways in an abandoned mine inside Mount Blue, and had been in the process of creating a thriving and almost self-sufficient community when the current shit came down.

So, yeah, they were used to being abandoned, making it on their own.

He was flying over the Marin Headlands now. Forest fires had broken out, but no firefighters were there to combat the spread of the flames. The funky multicolored homes of Sausalito, the lush millionaires' homes of Tiburon, all going up in smoke.

He flew alongside the most famous bridge in the world.

If you looked at the top of the Golden Gate Bridge, you could almost believe for a second that life was normal. There it stood, tall and red and elegant. But as he paralleled the bridge into San Francisco, he could see the roadway below clogged with abandoned tanks and military vehicles, several with smoke still pouring out from the engines. The roadway was clogged with bodies, too, some unrecognizable, just a red mass of protoplasm.

At the city end of the bridge, the access road had been blown up, leaving an inaccessible fifty-foot hole in the ground.

Back in Haven they'd been glued to their monitors, watching breaking news. The Marines had held the Golden Gate and the Bay Bridge, effectively quarantining the city. But apparently a few infected got through and each infected person became a vector, infecting ten or even hundreds in turn. It was exponential and it was fast.

One tank had crashed through a railing and hung half on, half off the bridge.

It was a good thing Jon wouldn't need to exit the city to the north from the bridge. It hurt to think that maybe no one would ever cross that bridge again.

No use thinking that way. It was what it was.

The beautiful white skyline of San Francisco drew nearer. Black columns of smoke resolved into flames at the base, whole sections of the city burning.

This is what 1906 must have looked like, he thought. Only no fire brigades were coming. No communal kitchens, no armies of volunteers helping the wounded. There would be no rebuilding.

He reached the outer arm of the marina, followed it in, crossed over into the city along the waterfront, alive with infected. No one looked up at his passage. Light was draining from the sky and his helo was a dull matte black with no reflective surfaces. And no one had the concept of helicopter in their heads anymore.

He flew over vicious street brawls, vehicles left askew, a cable car at the turning station lying on its side. He crossed the grassy expanse of Ghirardelli Square, hovering for a moment over the roof of the Ghirardelli Building, then landed lightly. He killed the engines and sat there for a moment, head bowed.

His hands dropped to his lap. They were trembling slightly.

Amazing.

Jon had spent his entire adult life either in training for combat, in combat or undercover. He'd spent two years undercover, pretending to be a dealer in the Cartagena cartel, where any second he could be unmasked and hung on a meat hook as reprisal and warning. Nothing fazed him, nothing scared him.

Or so he'd thought.

Turned out that the end of the world scared the shit out of him.

So though the city was burning around him, though time was pressing—because who knew if, even at this moment, Sophie Daniels was being torn to bits, the case with the vaccines kicked into the bay—Jon sat still in his little helo, a marvel of technology and engineering, and waited for his hands to stop shaking.

Screams came from the streets below. Bellows, really. Of rage, of fury. Something crashed heavily.

This wasn't getting any better.

Time to go.

He had his backpack already at the helo door. With an almost silent hiss of hydraulics, the helo door opened and Jon stepped out onto the Ghirardelli Building roof. From up here, where he couldn't see the street level, he could almost pretend that nothing had happened. If you ignored the smoke, you could almost think that it was two days ago and mankind was still rolling along in its lying, cheating, thieving ways, where, however, in the interstices and almost as an afterthought, some people got medical care, some cops were able to stop crime, some kids got educated.

Someone played music, wrote books, painted canvases.

He stepped to the edge of the building and the fantasy disappeared. Down on the street it was a jungle. Worse than a jungle. In the jungle, animals didn't try to exterminate their own species.

He strapped his scanner to his wrist and adjusted it to IR. Immediately, red human-shaped splodges appeared on the screen, crazy even in IR.

It was getting darker now. Jon watched the street carefully, looking for breaks in the patterns. He couldn't tell if the infected hunted in packs systematically or whether packs formed spontaneously. A snarling, crazed group of twenty creatures would go by, then nothing for a minute or two. Did they slow down with the darkness? Did they hunt at night? Did they sleep?

He had no idea.

His entire life as a soldier he'd pitted himself against enemies of different cultures. Pakistanis, Afghanis, Chinese, Mongolians, Colombians. All different, but now he realized they were more similar than different. Because they behaved according to human rules—the rules that were ingrained in our DNA.

Another pack passed by. And another. Then three separately, snarling down the street.

Fuck. There wasn't going to be a break in these creatures.

The math was against him. Almost by definition anyone on the street was infected. The few who weren't—and there was no way to tell how many of the uninfected were left—were locked indoors, frightened and trapped.

Like Sophie Daniels.

It was that thought—of Sophie Daniels trapped and terrified—that galvanized him.

He'd never met her, but he'd seen her photograph. She was beautiful, but beyond that she had the look of Mac's wife, Catherine, and Nick's woman, Elle: very smart and very kind. The kind of woman who had a glow about her. They didn't grow women like that on trees.

She'd been kidnapped by the goons of the company that had unleashed this virus, Arka Pharmaceuticals. Before being caught, she'd had the presence of mind and the courage to take a few moments to warn Elle. Elle had escaped, rescued by Nick, but Sophie had been caught. Maybe those moments had been just enough to have her fall into the hands of the fuckers who wanted to test her like an animal. Elle had been scared sick for her friend. The three of them—Mac, Nick, and Jon—had gone to Arka's headquarters to free the people being tested, including Sophie, but she was gone by then.

By some miracle, Sophie had escaped from the prison lab in the chaos of the infection; and instead of immediately getting the hell out, she'd gone back into the offices of a building full of monsters to hunt down and steal the vaccine. On the off chance that her bravery would give humanity a chance.

It was very likely that the fate of humanity rested with one lone, brave scientist trapped on Beach Street.

He looked east, to where Beach Street began. It was clogged with infected, looking like crazed cockroaches from his vantage point high on the roof of the Ghirardelli Building.

The salvation of humanity might be on that street.

Jon wasn't too fond of humanity. To his mind, it was already barreling toward disaster before the infection exploded. Most humans were petty and mean, with streaks of greed and cruelty running through them.

But there were exceptions. To his vast surprise, he'd found out that there were many who were good and brave, talented and selfless. Haven was full of people like that. People who deserved saving.

Okay.

He looked down from the parapet of the rooftop, checking his scanner, checking the writhing masses of red and yellow that appeared on his monitor. They were everywhere. There was never going to be a break. San Francisco was a city of 600,000 people and he had to assume that something like 80 to 90 percent were infected. Maybe more. The city was teeming with infected.

He had to go.

Now.

Without a second thought, he anchored two steel ropes, threw them over the side, grabbed one and rappelled down the building fast, kicking away a snarling infected before landing lightly onto the paving stones and taking off at a run for Sophie Daniels.

It was going to be a run for his life. On Jon's side was that he was a highly trained warrior, and bristling with weapons. But he was one man in an area bristling with . . . *meat*. Tons of it. Looking down Beach Street he could see at least a hundred people. Say an average of 80 kg a head, he was looking right now at 8,000 kg of lethally deranged humanity that could overwhelm him in an instant.

The only thing that was going to save him was speed.

At first, it was basically a slalom around the infected, at top speed. By the time one of the fuckers realized he was coming, he was past them. He was at the corner of Beach and Jones, sorry to see the Buena Vista Café torched and charred, when he had the first problem. A big motherfucker, watching him coming, light blue eyes filled with empty madness. Dressed like a chef, bloody toque and all.

The guy reached out with a blood-flecked hand as Jon raced past and the hand bounced off Jon's shoulder. He gave a huge yowl that lifted the hairs on the back of Jon's neck, and then the creature launched after Jon.

This seemed to stir some kind of primitive pack instinct. Ten creatures started running after Jon. They might have lost their intelligence and humanity, but their muscles worked just fine. They were fucking *fast*.

Jon turned, gave a wide blast of his stunner set to lethal, saw the big guy and four others fall dead. The pack instinct didn't run to helping one's fellow monsters. The fuckers behind just vaulted over the dead bodies and came after him.

The lethal stunner worked. It worked real well. It's just that there were so goddamned *many* of them. One of them reached out, hand sliding over the tough material of his ar-mored jumpsuit.

Damn.

He was close now. Sophie Daniel's apartment building was across the street and ten meters down.

Without looking, Jon tossed a grenade behind him, sprinted across the street to the apartment building, slamming open the street doors, pulling them together and throwing the bolt. It held against the dozens of bodies that piled up against the glass doors.

Most buildings had shatterproof glass in the doors, and Jon sure hoped the building was up to code because the mother-fuckers kept slamming against the now blood-smeared glass of the doors—bodies thumping, fists pounding, mouths gaping open, unearthly howls coming out of them.

They looked . . . astonished. They could see him but not touch him. One man bashed his face against the glass doors so hard his teeth flew out of his mouth.

They'd lost the notion of glass.

His skin crawled.

Sophie Daniels lived on the third floor. Jon moved fast, taking the stairs three at a time, grimly resolved. The stairs were slick with blood.

The third floor was miraculously clear. The building was a big one, and the corridor went right and left at the end. Jon rushed down, leaping over the corpses, counting doors. 312, 313, 314 . . . 315!

He looked at the lock. Oddly enough it was a pretty good one. One it would take even him a minute to pick. He was vul-nerable out here, goddammit.

He knocked softly on the door. Put his mouth close. "Dr. Daniels? Dr. Sophie Daniels?"

Silence.

He pressed against it, knocking softly again. "Sophie? Elle sends me. It's Jon Ryan, she said she sent you an email—"

Oh Christ. A loud sound around the corner at the end. A blood-flecked face peeked around the corner. A big guy dressed in a suit now torn in tatters. When he saw Jon, he lifted his head and howled. Like a wolf.

Goose bumps broke out all over Jon's body.

The guy started coming at him at a run.

"Sophie!" The rap was harder this time, still met by silence. Jon put his back to the door, took aim with his Glock 310, finger on the trigger, aiming at the neocortex—because he wanted the fucker to go down and stay down—tunnel visioning, finger tightening, the infected barreling down the corridor screaming—

The door at his back opened, a hand grabbed him around the throat from behind and pulled.

Taken off balance, still concentrated on the shot, Jon stumbled into the room, his shot gouging a hole in the wall next to the infected, who kept on coming. He fell down onto something soft, warm, fragrant.

Jon kicked his booted foot forward, slamming the door closed. The snick of the automatic lock sounded just as he heard a heavy body hitting the door.

Safe.

Safe in some soft, aromatic place.

With a beautiful woman.

He turned over.

He found himself on top of a woman with a heart-shaped face surrounded by a cloud of dark hair. Her skin was pale in the darkened room, but glowed in the dim light. Dark blue eyes, a small, straight nose, soft pillowy lips.

A face that was etched in his mind since he'd seen her photograph back in Haven among a list of scientists and test subjects who'd been kidnapped. The idea of her in the hands of Arka Pharmaceutical, which had tried to have him, Mac, Nick, Catherine, and Elle killed, had haunted his thoughts.

"Sophie Daniels," he said to the woman underneath him.

She was pale but all of a sudden her face turned rosy with a blush.

Because something else was happening. Totally out of his control. The adrenaline of the chase and the hunt had given him a hard-on. A combat boner big as a house.

And she could feel every inch of it.

# Chapter 2

San Francisco
Beach Street

Sophie peeked out from between her blinds at the violent chaos below. Her instinct, coming from the deepest part of her, was to shut them again and block everything out. But she was a scientist and every single thing she learned about this infection and the infected was useful.

It was easy to hate the creatures below. They were worse than animals. Animals went into feeding frenzies only when starving. They did it for food, for survival. The creatures crawling and running and biting and clawing below her window on Beach Street were motivated by some kind of insane, mindless lust for violence. Not hunger, not territoriality, not dominance. Sheer, mindless rage.

But . . . they'd been people once. And not long ago, either.

Only a week ago, before the security goons of Arka came for her, she'd been looking down onto Beach Street just as she was now. She often people-watched from her window.

Tourists and locals blended happily on her street, the tourists distinctive for their outlandish dress, broad grins, and sunburned foreheads. Many of them had just come from the Buena Vista Club down the street and had downed a couple too many delicious Irish coffees.

They'd been taken, all of them. Taken away somewhere, leaving behind these monstrous carapaces that had nothing to do with the souls that had inhabited them.

The world was burning.

What kept her going, what kept her from falling into the blackest pit of despair was that maybe, just maybe, some could be saved. Some small corner of the world could remain human. So she recorded. Watched, observed, took notes—noting hemorrhaging times, reflexes, reactions. What triggered the highest ferocity. How fast they ran, how impervious they were to pain. How they died, how they survived.

It was all stored in her computer, in her written notes, and she'd video recorded the accompanying scenes. It was getting to be too dark to film anything in the detail she needed. Crazily, she hadn't downloaded the IR app; so now that it was dark, she was stuck with what her eyes told her.

The city lights were still on. Who knew for how long? They had come on an hour ago, but several were flickering. This time tomorrow or the next day, they could be gone.

She could be gone too.

Her door was stout but conceivably a concerted attack by a couple of heavy men could break it, or at least unmoor it from its hinges. That was one possibility. She could starve to death or die of thirst if she was trapped for too long. Nasty thought, that one. If it looked like that would be her end, she had an entire bottle of Nobital. Crushing all the tablets, dissolving them in water, and drinking it would put her to sleep forever. Many times throughout the long day, while the city fell, she longed for that bottle, had to almost physically wrench her thoughts away from it.

But that was crazy thinking, and it had to stop, immediately.

She was alive right now, and in her right senses, and she was a scientist. She had a duty to observe, record, even postulate theories, however much on the fly. Science didn't work that way; it proceeded at its own stately pace. But this was different. The World of Science had waned and the World of Blood was rising. Hers might be the last scientific observations on earth.

She shook her head sharply. No thinking like that. Observe and understand. Keep your emotions out of it. Leave something behind in the hope that, at the end, there would be human beings to come across her findings.

A pack ran down the street, fast. She watched, observed.

She tapped her wrist to turn on the audio recording function.

"A group of infected is running down Beach. It is 5:25 P.M. It is almost exactly six hundred feet from the corner of Jones to Lorraine's Pet Shop. The pack covered the distance in thirty seconds, which means the infected can run a four-minute mile. One of the pack is an obese man. He is keeping up but shows signs of cardiopathy. His breathing is irregular, coloring ruddy. He has stopped and is looking around bewildered, holding a hand to his chest." Sophie watched as the man fell to one knee, still looking bewildered but not afraid, then pitched forward onto his face. No one in the pack stopped or even looked around. Eventually, his chest stopped moving. "Subject died at 5:37 P.M., presumably of a heart attack."

*No one will do an autopsy*, she thought. There wouldn't be a functioning morgue anywhere in the city. And what was one heart attack in the midst of so much death?

Sick at heart, Sophie turned away from the window. No more of this right now. She needed a short break. Watching the world go mad outside her window all day was breaking her heart, her spirit.

There was another factor. She was a healer. Had been, all her life.

This was well beyond anything she could fix.

One of her first memories was of holding a bird that had fallen to the ground. She remembered how it lay listlessly in her hands as she cried. Her mother had started gently curling her fingers away from the small body when suddenly there was a flutter in her hands and the bird flew away.

Then Nana Henderson had come for a stay when Sophie was seven years old. Nana suffered from rheumatoid arthritis and had walked with two canes, her face often disfigured by pain. Sophie sat on her Nana's lap for a while every afternoon, and when Nana left, she was walking normally.

Sophie had missed a lot of school that semester because she'd always been sick.

Pain, disease, afflictions. As she grew older, Sophie had felt these things in her fingertips when she touched someone. She could feel her hands grow warmer, could feel muscles bunched against the pain relax in the other person. Could *feel* sickness departing the body.

And entering hers.

With hindsight, she realized her parents had worried about her.

A healer. If word got out, every sick person in the world would show up on the doorstep, begging for help. And it would kill her. Because the other side of the coin was that she had to rest for several days after touching someone who was sick. She was weak, feverish. Depleted.

Both her parents were scientists and they threw her into an accelerated program, a scientific fast track, where she found herself studying biology, then virology, because both were so fascinating. Her parents had wanted her to go into computer science, engineering, or pure math. Something as far from medicine as possible. But Sophie was fascinated by viruses, those minute segments of protein that seemed to hold such immense power over human beings. Such terrible diseases. Rabies, Ebola virus, hantavirus, the 2021 bird flu that killed two million people. Certain cancers were caused by viruses.

She wanted to make that better. She wanted to *fix* that. She couldn't cure the world herself, but she could have a hand in finding out how to help the world heal itself. Virology proved to be a natural fit for her and she was recruited to Arka Pharmaceuticals directly from the Stanford PhD program.

Stanford was where she met her best friend, Elle Connolly. They were young and bright and were making names for themselves. They had something else in common too. Something deeper, something darker than shared courses and an inability to find decent dates.

Powers. Gifts. Curses. Whatever you wanted to call them.

Arka was funding a major study on psychic phenomena and by some principle of the drift factor, they'd both ended up in it. Elle as both a subject and researcher, which was a big no-no. There were a lot of no-nos in the program, it turned out, including human sacrifice. Research subjects were disappearing; and it just so happened that the ones who were disappearing were the most gifted with extrasensory powers. Those were the ones who ended up in an enormous black hole, nowhere to be found.

She was piecing together what was happening when they came for *her*. Men in black, in the night. Just like in a holo-movie, only for real.

When they came, she had managed to get a call to Elle to warn her. She hacked into the computer of the head of Arka Pharmaceuticals, Dr. Charles Lee, and read, with horror, about a virus he had been bioengineering—a virus designed to enhance warriors. Only he was having trouble keeping the enhanced soldiers on this side of sane. Then he'd taken some of the test subjects from the study on psychic phenomena, injected them with the virus, and harvested their brains. From the notes Sophie had read, he liked what he'd seen, so he upped the dosage.

There had been some animal tests with bonobos, a peaceable breed of primate. The virus turned them into killing machines. She knew then that she had to get her hands on the virus. When they came for her and locked her up in the underground test labs, she looked for an opening, any opening at all, to escape, to get her hands on the virus. But by that time, the virus—rendered insanely virulent—had escaped from Arka's control and spread to the employees in the Arka skyscraper.

It turned out she didn't need for one of the men in black to glance in the other direction, or let down his guard. Turned out that two lab techs, Carla Stiller and Robert Krotow, two of the gentlest, smartest people she knew, had become infected. They basically ate the two men in black. Arka's security guards, who she'd read had been recruited exclusively from U.S. Special Forces, didn't stand a chance.

Sophie hid in a supply closet until the carnage outside was over, opening the door only when she saw the two blood-stained lab rats lope down the hall for other victims, leaving behind two men in black in six distinct pieces.

The concept of door handles proving too much for the infected to conceptualize, they'd forgotten all about her. It was now or never. Sophie took the elevator to the twenty-first floor of the Arka offices, where the big boss himself, Dr. Charles Lee, resided. It had been the slimmest of chances, and her heart had pounded every second while her body was screaming at her to get out.

But something told her she needed to have samples of the viruses and the vaccine that had been in Dr. Lee's notes. She'd gone up to the administrative offices floor, hoping her Arka pass would let her through.

Her Arka pass didn't made any difference at all. All doors were open, there were four dead bodies in the corridor, the fire alarm was booming, smoke was in the air. The door to Dr. Lee's sumptuous office was open, a big Halliburton case on the floor. She snatched that and the 360 terabyte flash drive on Dr. Lee's desk and ran for the stairwell, reaching the bottom winded and desperate.

Chaos reigned. Several buildings had their fire alarms booming, up and down Market people were fighting, screaming, dying. Sophie had leaned with her back against the wall of the Arka building until she saw a taxi driver slow down. Without thinking, she wrenched open the door, threw in the case then herself after it.

"Beach Street," she gasped.

The taxi driver turned a terrified dark face to her. "Hey, lady, I'm not in service! I'm getting the hell out of here. Whatever's happening here, I don't want no part of it."

"Get out of town. Fast. The Bay Bridge is closed." She'd seen that on Google news. "The Golden Gate will be open for a few hours more. Let me off at Beach Street and I'll give you a hundred dollars."

The taxi driver's jaw worked. Something really awful was going down. But . . . a hundred dollars.

He stepped on the accelerator and they shot up Market. The further away they got, the less chaos there was. Sophie planned to get her car in her building's underground garage and head out. At Beach and Jones she had the driver stop a second, threw a hundred-dollar bill at him, and scrambled out. The case was so heavy she had to practically drag it, two-handed, home. She was wheezing by the time she made it to her building. She swiped her key, planning on descending to the garage, when a pack of monsters came unexpectedly around the corner, screaming and raging, caked with blood.

Two people at the head of the pack howled when they saw her. Heart pounding, she pulled the heavy front door behind her and ran up the stairs. The idea of being caught in the open spaces of the underground garage was too terrifying for words.

The stairs were clear and she managed to lug the heavy case to her apartment, slamming the door and leaning back against it, panting. The goons of Arka would look here for her first, of course. But somehow she was sure that the chain of command had broken now that the world was burning around them. Security would have no way of knowing she had the virus—and anyway, they were probably already dead or infected. Either way, she was sure no one would come for her.

She was safe.

But she was trapped.

That was yesterday. She'd spent a sleepless night shaking, listening to the sounds of screams, explosions, the city falling apart. And she'd spent the day watching the carnage outside her windows.

Her building had photovoltaic solar panels on the roof. At least she'd have electricity until the end. Probably. Maybe.

She made herself a cup of tea and sat on the sofa. It was the new Frau model with a digital music player in the arm. She plugged in her new noise-canceling earbuds and sat back, eyes closed, savoring the utter silence for just a few minutes.

The day had been filled with the cries of the enraged and the dying. Fire and car alarms going off all over the city. The sounds of feet pounding on the pavement, glass shattering, a few far-off explosions as gas mains went. Howls. Terrifying sounds of utter destruction.

Now the noise-canceling earbuds gave her the gift of silence, a moment of weary peace. She loved silence. Sometimes after a stressful week, she'd head up to the Marin Headlands for a long walk. Something she'd never be able to do again.

The last of the TV announcements had said that both the Bay Bridge and the Golden Gate were closed off and that Marines were stationed at the San Francisco ends. Earlier today, there'd been a huge explosion, a column of smoke rising from the west. Her windows gave out onto Beach with no view of the Golden Gate Bridge, but it sounded as if they'd blown it up. Or maybe they'd blown up the access roads?

Maybe she could never leave San Francisco ever again.

Unless . . .

Before the Internet had gone last night, her best friend Elle Connolly had emailed to say that someone named Jon was coming for her, would be there in a few hours. Elle had made only the vaguest mention of where she was—somewhere up north. And no mention of who this Jon was.

Then Sophie lost her Internet connection and was left only with this thin thread of hope.

Something about the way Elle had written the email—*Jon is coming*—had given her a rush of hope. Jon was coming. She had no idea who this Jon was, but it felt as if, even though the end of the world was here, Jon was coming and maybe, just maybe, things would get better.

That was twenty-four hours ago, and Jon hadn't come.

Jon was dead somewhere, torn limb from limb. Or, worse, Jon was now roaming the streets of San Francisco or wherever he was, with madness in his eyes, covered in blood, killing as many people as he could.

Sophie leaned back, enveloped in the cool embrace of the silence, wishing there was some kind of image-canceling mechanism too, something that would cancel memories the way the headsets canceled noise. But some things, once seen, could never be unseen.

So much violence, so much blood. So many dead.

She tried visualizing other things. Better things.

After all, her life had given her plenty of wonderful images. Her parents sneaking downstairs on Christmas Eve, placing presents under the ten-foot Christmas tree, relaxing with a glass of wine, making out on the couch, pretending with a perfectly straight face the next day that Santa had arrived.

Playing in the snow with her gorgeous, dumb-as-a-rock

cocker spaniel Fritz on the lawn of their house outside Chicago. Pajama parties. Piano recitals, her first kiss, her first lover, Allan Mercer, who'd been just as gorgeous and just as dumb as Fritz.

She smiled, eyes closed.

Lots of good things.

Lots of not-so-good things too. The death of her parents in a car accident when she was twenty-four. It was the death of her family. No siblings, and her parents had been only children too. They'd been a close, charmed circle, untouchable until the hand of fate swatted her family away.

That same hand of fate was going to swat her away, too, together with the rest of humanity if she died here and no one found the vaccine and the original virus.

Oh God.

Without even thinking about it, a tear trickled down her face. She opened her eyes and sat up straighter. Tears weren't going to change anything. If there was ever a situation in which tears couldn't help, this was it.

Maybe wine would help. Yes, a glass of that really good Damoy Chambertin. She'd bought a case of the ridiculously expensive wine because she was enchanted with the origin name—Côte de Nuits. The Night Coast. Turned out it wasn't a coast at all, but by that time the vendor had charmed her out of four-hundred dollars. But it was okay, because it was fabulous stuff.

Right. She had twelve bottles of it.

A bottle a day . . .

Would the world last twelve days?

Probably not.

*Don't think like that.* Don't think at all.

Yes, a glass of wine would do her good. She lifted the headset away and frowned. Was that a sound at her door? . . . Something was there . . . just as she removed the headset. More an echo of a sound than a sound itself.

Was she crazy?

It couldn't be an infected. The infected didn't make soft noises. They bellowed and staggered and crashed into things.

Suddenly there was the softest of sounds, a gentle rap-rap-rap. Someone *knocking!* An infected could never knock, they'd just beat themselves bloody against the door. Her heart was pounding. She rushed to the door, tapping out the security code to unlock it just as she heard a deep male voice say, "Dr. Sophie Daniels?" There was another sound now, a deep bellow, the sound of a heavy body crashing against something.

Oh God, an infected!

The monitor came to life. Most of the wall sconces had been ripped away, but a couple still functioned. There was a little bit of light, enough to show a tall man outside her door. Very tall. Too tall for her monitor. She could see a strong chin with blond stubble and not much more. He brought his mouth close to the intercom on the monitor. "Dr. Daniels? I'm Jon, Elle said—"

*Jon!* Oh God, not dead! Alive, right outside her door!

On the monitor, she saw his head swivel to the right. There was another bellow, pounding footsteps . . .

Sophie pulled the door open, yanked the man in and fell backward, and a ton of man fell right on top of her. He kicked out and slammed her door shut. It automatically locked just as the thuds of an infected's fists could be felt as well as heard. From what she'd seen on the street, the infected could beat themselves to death against doors and walls, like the bonobos. Butting their heads, banging fists and feet until they broke bones and teeth. It was terrifying to see.

One of the infected seemed to be doing just that. Massive thuds and terrifying screams, sounds no human should ever make, filtered through the heavy door. The vibrations carried through the floor, though, arguably, Sophie would be the only one feeling it. Jon was on top of her and the only thing he was feeling was her.

Another massive thud, two, and the infected sped off, screaming. Presumably he'd seen another victim.

Sophie let out her breath in a rush. The danger was over. She shuddered. It had been such a close call. When she'd pulled Jon in, the infected monster was reaching out and had almost touched his shoulder. The man who was lying on top of her was heavy with muscle, visibly strong, but infecteds didn't fight fairly. One bite and Jon would be gone.

So he was here on top of her by a split second miracle.

Breathing and *alive*.

All those hours staring out the window at the world ending, wondering where Jon could be—and here he was.

A living, breathing ray of hope in a world where hope had fled.

She could feel her body pulse with hope, could feel the blood rushing to her face.

"Jon," she breathed, tears springing to her eyes. "You made it!" She threw her arms around his neck and hugged him tight, burying her face in the crook of his shoulder to hide the tears.

It was no time for tears. Tears were weakness and weakness killed.

His body was stiff for a second, the tension of battle. The tension left him in a rush. He relaxed and hugged her back.

The world was burning outside her door, but inside her

apartment, right now, for just a second, there was life and hope as she and Jon desperately held on to each other.

Oh God. He was so big, so strong—the strongest man she'd ever touched, ever seen. She was touching something hard, resistant. It was only when he tapped something on his forearm and hard panels fell away with a thunk that she realized she had been feeling body armor.

But—even after the body armor fell away—he was still seemingly just as hard. Muscles, thick and unyielding; her arms wouldn't meet around his enormously broad shoulders. He was wearing some kind of slick flight suit, and it did nothing to hide what he had underneath. Every inch of him was huge, hard as steel.

Something else was huge and hard too.

He'd fallen backward, but must have flipped in midair onto her. In the twisting, turning movements, somehow she'd opened her legs, and now he was lying on her in the most intimate fashion possible. Mouth to mouth, breasts to chest, hip to hip. If they hadn't had clothes on, they'd be making love . . . because he had the biggest erection she'd ever felt.

He was so *heavy*. She had to work to inflate her lungs, bringing her breasts even closer to his chest—and it had an immediate effect on him. His penis moved, and somehow lengthened further and became harder.

From her breathing in.

Oh God.

She breathed out heavily, mouth against his ear, and that made him lengthen another bit. It would seem impossible, but there it was. Between them, his penis surged with every movement she made.

Usually, a man's penis rising signaled pleasure, but there

was no trace of that in his face when he lifted his head from her shoulder. If anything, his expression was grim, harsh, pale blue eyes blazing into hers. He moved, and big callused hands cupped the sides of her face.

It was as if he were two people. A big man grimly frowning, and a happy penis ready for action.

"Are you okay? Did I hurt you?" His voice was so deep she could swear she heard it in her diaphragm.

*Was she hurt?* Yes. No. Maybe.

Sophie was so transfixed by him, she had to actually think about it. Take stock. She wriggled fingers and toes. No damage to her extremities. So probably no nerve damage. It was hard to breathe, true, but then she had a huge man lying right on top of her. No pain anywhere, though it was hard to tell because she was so mesmerized by the man whose nose was half an inch from hers.

She'd probably have to have a compound fracture to register pain over the fascination he held for her.

He was beautiful. That was the only word for it, yet it was the wrong word.

Beautiful because his features were pure Nordic-god perfect. Ice blue eyes, sharp high cheekbones, straight, narrow nose, sculpted jaw, firm full mouth. That gorgeous face framed by longish sun-streaked blond hair. If not for the lines of stress bracketing his mouth, the weather-beaten skin, and the crow's feet around his eyes, he could have been a Calvin Klein model. But beautiful couldn't be used to describe a man whose face wore that expression of grim awareness, of unspeakable weariness.

Beautiful also didn't cover his extreme . . . maleness. Few men nowadays didn't color their hair, shape their eyebrows, laser away wrinkles, use moisturizer. The usual enhancements. That was what was considered male beauty—someone who worked at his appearance. That wasn't this man at all. He looked like he'd time-jumped directly from a Viking boat in AD 1100.

He was beautiful. And hard and dangerous.

And he'd come through hell to find her.

She couldn't even imagine how he'd gotten here from somewhere in Northern California. She'd been at her window on and off all day and hadn't seen one healthy man or woman. The healthy had deserted the world and left it to the infected. She couldn't imagine how a noninfected had been able to walk for more than a minute with all the monsters out on the streets, let alone make his way here from far away.

And yet, here he was.

The despair that had gripped her heart eased, just a fraction.

"I thought you were dead," she whispered, eyes locked onto his. Dead, or worse. The thought had been tearing at her all day. That the man coming to her rescue would fall, and turn. Another tear slipped down her cheek, completely against her will. She wasn't crying. The stress of the past two days was seeping out of her eyes, that was all. "I thought you would never come, and that I would die here alone."

Those strong arms tightened around her. What with his weight and his arms crushing her to him, she could barely breathe. She didn't care. Who cared about breathing when she held life itself in her arms? She thought she'd go out alone, but now she had this amazing man, alive down to his fingertips, strong and vibrant, and she wasn't alone anymore.

"No," he whispered back. "I wouldn't let that happen. I was coming for you. Nothing could stop me."

Their eyes met and held. His eyes blazed with light and

purpose. Beyond the vivid coloring and movie-star good looks, there was something deeper there. Strength, power, determination. Her gaze drifted over his face, the tight features holding back some strong emotion she couldn't identify.

She was so intent on his face that his words penetrated moments later. *Nothing could stop me.*

And nothing had.

Sophie knew what was out there. She'd spent the past day watching the streets. What was out there was chaos and danger on a level so outrageous it would have been safer to walk down the streets of Baghdad during the Iraq War twenty years earlier than along pretty touristy Beach Street in downtown San Francisco.

How had he arrived here? However it was, he'd undertaken a monumental task, an impossible one. As far as she had been able to tell, no normal survived out there, *could* survive out there.

And yet here he was and . . . she might not die today.

More water leaked out of her eyes. "Oh God," she whispered and tightened her arms around his neck again. Was she touching the last human left? Was she holding the last sane man in the world?

Sophie shuddered, an uncontrollable shiver raking her body, and he tightened his arms even more, as if in taking her shudders into him, he could absorb her fear and panic and despair.

His hold spoke of comfort. What was between his thighs spoke of desire.

Desire.

Desire. Heat. Life.

Heat was bubbling under her skin. She'd spent the past twenty-four hours encased in ice, cold down to her bones—

scared and huddled into herself to give herself warmth and comfort because no one else ever could.

Now there was someone who could. Not a girlfriend, not even someone she knew. A complete stranger, handsome and focused on her with an icy blue laserlike gaze.

*Nothing could stop me.*

He'd battled his way to her. "How did you—" she began and he kissed her.

And kissed her and kissed her.

Not a tentative first kiss, no. His big hands held her head still as his eyes dropped to her mouth. It was instinctive, she could feel it. That intense blue gaze turned sharply heated as he looked at her mouth, then his gaze rose. Not tender, not the look of a lover. More the look of a conqueror. The look of someone who'd traveled a long, hard road for something, and now here it was.

Yes. Here she was. She'd spent the day preparing for death, and, inevitably, she'd looked back on her life. A life well spent, oh yes. She'd studied hard, loved her parents, gone into science wanting to do good. She'd been a good girl every step of the way. Even her few lovers had been good guys. Boys, really, even if they were technically men. Other scientists like herself, from good families, like herself.

But she'd kept her healing abilities from them. Out of self-defense. It was hard, though, to keep such a big chunk of herself out of a relationship. You ended up handing over a truncated version of yourself, almost a cardboard version, everything external. Never letting anyone get too close. And no one ever had.

Jon lifted his head, eyes blazing, face drawn.

Certainly no man had ever looked at her like this—intently, as if that ice blue gaze could read inside her head. He closed his eyes, the intensity seeming too much, and so did she—because it was.

And then his mouth was on hers once more.

Soft. Hard. Soft. Hard.

Soft touches, fingertips callused but gentle as he touched her face, her neck.

Hard muscles, immensely strong. She dug her fingernails into his shoulders and felt no give whatsoever.

Soft. His lips were so soft on hers.

Hard. His erection was like a steel cylinder between them.

Wild screams erupted outside her window. Someone dying, badly. As so many had done today. So much pain, so much death.

And yet she had life itself under the palms of her hands. Life. Such a precious thing, so taken for granted.

Another scream and she held him more tightly, pushing up against him. Immediately, his huge hard penis somehow lengthened even more. From her movement against him. She'd done that to him, to this hard and powerful man.

The change wasn't only in him, though. When she felt his penis surge with blood, it echoed inside her. He couldn't feel it, of course. But Sophie felt it. A bolt of heat in her groin so strong she turned liquid, so strong she undulated against him and immediately felt again how that affected him. He lifted his head for just a second and she missed his mouth against hers. Every time his tongue touched hers, a line of heat went straight to her womb.

Such heat, such life. The world was drowning in blood and pain and here was this magical man, come to save her, giving her such pleasure she nearly sighed with it.

"Sophie," he whispered. There was a question in there somewhere. She was shaking with emotion, with relief and joy. She had no idea what that question might be, but the answer was clear.

"Yes," she whispered back.

His big hands moved down to where her robe crossed her breasts. She was naked under the robe; he must be able to feel that. He lifted slightly on his elbows to untie her robe and open it, slowly, like a kid opens a long-awaited present. His hands covered her breasts, hands hard, strong.

He wasn't using his strength, oh no. Every movement was careful. He didn't talk to her—how could he, he was kissing her senseless. But his body did. His hands were gentle, cupping her sides, thumbs stroking her nipples. Each touch of his thumbs sent blinding pleasure to her groin and her vagina contracted.

Oh God! An orgasm! She huffed out a breath and shuddered. It was like she'd lit a fuse under him. The movements that had been so controlled before, so slow and tender, speeded up. His hands became harder, everything became harder, including his penis. She could feel it moving against her mound, lengthening even more as he slid up and down along the lips of her sex. She moved under him and her sex opened up. She arched against him, as if she could somehow be even closer to him.

In a world gone mad and dark and cold, he was life and heat. Such strength, transferring from him to her. She felt strong, her whole body working to envelop him. Arms tightly linked around his neck, torso pressing upward, legs opening to twine around his.

A strange ripping sound that she only deciphered later as the Velcro of his flight suit opening, a shrug and it was off.

Sophie desperately wanted him naked, wanted to touch that hard warm flesh she'd only felt beneath his clothes. He lifted slightly, holding his arms out, and she pulled a light cotton tee over his head, long, dark blond hair lifting around that perfect face and—*Oh God!* He looked like Thor, like a Nordic god, larger than life, shoulders so broad they shut out the world, encasing her in a world that had contracted to only her and Jon.

He eased her back down with a hand to the back of her head and caught her mouth again. Now. Now she could touch him, touch his naked flesh. She hooked her hands around his back, all that golden skin like steel, only warm.

She dug her nails into his back and it was like she'd kicked him into another gear. His thighs opened hers, he positioned himself at the opening of her sex and she hesitated. He was enormous and it had been a long time for her.

It was like he could read her, read her body. Instead of entering, he shifted so one hand could drift down her chest, over her belly, down to cup her mound. He was kissing her hard, tongue deep in her mouth, stroking.

Her sex contracted again. He felt that. He must have felt it against his hand, against his loins as her hips moved. He could feel how wet she was, how ready.

He didn't have to ask because her body was talking to him. He knew.

When he slid into her, hot and hard and deep, they both moaned.

She lifted her thighs, opened herself up to him even more, and he began moving. Long, deep, slow thrusts. She was holding him so tightly she felt all his muscles in motion as he moved in her. Lean, incredibly strong muscles, with no give.

She'd taken an anatomy class once and could identify each muscle in his back by touch. Trapezii, deltoids, lats. She moved her hands down lower. Glutei. Mmm. All those muscles shifting and bunching and moving like a well-oiled machine, only warm. And alive.

God, he was alive, down to his fingertips, and he infused her with life. He was strong enough for the two of them, such incredible power under her hands. He surrounded her completely, on her, in her. So close she could see only him, smell only him, feel only him.

Nothing bad could happen to her while he was making love to her. The world outside—that terrible world of death and destruction—receded with every stroke. Nothing else existed, only this powerful man moving in her. He was incredibly heavy, but she liked that. Proof of how powerful he was.

He pressed into her deeply, holding her head between his two large hands, kissing her as if someone was about to come and separate them. No, nothing could separate them. She wouldn't let it. Her hands moved slowly up his back, up over those strong, slick muscles until she curled her arms around his neck, holding tightly.

*Never let me go*, she thought. The very notion of him leaving her body, of not feeling that heavy weight on her acting as a wall between her and the rest of the world, made her panicky. She tightened her arms around him.

He pulled out of her slowly, so slowly she thought she could feel the emptiness in her womb that he left behind. He held himself at her opening, the big head of his penis stretching her; but if he pulled back even a touch more, he'd leave her body.

*No!*

She instinctively rebelled at the thought.

She freed her mouth, placed her lips against his ear. "Don't leave me," she whispered and felt him jolt, as if in shock.

"God, no," he muttered, lifting his head. His eyes were slitted, only a shard of ice blue showing. They were both trembling, panting. He moved back into her, just a little. God, he'd somehow become even larger. "Does that feel like I can leave you?"

She stared into his eyes, aware of him over every inch of her body. Cheeks flushed, face grim, he looked as if he were almost in pain. She felt the same way. They were barely making love and it was the most intense experience of her life. He pressed forward just a little and her vagina clenched hard.

She shook, on the very edge of orgasm.

"Jesus." Jon closed his eyes, then opened them again, staring into hers. His jaw clenched so hard she could hear his teeth grinding. "I need to move fast now," he panted. "Is that okay?"

Those words, and the image they evoked, set her off. She clenched around him, arching her neck back, breath leaving her lungs in a burst.

"I'll take that as a yes," he said, moving hard and fast inside her.

# Chapter 3

Eyes closed, Sophie drifted. She was wiped out, completely depleted. Every cell lax, ripe with pleasure, a pleasure she thought had left the world. Apparently not. Apparently there were small pockets of mind-blowing pleasure still around.

And the source of one was lying on top of her, heavy as an elephant.

A tap on her cheek. Her eyes fluttered, but she couldn't open them. Too much effort . . . she drifted again.

Another tap. Annoying. "Sophie," a deep voice commanded. "Open those beautiful eyes."

"Mmm." She tried to breathe in but he was so heavy he was bending her ribs. But still, it was a wonderful sensation. A heavy male body, brimming with heat and life. Her arms tightened around him, then slid away as he lifted himself up off her, resting on his forearms.

"Sophie!" It was a barked command, in a voice used to command.

Her eyes popped open.

"God." His own eyes closed for a second, then opened again, narrow and intense. Was he—was he angry? "Don't do that to me."

"What? Do what?" Her senses were muddled. How could she think when that intense icy gaze was locked on her? When she was held in a cage between incredibly brawny arms? She had good peripheral vision and those arms alone were worthy of contemplation. Not huge hunks of meat like body build- ers' or wrestlers' but rather long lean supertoned and tanned muscle. Big raised veins that you had to build to carry oxygen to all that brawn. The ceiling light picked out the blond hairs on his forearms, thick and wiry. She could feel the strength of the hands holding her head. He wasn't using his strength in any way against her, no. She felt safe and protected. But the power in those hands somehow seeped through skin and bone, per- ceived as an elemental force with just the lightest of touches.

"Disappear."

She blinked. "I disappeared?"

She most certainly had not. If anything, she was pinned, like a butterfly, to her hardwood floor. His weight on her from the waist down, long strong legs next to hers, taut abdominals right on top of hers. His torso was held away, but those large hands curling around her head ensured she couldn't move, couldn't even breathe without him knowing about it.

And, of course, he was still inside her. Talk about being pinned.

Sophie squirmed a little, just enough to make the point that she couldn't go anywhere, not with him on top of her, *in* her.

"I can't go anywhere. You can feel that I can't go anywhere."

That grim expression hadn't changed. "You were drifting. With your thoughts."

Without her willing it, her hand lifted from the floor and caressed his cheek. It was warm, slightly bristly. His beard was blond, heavy. "No," she said softly, looking into his eyes. "I was savoring. I thought . . . I thought I would never touch another human being again."

He let out a long sigh, touched his forehead to hers. "Yeah. That's why I wanted you with me, not drifting away."

"It doesn't make any difference anymore, given that society has collapsed, but . . . I just want you to know that I'm not in the habit of making love to the first guy who falls on top of me. Just for the record."

He lifted his head at that and stared into her eyes. "Oh yeah. I got that. You're very tight."

Yes, she was tight. Her last lover had been—what?—two years ago? She gave an inward sigh. They were all going to die, and soon. Why, oh *why*, hadn't she had more sex? Why had she been so *picky*? All her girlfriends had complained about it. Everyone except Elle, of course, who had an even more pathetic love life than she did. There was some guy in her past she was still in love with even though he'd dumped her, brutally, ten years ago.

Sophie didn't have that. Didn't have anything like that in her past. No star-crossed loves, no yearning for someone. All she'd had was safe, mild-mannered men who cared for her more than she cared for them, and wasn't that sad?

Right now she wished fiercely she'd spent her college years sleeping around and having a good time like her roommate Sharon. Sharon had majored in men and Sophie had majored in biology, and they'd both been A students.

She should have had more sex, oh yeah. Except . . . it would have to have been like what she'd just had, right now. With the guy who was staring at her intensely. With the guy who was still erect inside her even after having had a climax. With the guy who'd made love to her so fiercely she thought her heart would stop.

There hadn't been any sex like that, ever. And that was why she hadn't had too much of it.

Jon shook himself. "You're on the floor and I weigh a ton. You must be uncomfortable. Sorry about that."

He slowly pulled out of her, his still erect penis sliding against supersensitized tissues. Oh God. Heat blossomed in her groin, a sensation so intense it was almost pain.

A burst of breath came from her. She could finally breathe properly, but having him withdraw was—sad. The breath came out as a sigh and she was instantly embarrassed. Who knew what he thought of her, and now she was sighing because their lovemaking was over.

Men liked that. They liked the idea that sex with them was overwhelming. It rarely was, but Sophie had learned the fine art of faking it. But that sigh had been real and it probably fed right into his ego.

A peek up at that suntanned Nordic god, though, didn't show a smirking male face. Not even a smiling one. He looked grim and tough and dangerous. Of course he had to be tough and dangerous to make it through even a couple of feet of infected, let alone hundreds of miles.

He stretched out a big sinewy hand and she took it. She didn't need help getting up, but refusing a hand would be churlish. He lifted her with astonishing ease, one-handed. And, surprisingly, she did need help. Her legs were wobbly, unused muscles stretched. His semen was wetting her thighs, the feeling so strange she staggered.

A big arm went around her waist immediately, his hold so

strong she could have let all her muscles go lax and he would have held her upright.

"You okay?" Those laser-bright blue eyes bored into hers, face pulled tight. You'd think he'd spent the past half hour beating her up instead of giving her the best sex of her life.

"Yes, of course." Sophie tested her legs. They could hold her up. She hoped. How strange to be so embarrassed with him, now that he only had an arm around her. When he'd been in her, making love to her, she hadn't been embarrassed at all. There'd been no room for anything but heat and the wildest sort of pleasure. "I'm sorry. I just—"

She couldn't even finish the sentence. His gaze was so mesmerizing, words fled from her head.

She was a scholar, a scientist. Words were to be used precisely, to describe natural phenomena. She'd always used words like a scalpel, and here she couldn't think of a one. He was still holding on to her, so tall he was bent over her a little, face close to hers.

He wasn't smiling at her utter inability to form a sentence, as any other man would be. Striking a woman dumb was probably every man's dream. That strong arm tightened around her waist as he lifted his head slightly to examine her closely. Not a lover's look. A doctor's look, making sure she was all right.

Okay, now she was embarrassed. Granted, the sex had been off the charts, but she had to come back from ecstasy, which wasn't as easy as it seemed. Her thighs were coated, slick with his semen, the lips of her sex felt swollen, incredibly tender. His big body curved over hers was so close she had to dig her fingernails into her palm to keep from touching him. She twisted slightly and came against his still-erect penis and heat flashed through her, unstoppable. A great, rolling wave of it, and her sex clenched.

Oh God.

"You just—" he said. With his chest so close to hers, that deep voice seemed to sink right into her diaphragm and vibrate upward instead of entering her head normally through her ears. "You just what?"

Sophie shook her head sharply. She placed her hands against that massive chest, palms flat against his pectorals. Oh God. She wanted to push him away slightly, gain a little breathing room, get away from this magnetic field he exerted, but her body betrayed her.

She had always been disciplined, focused. Right now she dug deep into her depths to find just a little of that discipline and pull away.

"I just need to use the bathroom," she said, finally pulling her dressing gown tightly around herself. With every ounce of her being she wanted her voice to be cool and matter-of-fact, but she was breathless. She didn't even know if she'd said the words or if she'd just mouthed them.

His arms opened immediately and she almost staggered at the sudden lack of support. A big hand shot out to her elbow, then he withdrew his hand when it was clear she was steady.

Or at least she looked steady. He watched as she walked across the room, tightening her silk robe again, as if he hadn't already seen, already touched, her naked flesh. In the bathroom Sophie leaned her hands on the rim of the sandstone sink, blew out her breath, and looked at herself in the mirror.

What she saw astonished her. She was expecting to see her usual pale face overrun with embarrassment. What she saw was a rosy version of herself, rested and relaxed, the exact opposite of the person she'd been seeing in the mirror these past few weeks.

Things had been very wrong at Arka Pharmaceuticals. Much as she'd tried to ignore it, concentrate on her work, which was both fascinating and incredibly challenging, warning bells had been clanging for some time before she allowed herself to notice anything. Orders from administration made no sense. The protocol timelines were increased—doubled, at times trebled. They'd be taken off one line of testing and put on an entirely new one and pressed for results. That's not the way science worked. Science worked by reason and slow deliberation, neither of which were present in Arka's leadership.

She and Elle had been deeply worried even before people started disappearing. It had been like doing science in a whirlwind. And then the disappearances started.

She had started losing weight, when she had no weight to lose. Hollows were appearing under her cheekbones because she found it almost impossible to eat, given that her stomach was usually in knots. She'd stopped sleeping and the purple bruises under her eyes were starting to look permanent.

Now she was looking at a woman with wild bedhead spiraling around her pink, flushed face. It looked like she'd put three or four pounds back on, all of them from eating fabulous food.

Here it was, the end of the world, and all it took was the best sex of her life to make her feel better. Shaking her head at her own folly, she stepped under the shower for a quick wash. Not much in the world worked, but her building still had hot water.

Who knew how long that would last?

It might be her last one in this lifetime so, though she was fast, she was thorough. The hot water revived her, except when she swiped between her legs with the washcloth. Everything down there was supersensitized, slightly swollen. It was as if the tissues themselves bore a cellular memory of Jon's presence inside her body. Her legs trembled when she washed herself and she had to stand for a full minute, arms braced against the tile wall, under the hot torrent until the trembling passed.

Sophie kept some yoga outfits in the bathroom so when she walked back out, in a thin T-shirt and yoga pants, she felt more in control of herself than when she'd walked in.

Jon was exactly where she'd left him, by the window, looking down at the destruction below with a drawn face.

"Jon?" she asked softly, putting a hand on a massive shoulder. *Oh God.* Touching him made all her senses flare. It was the lightest touch, her palm lightly pressed against his shoulder blade. Under her palm was warm hard muscle and a sense of vibrancy, of unusual power and strength, like the engine of a racing car temporarily idling.

"Would you like to shower at some point?"

He pulled in a sharp breath and turned, his ice blue gaze so very sharp and intense. "Do I dare? What if we run out of water?"

Sophie didn't have many answers to what was going on, but she did have an answer to that. "The building has a huge reservoir on top and I don't think too many people are left"—her voice wobbled as she thought of all her neighbors—"are left alive. The building has a mini heliostat, so the electricity will keep pumping the water until it's finished. I have a second bathroom with a hip bath and that is filled with water. I have filled every large pot and pan and bucket with water. The water will last at least a week. The water will outlast—"

*Us.* She stopped herself before the truth could come tumbling out. The water she'd stored would outlast humanity, at this rate.

She tilted her head, studying him. He was tall, visibly very strong. There was a stunner in a holster on the floor next to his Superman suit, some kind of gun in a shoulder holster. But still—

"How did you make it here?" she asked.

Someone screamed. A woman. Not close, maybe from a building across the street. It wasn't a scream of fear but of rage. Sophie waved a hand at the window, encompassing the fallen world outside. "How can anyone survive out there?"

It wasn't an idle question. He was here to rescue her and get the case with the live virus and the vaccine, but unless he had a tank right outside her front door, she had no idea how they could manage to get five feet without dying or, worse, without being turned.

Something of her terror must have been showing. He lifted a big hand, cupped the side of her face. His deep voice was soft, almost tender. "I'll keep you safe."

She nodded, though of course that was an insane comment. Nobody could keep anybody safe. Not in this new, broken world. "How did you make it?" she repeated. She shivered.

Jon looked down at her. "I have a helo."

She blinked. For a second she thought he said—*I have a halo.* He was an angel? What?—and then she understood. A *helicopter.* He had a helicopter.

A little shiver of hope went through her, the first in three days. A helicopter! Helicopters could land almost anywhere. And they took off, could just fly right over the chaos and violence.

"Here?" she asked eagerly, looking up toward the roof. Could it be that easy? Somehow make it up the stairs and away? "On top of my building?"

Jon sighed, that big chest expanding. It was a sigh almost of sorrow. "No, sorry. We checked your rooftop, and though my helo doesn't need much of a helipad, there was some equipment taking up most of the roof. Couldn't land safely."

She bit her lips. "Oh no. They are making repairs, the whole condo voted on it. The workers must have just abandoned their equipment." And she'd voted for the repairs too. "So where did you land? Not on the street, I hope."

"Nope. I landed on top of the Ghirardelli Building. Biggest high, clear space around. And I looked carefully as I flew down. The . . . infected aren't on rooftops. I don't know whether it's because they don't like stairs or heights or what."

"But . . . on top of the Ghirardelli Building." Sophie tried to keep dismay out of her voice. She loved strolling over to the Ghirardelli Building on weekends, checking the shops. Sometimes she and Elle would indulge in a hamburger at Sara's Diner, overlooking the Bay. It made for a nice walk. Running there, dodging monsters, lugging that heavy case . . . "If we make it, it would be a miracle. And the case is heavy."

"I'll take care of the case." Jon reached out with his thumb to smooth the crease between her eyebrows. "I'm not going to insult you and say it's going to be easy, but I have a stunner and a pistol and some grenades. And I'll give you my suit. We'll roll up the sleeves and pants. It's scratch and bite proof. And—"

"And we'll douse ourselves with perfume. I have plenty."

His head jerked back. "What?"

"I've been observing them." Her eyes slid to the window where she'd watched for hours, brokenhearted at the violence and bloodshed on her street. "I'm a scientist. That's what I do. Observe. I think that their olfactory sense has strengthened. I've often watched as an infected stops and sniffs the air, like a dog would. Hunting for a particular scent. I think that's what's happening." Her throat tightened. She had to swallow to get rid of the lump that had suddenly appeared. "I think they are hunting . . . humans."

He made a low noise deep in his chest. "Yeah. So—what? Dousing ourselves with perfume would help?" He turned his head, looked at her door. "That's all the scented candles at your door."

She nodded. "Yes. It can't hurt. You can have my Chanel N° 5. It's real perfume and it costs the earth." She smiled a little at the thought of him doused in her Chanel. He didn't look like the Chanel type.

"What else? What else have you observed, Sophie? Anything at all. Any information is better than none, it ups our chances of survival."

She didn't need her notes, though she'd take them with her in her laptop. Everything she knew was seared into her mind. "I think their eyesight is diminished. Perhaps the virus affects the optic nerve, perhaps their brains are no longer equipped to process all the data that comes in through the eyes. Smell is the oldest and most primitive of the senses and that is why it is strengthened. I think the virus amplifies the limbic system, hence the savagery, the inability to reason. I haven't seen an infected be able to open doors with handles and they have great difficulty navigating stairs. Eyesight is diminished, as I said. At twilight they start bumping into things. I think they might be essentially blind in the dark. But they'll still attack if they touch someone."

"Shit," he swore in a vicious tone. "They're like fucking zombies."

"No," Sophie said. "They seem like zombies because it appears they don't feel pain. I think the pain receptors are wiped out. That's very dangerous to them, by the way. You've heard the stories of people who have no pain receptors and who sometimes burn to death because they can't feel pain. The same with the infected. They have absolutely no sense of self-preservation. And they are dying. Let me show you. Do you have a thermal scanner?"

He took a scanner and tapped the side. A hologram popped out. Their two bodies showed, glowing pale yellow.

"Now aim it out the window."

He held his arm up and the hologram showed the street scene outside. There must have been a hundred infected outside on the street, showing up crimson with trailing tails of red when they moved fast. They were so hot, they managed to heat the air in their wake.

"Let me show you something else," Sophie said, swiping her finger left to right along the bottom of the hologram. Instantly the outline of the bodies darkened, but digits appeared above their heads, following the infected in their almost Brownian movements. The digits ran from 99.5 to 104.

"Whoa." Jon frowned. "I didn't know it could do that."

She looked up at him briefly, then concentrated on the scanner's image. "We have these in the lab." She closed her eyes in pain. "*Had* them in the lab."

For an instant, Sophie allowed herself to mourn the lab. Except for the past few months, which had been weird, she loved her job. Loved the camaraderie of science. Everyone striving for the same goal: knowledge. Everything orderly and rational, everything this new world was not. Maybe science as she understood it was gone. Maybe the generations that would come—*if* there were to be any generations and mankind didn't simply die off—would worship the moon and the stars.

She trembled at the thought. Jon put a big hand on her shoulder, almost as if he could read her mind. It steadied her, stabilized her. Science wasn't quite dead. Not as long as she was alive. And if Elle was emailing her, she was somewhere safe. Elle was a brilliant scientist.

"So what are we looking at?" Jon asked.

Sophie shook her thoughts off. This was no time to be mourning what was lost. Now was the time to fight hard to keep what was left. "The infected's temperatures."

Jon's eyes widened. "They've all got—"

"A fever. A raging fever. It's why they show up so red on your scanners. There's obviously been massive damage to the hypo-thalamus, which is the body's thermostat, regulating body tem-perature. Everyone out there is close to heatstroke. I've seen a couple of infected fall down suddenly and twitch. I didn't have my scanner with me, but it looked like they were having a seizure; and if their core temperatures reached 105 degrees, it was a seizure. One way to fight a high temperature, besides pharmacologically, is fluid and electrolyte replacement, but I don't think they have the brains to look for water. A fever this high for any sustained period is incompatible with life, as medi-cal texts say. The infected are not doing anything at all to bring their temperatures down. There's nothing they can do in their state. So they are all dying. It's just a question of time. So we need to set your scanner to scan for bodies with a temperature of 98 degrees and up. That way we are almost sure to capture only the infected. Another thing . . ."

Sophie swiped from left to right again and the digits above the glowing outlines showed different figures ranging from 140 to 200.

"There," she said, pointing. "Look at those numbers and then look outside."

"Okay." He studied the hologram, then watched the scenes below carefully. "What am I seeing? What are those numbers?"

"What you are seeing, first of all, is an exclusively young population. I'd guess there isn't anyone over forty down there."

Jon's face tightened as he observed more closely, watching in silence for five minutes. "You're right," he said finally. "No old people at all."

"Beach Street is a tourist street. At any given moment, there will be lots of people sixty-five or older. Lots of retired people on vacation. But not now. Not with those numbers. What you're seeing are heart rates. Their hearts are pumping painfully fast in their chests. The maximum heart rate you can survive is 220 minus your age. So if you have a sixty-five-year-old whose maximum heart rate should be 155, and it's 190, that heart is going to explode in his or her chest. Soon. They're dying, Jon. All of them. Even the hardiest won't survive more than a month, unless they can learn some basic skills like looking for water. And that's being generous. The people outside on the street right now? They're the walking dead."

His jaw muscles clenched. "A month? That's enough to break down civilization. Reduce us to rubble. Reduce us to the Stone Age. Wipe us out."

"Yeah." Sophie's voice wobbled. She cleared her throat. "That's what we're going to prevent. We're going to produce as many doses of vaccine as possible and inoculate as many people as we can as fast as we can."

"How fast can that be?"

"I don't know what the lab facilities are . . . where we're

going. Where Elle is. If you don't have the equipment we'd have to—I don't know . . . invade a lab, secure it, and produce the doses on an industrial level."

"Do you want to talk to Elle? She's with another scientist, Catherine Young."

Sophie's eyes widened. "*The* Catherine Young? She's a genius! Oh my God! With Elle and Dr. Young we might really have a fighting chance!"

Sophie was practically hopping with excitement. Elle was superb at lab work and Dr. Young—she was an expert on dementia. The virus inflicted huge neurological damage, which was Dr. Young's specialty. And Dr. Young knew a lot about virology. The three of them were like a sports Dream Team, only for viruses.

Jon's mouth lifted at the corners. It wasn't quite a smile, but it lightened his features. "So. Would you like to talk to Elle? And Catherine?"

*Oh God, yes!* She almost shouted the words when she remembered and her heart sank. "The Internet's down. The heliostat will keep the electricity on as long as it remains undamaged, but I lost Internet contact yesterday."

Jon had reached down to pull out a flexible tablet that had been rolled up in a pocket of his magic suit and spread it out. "We have our own Internet, no problem." He unrolled the tablet, tapped it, the hologram bloomed in the air and—

*Oh my God! There she is!*

"Elle!" Sophie instinctively reached out to touch her friend, her hand going right through Elle's cheek. Elle was flanked by a tall, tough-looking guy. Dark-haired. Grim.

The image was so lifelike, it was as if Elle were right here in the room with them. Sophie realized she'd had low-level anxiety that Elle hadn't made it. Elle had sent an email, but that wasn't the same as actually seeing her.

Elle held her hand in front of her mouth, stifling a sob. "Oh my God, Soph, you're alive! I was so worried!"

The tall dark guy put his arm around Elle's shoulders, hugging her to him. *Elle had a boyfriend?* Elle was even pickier than she was. For just a second, Sophie forgot the marauding infected, the violence on the streets, the end of the world. Elle had a boyfriend!

Then she dismissed the guy and concentrated on her best friend. "Elle, I've got the virus and the vaccine. Do you have any lab equipment where you are?"

"Oh yeah." Elle glanced up at the man gripping her shoulders, and even in the hologram Sophie could see Elle's pale skin flush. "There are some . . . guys here who are very good at, um, liberating things."

She meant steal. Very cool.

"What equipment do you have?"

"We have it all. Including a Step Facility."

"Wow." The Step Facility was brand-new, revolutionary. A system that cut the production time to less than twenty-four hours and allowed for immediate mass production.

Another woman stepped to Elle's side. Pretty, slender, dark-haired. "Dr. Daniels, I am Catherine Young. If you can get the vaccine here as fast as possible, we can start mass manufacture immediately."

Wow. Catherine Young in person! Sophie had never met her but had read her papers. "Dr. Young! It's an honor to meet you!"

A huge man stepped to her side. If he hadn't put a protective arm around her, Sophie would have shouted at Catherine Young to run like the devil. He was enormous, even more heavily muscled than Jon or the guy with an arm around Elle, and had badass, scarred features. He looked like something out of a horror movie. The kind of guy you ran from the instant you saw him.

Dr. Young didn't look afraid, though. She reached up to touch the huge scarred hand cupping her shoulder, glancing up at him and smiling. She didn't look like she was running away from him any time soon.

"Please, call me Catherine. And I'm hoping I can call you Sophie."

"Of course. It would be an honor."

"And the two gentlemen here are Mac and Nick." She gestured. Mac was the Hulk and Nick was the Brooder holding Elle. Sophie noticed that no one mentioned last names.

"Sweetie." Elle leaned forward, her pretty face filling the hologram. "I can't thank you enough for warning me the other night. You saved my life. You gave me just enough time to get away. Arka goons were after me and after the whole project group."

"I know. I think they got Les, Moira, and Roger." It pained Sophie's heart. The only saving grace was that they had probably been killed before the virus was released and had been spared the end of the world.

"No, no they didn't." Elle looked up lovingly at the dark man holding her tightly. "Nick and Mac and Jon rescued them. They are actually here with us."

"Oh my gosh!" Tears sprang to Sophie's eyes. This was the first piece of good news in . . . forever, it seemed. She swiveled her head up to look at Jon. *Thank you*, she mouthed and he dipped his head. "So . . . where is here?"

Silence. Elle bit her lip and the two men in the hologram looked even grimmer.

Catherine Young answered. "'Here' is a community situated on, or rather in, Mount Blue. About 450 miles from where you are now." She looked at the huge man holding her, narrowing her eyes at him. She spoke directly to him. "She has a right to know. And with any luck she'll be here soon. So I don't want any flak from you."

Sophie would have felt a little scared of the huge scowl she got, but it didn't seem to faze Catherine any.

"So, Sophie," Catherine continued, "our news is that as soon as you get the vaccine here, we are fully equipped to start incubating and then mass producing. We've had an input of new arrivals and plans are being made to go out in armored vehicles to reach the uninfected and inoculate them. So you guys get here as soon as you can. For the rest, I think Mac and Nick here want to give Jon the latest news."

"Sitrep," Jon barked.

Sophie's head swirled. These guys, together with Catherine and Elle, were equipped and had plans, whatever they were. Oh God. She clung to that thought. That someone somewhere had a *plan* and that she could play a part in it. That somewhere reason and will survived. And might even prevail.

Jon was exchanging news with the two men. She barely followed, but then he suddenly shouted, "*What?*"

"You heard me," the man called Mac said. "We've got General Snyder here. Together with about three hundred civilians. Some are ex-Marines, so we're looking good security-wise."

Jon looked at her, then back at the hologram. "You know the score, Mac," he growled. "General Snyder is our enemy."

"He's not the enemy. Never was. He had to take early retirement because he didn't believe the story about Cambridge and kicked up a fuss. The Pentagon Internet is still up, I checked, and it's true. So he's now Robert Snyder, and he retired to a community about 150 miles from where we are now. The captain talked to him. The community where he lives is a gated community with a lot of former military people and they took security seriously. So when the shit came down—"

Catherine Young elbowed him and his eyes rolled. He blew out a breath, looked straight into the camera, dipped his head. "Begging your pardon, ma'am."

Sophie waved that off.

Mac continued. "So when the virus hit, they were able to close themselves off fast. There are no infected in their group. We heard them issuing a general SOS. I didn't want to contact them at first because, fuck—" He rolled his eyes and sidestepped another sharp elbow to his side. "Sorry. I didn't want to contact them for reasons you can imagine. But the captain overrode me. He said Snyder had always been a good guy. And you know, Jon. It's a whole other ball game now. Anyway, we gave them directions. There were enough secure vehicles to evacuate the entire community—almost a hundred families. They also came with provisions and weapons and they are now part of Haven. And we're happy to have them. They are also happy that there is the possibility of a vaccine. And that's that, Jon. End of story."

Mac's voice had turned hard at the end, as if knowing that Jon had objections. Whatever objections he might have, they were overruled. Jon stiffened. "Yes, sir," he replied.

"The group also has some useful skills. Military-trained men and women for defense. Four armorers. Eight nurses, two with emergency training, two medics, eight cooks. We're in touch with other groups who've barricaded themselves against the infection. We're estimating at least three thousand people within an hour's radius. Get that vaccine to us fast, Jon, and we're going to save some lives. Maybe even civilization while we're at it."

"Yeah, there's something else, too," Nick said.

Sophie was interested in what he had to say, but she was also interested because of Elle. Though she and Elle were very good friends, Elle had spoken very little of her love life, maybe because she had even less of one than Sophie did. But Sophie had had the impression that Elle had loved someone very much in the past and that the memory was painful. There was a feeling that Elle had been brutally abandoned.

Could this possibly be that guy? Though . . . Elle's body language wasn't one of anger or resentment. She loved this guy, and Elle wasn't the type to fall in love overnight. So maybe this was the guy she'd been secretly in love with all this time?

Sophie tried to focus on what the guy was saying.

"Jon, we've analyzed the situation and we think you shouldn't move until tomorrow. Here." Nick made a movement off screen and suddenly Sophie was looking at . . . she had no idea what she was looking at. She tilted her head. Masses of fiery red blobs moving in a sort of Brownian motion. Nick made another movement and a map was superimposed and suddenly it made sense. A terrible kind of sense.

Sophie gasped, heartsick.

What she was seeing was a thermal image of an area a couple of miles from her home, in the Western Addition. It was teeming—*teeming*—with infected. "Fuck," Jon said quietly.

"Wait," Nick said and manipulated the image. "It's not all bad. What you're seeing is—I don't know what else to call it but a swarm. Like of insects. We checked our drone tapes and went back about ten hours and it looks like there was a locus of infection in Richmond during a big street fair and a whole *nest* of the things spent a lot of time killing everything in sight, then they started moving. They seem to be moving counterclockwise. Here, let me show you."

The hologram switched to daytime, on fast forward. It was an area she was familiar with, made up of funky wooden houses, most at least sixty years old, and tiny little shops. She'd been to that street fair many times. At first, the streets were full of happy tourists and locals, going from stall to stall. In fast-forward, the infection looked weird, like an old-time movie. Somehow, it was less horrible on fast-forward. A few blood-stained infected erupted into the crowd, which ran away. But not fast enough. From a few infected, within the space of three hours, according to the timeline at the bottom of the hologram, it looked like tens of thousands of infected crowded the streets.

At first, they moved completely separately, but as soon as a critical mass was achieved, which Sophie judged to be about four hundred infected, they started swarming behavior. It took hours and hours for the swarm to form, and the outlying edges of it showed anomalous behavior, but the center held. And a few hours after that, they started the trek east, then as they hit the water, doubling back northwest. It was a swarm about two miles across and it was terrifying. It moved slowly, but it left utter devastation in its wake. The images had quickly followed the day into night. Judging from the footage she'd seen, they'd come to her part of town some time tomorrow.

"Swarming behavior," Sophie murmured.

Elle and Catherine nodded.

"So." Mac's eyes narrowed. "They've become insects?"

"Sort of." Sophie looked up at Jon. He tipped his head in a *go ahead* gesture.

Jon turned to the hologram. "Sophie's been observing the—

the infected. They're right outside her window. She has some interesting theories."

"Please, Sophie," Nick said. "Any information you have is useful. Could save lives."

"Okay. This is anecdotal, you understand." She tried to gather her thoughts, resisting the urge to stay quiet until she had further data. Science moved slowly, but thoroughly. Each hypothesis tested and retested to make sure it could bear the weight of other facts being loaded onto it. A little like walking across a frozen pond, testing each step before putting your full weight on it.

It was what she loved about science. It was not random. Her parents' deaths had been random, completely unexpected and it had cracked her faith in the world as a knowable entity. Science had saved her from plunging into despair. Most things were knowable, if you approached everything using the scientific method.

This was the opposite. Random observations over a couple of hours were nothing. But they had nothing else to go on. And perhaps science had fled the world, anyway.

The holograms were positioned in such a way that the two images were on a parallel axis. It felt like she was looking straight into Elle and Catherine's eyes. "Go ahead, Soph," Elle said softly.

Sophie drew in a deep breath. "Okay. I think we can safely say that the virus knocks out the neocortex." Both women nodded. "Catherine, I'm going to make some assumptions about neurological damage, but of course, you're the expert—"

Catherine waved her hand. "Not about this, my dear. I think we're all in the dark. This is something entirely new."

Sophie nodded. Yes, it was.

Okay. She was going to lay out her observations. "I suspect the virus knocks out the neocortex and also the cerebrum. Essentially what is left is the limbic brain. It's reverse ontogeny. Basically they are almost insects, hence the swarming behavior. Their behavior, no longer human, is essentially stigmergy."

Catherine and Elle were nodding thoughtfully.

Mac, Nick, and Jon all said, "What?"

"Stigmergy. It's a sort of indirect coordination. An action in a crowd stimulates emulation and reinforces crowd behavior. Some headed instinctively north and others followed suit, though they are unaware of following any of the other infected consciously, because they no longer have a consciousness. They only have primitive instincts. But if there are enough of them— and I postulate about four hundred in one place at one time— they will unconsciously coordinate their actions.

Jon was looking at the scanner, basically a field of red, the number of infected with raised temperatures almost beyond the scope of the drone. He tapped the scanner, the field widened further, without reaching the edges of the field of red. "I'd say we're looking here at about ten thousand people. Ten thousand . . . things," he corrected. He nudged her with his shoulder. "Tell them about the other things you've observed."

Sophie nodded. "I suspect they have lost some of their vision, particularly in the dark. Conversely, I think their olfactory sense has increased exponentially. I think they smell the uninfected. Therefore, any masking odors could be protective. Perfumes or anything that covers our natural body odor might help."

"That's really useful," Nick noted. "Thanks."

Jon nudged her lightly again. "Tell them what you think about their life expectancy."

Sophie nodded. "I think there's a definite limit to how long they can live. Their metabolism is out of control. Median body temperature is 101 degrees—a high fever—and median heart rate is 180. There are very few elderly infected left on the streets. At least, I haven't seen any elderly in a full day of observation. Their bodies couldn't sustain the high fever and the increased heart rates. They are also starving. They are unable to feed themselves, except"—she swallowed and waited a minute for her voice to even out—"except for the bits of humans they are biting off, which seem to me more acts of uncontrollable aggression than hunger. Actually, I haven't seen any feeding behavior at all. I don't even know if they are smart enough to drink water."

"They have no instincts for self-preservation?" Mac asked.

"None, from what I have been able to ascertain. They're walking time bombs. Walking dead, actually."

"Zombies," Jon muttered.

She shook her head. "No, they are *not* zombies. They are very much alive—but they are dying, all of them. Quickly. We just need to save as many people as possible from the infection and hope that when the last one is gone . . ." Her throat hurt. Her voice wobbled. She cleared her throat. "When the last one is dead, let's hope there's still something there for us to rebuild."

"Well," Mac said briskly, "we're working really hard on that. Jon"—he switched his gaze to the man standing beside her—"we're monitoring all radio bands. The civilian Internet is down. Ours is still working of course but that doesn't help people outside our network. But we're finding pockets of uninfected almost hourly and some of them have radios. Lucius has been advising them on how to make their homes as secure as possible. We've got a map of everyone and we're scheduling pickups. The more people arriving here, the more people can go out in secure vehicles to rescue them."

"You have enough food for everyone?"

"Yeah. And Snyder and his men are going to go back down to their gated community and make it impregnable, so that can be a staging area for the refugees. They have stocks." Mac's eyes went back to hers. "So, Dr. Daniels—"

"Sophie, please," she murmured.

He dipped his head. "So, Sophie. You bring us that case so we can start manufacturing the vaccine and we'll start a mass-immunization campaign. Let's see if we can save the world."

Save the world. Sounded good. "Yes, sir."

"We have projections that the swarm should hit your area around fifteen hundred hours tomorrow. There are still lots of infected in your area and we think they will join the swarm. Once it's past, you should have a clean shot at getting to the helo. Everything will be waiting for you when you arrive."

"Boss—is the infection spreading to other states?" Jon asked.

All of a sudden, Sophie realized that she had no idea whatsoever what was happening outside California.

"Unclear. Marines are stationed all along the border. Our drones show us they're stringing barbed wire along the border too. They're going to contain the disease at the cost of writing California off."

"What's the rest of the country saying about that?"

Mac gave a huge sigh. "Not much. There's been a massive news blackout. No reporters are allowed near the borders, and the governors of Oregon, Nevada, and Arizona have instituted a curfew. Also, residents within a fifty-mile radius of the border are being evacuated."

"What about boats? California's coastline is 840 miles long," Sophie asked.

"From what we can see, there are Coast Guard cutters from one to three miles out along the coast. All boats are being turned back. "

Anger flashed in her. "If people are operating boats they are not infected!" Sophie said angrily. "They are turning back people fleeing from a massive pandemic! That's cruel."

"Yes, ma'am," Mac and Nick said at the same time.

"We're being abandoned to our own devices." The truth sank into Sophie. Her entire country was deserting her.

Elle huffed out a breath. "Well, it looks like we're not going to have any help. We're on our own here. We're going to keep locating uninfected and bringing them up to Haven, just as quickly as we can. And you, Jon, you're going to bring us what we need to make a vaccine."

Elle's eyes brimmed as she looked at Jon. She reached out a hand and Sophie ached to take it though they were separated by hundreds of miles. "And Sophie. We need her. She's a brilliant virologist." Two silver tears tracked down her pale face. "And my best friend. Bring Sophie back to me, Jon."

Jon's hand cupped Sophie's shoulder. He was holding her so tightly it almost—but not quite—hurt. "Count on it, Elle. We'll make it, I promise."

That was crazy. It was going to be almost impossible to make their way out of the city. Sophie doubted whether they could make it across the street. Jon was in no position to make such an insane promise. They were going to do their best, but the odds were almost outrageously stacked against them. On principle, Sophie didn't like to make promises she wasn't absolutely certain could be kept, and she opened her mouth to say so, but the look of relief that flooded Elle's face kept her back. Elle believed in Jon, absolutely.

Actually, all four of them looked . . . relieved. As if something had happened and they could lay at least this problem to rest. But nothing had happened except that Jon had promised the impossible. How could they look so relieved?

And then she looked up at him, at his perfect but cold and hard features, the look of a man who was absolutely certain of himself and his abilities and for an instant, even though she knew better, she was relieved too.

"Okay," Mac said. "We have the swarm leaving your area around 1800 hours tomorrow. It will be nautical twilight, and night vision can be used, so that's when you exfil to the helo, Jon. We clear on that?"

"Yessir." Jon's deep voice was so certain. Sophie took in a deep, shaky breath. Everyone seemed so certain they had a fighting chance. She wasn't going to jinx this. If there was even a chance in a million they might make it to the helicopter and then might make it back to where there was a lab that might have everything they needed to produce a vaccine quickly and they might distribute it . . .

A lot of mights there. But if there was a chance that it could be done, she had to believe it could be done. Otherwise . . .

No. The alternative was too horrible to contemplate.

Mac nodded. "Bring Sophie and the vaccine back home, Jon. We're counting on you. Over and out."

A big hand reached out to switch the hologram off and suddenly there was silence in her living room. Only a few screams could be heard, from a distance.

# Chapter 4

*Mount Blue*
*Haven*

Elle Connolly sat on the couch in her comfortable living quarters, arms around her knees, trying to control the trembling. She waited until she was sure of her voice. "How can he make it, Nick? Did you see those images?" A shudder shot through her.

A mass of writhing red creatures in IR, whole city blocks long and wide. Thousands and thousands of those . . . things. Not human anymore. Merely claws and fangs and rage. That's what Jon and her best friend, Sophie, had to battle their way through.

Nick sat beside her and picked up her hand. His hand was huge, scarred. Across the back of his strong, wide wrist was a jagged-looking scar. Catherine had Dermaglued it shut, but it had been deep and had bled badly. Nick was lucky he hadn't sliced a tendon.

His body was full of bruises, too, from the grenade he'd thrown in the basement of Arka headquarters, where friends and colleagues of hers had been held prisoner. And where her spirit had been trapped in a Faraday cage.

They'd all been very special prisoners, with special powers, and were now safe here in Haven. As was she. Elle could astrally project, a power she was only coming to grips with now, at the age of thirty. As a child, her dreams had scared her. And even when she discovered that what she thought were very vivid dreams was actually her ability to project herself to other places, it had been hard to control the ability. Only at Arka had she found people willing to study the phenomenon, together with other extrasensory abilities, scientifically. But Arka had betrayed the people with abilities. Caged them.

They'd trapped her in the Faraday cage when she'd accompanied Nick and his warrior friends to the headquarters in San Francisco to free the gifted prisoners. When her astral projection had been trapped, her body, back here in Haven, had started dying.

Nick's grenade had shattered the cage, setting her free. He had refused to leave until he'd freed her spirit. The virus had just erupted, and crazy violent monsters were running screaming down corridors. Mac and Jon had left him, but Nick hadn't left Elle. He wouldn't budge until he found her, and find her he did.

He loved her.

They'd lost each other ten years before, but now they were together—forever.

Or maybe until next month, when everyone died.

Who knew?

Nick rubbed a thumb over her knuckles, then brought her hand to his mouth. He was always making romantic little gestures like that, and Mac and Jon kept looking at him as if he'd grown two heads. Because, well, until he'd found her again, apparently romantic gestures hadn't been Nick's thing. Not much had been Nick's thing beyond soldiering and, after they'd been betrayed by a four-star general for money, the creation of Haven, a hidden high-tech city and now, possibly, the last hope of mankind.

He kissed her hand gently then brought both their hands down to rest on his massive thigh. But today, not even his thighs could distract her from her misery.

"I know you're worried, but Jon's the best, honey. Simply the best. At this kind of thing, maybe . . . maybe he's even better than me."

Huh. She blinked at him. "Did that hurt?"

A corner of his mouth went up. "A little. I'm a shooter. One of the best. But Jon—Jon's a strategist and he is cold as ice. He was undercover for two years in a Colombian cartel known for its brutality. He impersonated a California dealer and they bought it, because he looks the part. If they had had even the slightest inkling that he was undercover, they'd have strangled him with his own intestines and it would have taken him a week to die. Or hung him on a meat hook till he bled out. They'd done it before; it was one of their specialties. But Jon kept his head, got tons of intel, and melted away one night. Two days later their enemies had enough information on their security arrangements to try to take the whole cartel down. The upshot was real satisfying. Bad guys were butchering each other all over the place and the DEA and the Colombian cops mopped up the survivors and put them in jail. You can thank Jon's intel for your fancy research lab too."

She'd been astonished when Catherine had shown her where she worked. They had absolutely everything in the lab, top of the line. "Yeah? How so?"

"Jon got their bank account numbers before getting away. The few members of the cartel that are left get their accounts depleted by a couple million dollars every other week or so. Keeps them agitated and suspicious of each other. Keeps us happy."

She searched his eyes.

Nick's eyes. It still thrilled her that he was here, that they were together. They'd come together again under such unusual circumstances—when he'd saved her life by a margin of a few seconds—that she couldn't help but think it was fate itself that had conspired to unite them again. She was a scientist and shouldn't believe in fate.

But there it was. She did.

"Sophie is very dear to me," she said.

Nick bent forward to kiss her cheek. "I know she is, honey. She'll be safe with Jon. That story about him undercover? It was to make you understand that he is smart and quick. He'll get them out of there. And once they're back here, you brainiac women are going to have to start working around the clock on that vaccine. At least enough for all of us in Haven. Then as soon as we're inoculated, we're going to start canvassing for pockets of normals to inoculate."

She nodded. "We can start mass producing right away."

"Good, we're going to need it. Snyder found another community that has fortified. So far the community's intact. They're well armed and they are vigilant."

"How many?"

"About two hundred."

"Are we okay on supplies?"

"So far, yeah. And Manuel's hydroponic vats are coming online. I heard there was a two-ton tomato harvest. Start counting on lots of pasta and tomato sauce."

She tried to smile, but it didn't quite work. "I'm so worried, Nick," she confessed.

"Yeah." He leaned forward until his forehead rested against hers. "I know."

"I'm scared they won't get the virus and vaccine to us and we'll live the rest of our lives behind ten-foot walls, terrified of strangers. I'm scared Sophie won't make it. I'm even scared for Jon, though I know he can handle himself."

"Tomorrow night Jon and Sophie and the virus will be here. Count on it. And you and your genius girlfriends disappear to the lab. So how about a little hanky-panky right now? Like a little advance payment?"

A laugh bubbled out of her, then a sob, then a laugh.

Love. Making love. In the middle of mass death. Yes. She and Nick had been separated for so long, and the future looked so dark.

Life in the middle of death, oh yes.

She ran her hands over his broad shoulders, loving the vital, strong feel of him. Life pulsed in him, strong and steady. She linked her hands behind his neck and pulled him to her.

"Now," she whispered against his mouth. "Now, Nick. Hard and fast. Make me forget all this. Make me feel alive."

He kissed her, hard, deep, one big hand holding her still for his kiss as if she would pull away from him. The idea was ridiculous. She would never pull away from Nick, turn her back on him. She loved him.

Nick lifted his head for just a second, the hand cupping her head becoming a cradle. Watching her eyes, his other hand slowly unzipped her hoodie, brushing it off her shoulders. It slid softly to the couch behind her. His large, warm hand brushed her back and in a second her bra was off too. She knew he loved seeing her naked and, truth be told, she loved it too. His dark eyes grew hot, his face tightened, the skin over his cheekbones flushed. Arousal was all over his face, but instead of a big grin—the grin of a man about to have sex with a woman he desired—his face was somber.

He held her, tightly, so tightly her ribs protested. His face dipped to her neck suddenly and she felt wetness on her neck. Tears? From Nick Ross?

His voice was muffled against the skin of her neck, but she understood every word.

"Nothing bad will happen to you as long as we're together, Elle. I promise you that. As long as I'm with you, you'll be safe."

*San Francisco*
*Beach Street*

"If you want to take that shower, Jon, go right ahead. There seems to be plenty of water."

He dipped his head. "In that case, I'd love a shower. I'll make it fast."

She smiled at him. "I don't have anything that would fit you, but I have the new FastWash combo. Give me your clothes and they'll be washed and dried by the time you get out. Then we'll eat something and talk."

Jesus. Hot shower. Clean clothes. Food.

Sex.

Jon tried to keep that last thought out of his head. He had to practically nuke it out because that's what he wanted, much, *much* more than the shower and the food. Just dive right back into luscious Sophie Daniels, slide right into that tight warm sheath and forget about the world.

Oh yeah.

Thank God he had a poker face. Came in real handy when undercover. Jon never let anything he didn't want anyone to see show on his face, so right now he plastered a pleasant, polite smile on it and thanked her. A proper hostess offering comforts to a guest. She didn't know that the guest was planning on getting back inside her just as fast as he could, that the shower was to make him more acceptable to her, and the food was going to be fuel because—the way he felt right now? . . . he was going to fuck her all through the night.

This might be his last chance at sex, which was okay because, man, after having a taste of Sophie Daniels, no other woman would do. The last woman he'd fucked had been—Christ. He couldn't remember. Maybe that lady he'd met at the diner in Bakersfield after spending the afternoon buying a consignment of servers with fake ID. Bottle blonde, a little sad, a little too eager for sex. For an uncomfortable moment there, he'd wondered if she was a working girl because that's where he drew the line.

But no. She'd been happy enough with him just buying her dinner. And spending the night with him.

All in all, it had been a depressing night. While fucking, he'd ended up thinking more about where to find extra computer servers for Haven than about the woman under him. He was a polite kinda guy, so he did wait for her to come before he did. Took a little effort too. He remembered thinking it was a real pity men couldn't fake it like women did because, man, he would have faked an orgasm happily, then hightailed it out of there.

He remembered thinking—*I'm getting too old for this.*

It was exactly the opposite of making love to Sophie. No thoughts had passed through his head at all. The only thing in his head had been heat and desire. She'd felt like hot silk in his arms. Plunging into her had been like plugging his dick into an electric socket and the whole world had disappeared. All of it. Monster zombies—no, she said they weren't zombies, but damn, it felt like the zombie apocalypse—San Francisco on fire, the end of humanity . . . it all went away. All dark terrible things replaced by silky softness, warm, fragrant flesh, and something else. Something he couldn't pin down, something he couldn't describe, but which he remembered perfectly.

Making love to Sophie Daniels had been the most joyous experience of his life. Granted, his life wasn't exactly teeming with wonderful memories, but thirty-four years on this earth and he had never felt anything like that before. Lust and heat, yes. Of course. It was sex, after all. But more. Joy and . . . and peace. That was crazy. Sex wasn't about peace, but that's what he had felt. It was as if light had entered his world where before there had been darkness.

It was nuts, of course. Probably some body chemical that was released when he'd landed safe and sound right on top of beautiful, delectable Sophie Daniels. Sophie would know which chemical. And Catherine and Elle would know too. They seemed to know everything.

He himself had no clue.

But . . . but there had definitely been *something*. Something incredible, something exquisitely beautiful. When he had lifted himself up and away from her, he'd felt suddenly desolate, as if the door to a new and better world had suddenly slammed in his face, locking him out.

He'd felt wonderful, hopeful and happy, while touching her. And inside her? Jesus, that had been like opening the gates to paradise.

He was crazy, imagining things. But even if it was false, some kind of construct of his mind, it had been fantastic. He couldn't wait to get back inside her.

"Jon?"

Sophie touched his arm and—*damn*. It happened again. Warmth, right where she touched him. A sense of absolute rightness in her touching him.

Fuck. This was scary shit.

"Here." She smiled and handed him a stack of fluffy towels that smelled fresh with a hint of lavender.

That was another thing.

All his senses were heightened in her presence.

He was a warrior. He would never have made the grade, risen up through the ranks of soldiering, if his senses hadn't been keen. He had perfect eyesight. His hearing was acute. He had a phenomenal sense of smell. He'd smelled human body odor in the jungle and had stopped his men from walking into an ambush.

But that Sophie Daniels thing made his senses even keener. He could smell everything about her—her shampoo, the fresh smell of her clothes, something nice that he just knew was her skin. Everything about her stood out. He could see every color in her hair. She didn't dye it, and she was right not to because it seemed every single hair was a different color that came to life whenever she came under the overhead light. Brunette, auburn, gold—they were all there.

Up till that point, it was all fairly ordinary. Not ordinary for *him*—one woman was pretty much like another in his experience. But still, he could put all of that down to the fact that he found her extraordinarily attractive. He'd fallen for her, fast and hard.

No, what was spooky was the other stuff. Woo-woo stuff that would have scared the shit out of him except it felt so frigging good.

He could fucking *hear* her heartbeat. Slow and steady now, tripping fast while they were on the floor having sex. He sounded insane even to himself, but he was sure he could also hear her blood rushing through her veins.

Okay. Officially crazy now.

He grabbed the towels, trying to make his mouth move up in a smile because that was the polite thing to do, never mind that he was clearly losing it. Cold, level-headed Jon Ryan, gone insane. "I won't use up too much water," he said and she smiled at him.

"Don't worry about it too much. We should be out of here by tomorrow evening. And like I said, the building's water supply is rated at a week of self-sufficiency."

Oh God. Sophie Daniels should definitely not smile, ever. It messed with his head, with his focus, his concentration. Having sex—yeah, he could sort of justify that. On the age-old male theory that getting your pipes cleaned made you more effective. But that smile—it just about wiped him out.

He backed away, in self-defense.

" 'Kay," he mumbled. "Thanks."

Her bathroom smelled like a billion roses and whatever other flowers smelled good. Fuck, he didn't have a clue. Did daisies smell? No idea. That was about the only other flower he'd recognize.

It would have been overwhelming if it hadn't been so good. Everywhere were small complicated glass jars and glass vials with stoppers and dried flower petals and silver doodads and candles. Pretty towels with lace thingies around the edges and flower-shaped soaps and creams for every hour of the day. Feminine overkill. You just wanted to pitch forward, face-first, into all that softness.

It was the kind of place where a man would lose a percentage of his testosterone for every minute he spent in here.

He would have, too, except—except for the hard-on of course.

That wasn't going anywhere, no matter how many feminine frills surrounded him. His dick felt like a club hanging off his front. This was all too much. Sensory overload. He had to get himself under control.

He'd jack off in the shower, that's what he'd do. Get some of his headspace back. Good old jerking off in the shower. Worked a charm, and had since junior high.

The shower fittings were pretty easy to figure out and didn't require a password to access 150 settings, as had the showers of the Cortez clan back in Colombia. Old Joaquin Cortez had spent half a million dollars each on his johns, and he'd had twenty-four of them. The fittings had been pure gold and each showerhead could run water, perfume, or champagne.

Sophie's shower ran water. A nice jet of hot water. He stepped under it and opened a small cabinet set in the turquoise mosaic tile. He pumped soap from the turquoise enamel dispenser and lathered up, then was nearly brought to his knees because it smelled of Sophie. On her skin, it had been so faint he only thought of it as the way her skin smelled. But in that concentrated form, it was like having a thousand Sophies spread over his body and, oh God.

His knees buckled.

Luckily there was a small marble bench running along one side. He sat down heavily. The showerhead must have had those new sensors because it automatically followed his movements. Sitting on the bench was like sitting under a waterfall. The water was warm and silky, just like Sophie's skin.

He looked down at himself. The hard-on was so full he felt tight, bursting out of his skin. He dropped a hand down, touched himself, then lifted his hand away. His cock didn't want his hand, it wanted *her*, Sophie. But Sophie wasn't here and he couldn't present himself to her like this, like some teenage boy who couldn't control his hormones.

Jon knew how to control himself. Control had been necessary with his family, otherwise he'd have sunk into the pit with them. At times, it felt like he was nothing but iron-clad control. But right now, his cock was dark and swollen, actually twitching. He had to get rid of this hard-on. He had to be presentable when he emerged from the bathroom, otherwise he'd scare her. And, man, that was the last thing he wanted.

The world was scary as shit right outside her door. Monsters, on the loose. The city on fire. Their lives hanging by a thread, hanging by his ability to be quick-witted and fast, his ability to navigate their way through monsters who could turn them into monsters themselves with one bite, one scratch. He was going to have to get a woman with no training several blocks to the Ghirardelli Building and then up onto the roof. It had been hard enough alone, sprinting and stunning and shooting. On the way back, he was going to have to go at her pace, carrying a case, holding a weapon, which meant he couldn't keep a hand on her.

Sophie Daniels was in shape. She'd felt lithe and sleek in his arms. But he knew the kind of muscles that heavy training built, and she didn't have them. She was in shape but not conditioned. She wouldn't be able to keep up with him so he'd have to keep up with her.

He'd be on point of course. And he'd give her his stealth suit, which would leave him pretty much defenseless. One scratch, one bite, and he'd turn into a monster himself. He didn't know the latency of the virus, but it must be very, very fast, judging from the way it had spread. Before he knew it, his mind would be gone and he would turn on pretty Sophie Daniels and tear her apart.

She could beg and she could cry, but he wouldn't be himself anymore. He'd be gone in the smoky ruined depths of his own mind.

Like his parents.

He shoved that thought away, but it stuck in his head like barbed wire.

His parents had been druggies. When high, there'd been nothing there for their son. He'd spent most of his childhood watching his parents clock out. It hadn't mattered at all to them that he was cold and hungry and lonely. He remembered telling his mother that there was no food in the house and that he was hungry. She'd looked at him blankly and at that moment, Jon realized she didn't know who he was.

He'd been five.

At the age of nine, a good-looking blond kid, his parents had sold him to sex traffickers for a fix.

His parents had been monsters. All his life had been dedicated to being a good guy. Fighting against people exactly like
them. Those two years undercover—a mission so dangerous
he had a box full of medals he could never show anyone—had
been all about that.

The idea that with one bite he could become a monster himself, hurt Sophie, kill her even, without feeling anything . . .
that idea *terrified* him. More than any battle he'd been in.

Well.

He looked down at himself. He was only half erect now, dick
drooping more with each passing second. That was a way to
get rid of his boner. Even better than jerking off, since his dick
didn't want his hand, anyway. Just think of becoming infected
and not only not being able to protect Sophie, but hurting her.

Guaranteed dick deflation.

He stepped out of the shower and into the air dryer. Even
that smelled like Sophie. His clean clothes were neatly folded
on a chair. He picked up his long-sleeved tee and sniffed it. It
didn't smell as good as Sophie, but then nothing did. He put on
the tee and jeans and walked out barefoot to see Sophie at the
kitchen door, smiling at him.

"Ready for some food?" she called out softly.

Hunger roared through him. Whatever she was cooking
smelled wonderful. She stood framed in the door, shiny dark
hair gleaming under the kitchen light, beautiful face lit with a
welcoming smile, and his heart skipped a beat.

He was a dead man. If the zombies didn't get him, Sophie
Daniels would.

# Chapter 5

*Mount Blue*
*Haven*

"If you don't stop right this minute, I'm going to throw you over my shoulder and tie you down to the bed," Catherine's husband Mac growled.

When Tom "Mac" McEnroe growled most people cringed. His speaking voice was naturally low and very deep. When he growled it was the same timbre of a bear in a cave. Match that with a huge, muscled body and an ugly, scarred face, and most people would be terrified.

Catherine McEnroe wasn't terrified. Not at all. She knew the good man inside the terrifying exterior and she knew, above all, that he loved her.

"Why Mac," she smiled and simpered, dramatically fluttering her eyelashes at him. "I had no idea your tastes ran that way."

He made an exasperated noise deep in his throat and she laughed.

They were in Haven's infirmary. There was a massive rescue mission under way and new refugees were arriving hourly. None of them were infected. Everyone who arrived was placed separately in secure rooms, in quarantine, subjected to thermal scanning for half an hour and spot tests of pupils and body temperature. Infection showed up quickly. As soon as they passed the test, they were admitted into their community.

Before the outbreak, Haven had been an outlaw community. Mac, Nick, and Jon had been members of a super-elite group of warriors known as Ghost Ops. But they had been betrayed, accused of treason, and had disappeared. Mac had known of an abandoned mine inside a mountain, and from there they built their high-tech headquarters, Haven. By some mysterious process, Haven had attracted a community of geniuses and good people, most of them on the run from something.

Catherine herself had found her way here, to the home of her heart, by bearing a message from Mac's commanding officer, Lucius Ward. The three men had thought Ward had betrayed them, but Lucius had been betrayed himself, together with three young soldiers of Ghost Ops. The four of them had been hideously tortured and experimented on by Arka.

Their nemesis.

The company was no more, but it had unleashed this terrible virus before dying, like a scorpion's tail delivering one last fatal sting.

"You are not going to joke your way out of this, Catherine," Mac said in his laying-down-the-law voice. To most everyone he came across, that voice was the voice of God. Catherine obeyed him too. When she wanted to. The other times . . .

She swept a hand at the infirmary. It was organized chaos. New arrivals were coming in hourly. Though there were no infected, there were plenty of people who'd been injured in the evacuation. Lacerations, broken bones, concussions were the order of the day.

They both sidestepped as a volunteer nurse rolled in a patient on a gurney, a young woman with a severely bruised face and a broken arm. Soon the infirmary would be full and they would have to start stacking them in the corridors.

Catherine looked up at Mac. "There's so much to be done," she said softly.

He closed his eyes and pinched his nose.

Catherine touched him, laying her hand on his muscled forearm. She had a gift. It had been a curse most of her life, but here in Haven she came into it fully and accepted it fully as a gift. She was an empath, and a powerful one. Each day refined her gift. She could feel people's emotions at a touch. And if she was close to the person, she could almost read thoughts. And in Mac's case, since she loved him, she *could* read his thoughts. He was an open book to her.

And she could read clearly, as if in a book, how much he loved her and how worried he was for her. How worried he was for the baby in her belly.

Mac had no family at all. Being without human ties had actually been a condition for joining Ghost Ops—a deniable team of elite warriors, completely off the books. They had to have no ties whatsoever, no family, no friends, no loved ones.

At the time, that had been fine with them. Mac had never

loved a woman. Had sex, yes. A lot—though he'd told her he hadn't had sex since the group's betrayal the year before. He thought they had been betrayed by a man he idolized and it had been nearly a mortal blow.

She had changed all of that. She came to him with proof that he hadn't been betrayed by his commanding officer, Lucius Ward, and it turned out she came with living proof that he could love.

The moment she and Mac had met—even though he had suspected her of being a mole, sent in to find him and his teammates—the relationship had exploded. And now they were married and expecting a child, and it unnerved Mac completely. He hadn't had a place in his head and his heart for love, had barely coped with the idea of falling in love with her, and now there was a new life coming, to love and to care for and—this still blew Mac's mind—that new life would be his blood relative. His only blood relative in the world.

Mac had no idea how to cope with all these feelings and the only thing that made sense to him was to make sure nothing harmed her or their child. He was a warrior, a protector, and that he knew how to do. And the way to do that, apparently, was to make sure that she did nothing more strenuous than sit on the couch and read a book. Maybe listen to a little music.

While the world burned around them.

Catherine loved Mac, and, more to the point, she understood him. Bone deep. So she cut him some slack even though he exasperated her enormously at times, like right now.

Refugees were streaming in hourly, their resources were strained to the limits, every hand with medical training was absolutely essential. If they ever hoped to survive this plague, everyone had to pitch in.

But fighting him would only get his back up. It was only the fact that Catherine understood deeply, bone deep, Mac's fear of losing her, which kept her from kicking him in the backside.

"Mac," she said softly, taking one of his big hands in both of her own. Under his skin she could feel the emotions skittering, something that would surprise people who thought of him as an emotionless hulk of a man, cold as ice. Her Mac wasn't cold, just controlled. She knew, too—and this was brand-new to her—that her touch soothed him, as if she were cool water poured over a burning wound. That had been his description of what happened when she touched him while he was upset. "My darling, we're fighting not just for our lives here, but we're fighting so that something remains when this—this thing burns itself out. We're bringing a child into the world, and I want there to be a world for her, or him, to grow up in. And you know that—"

"*Make a hole!*" Larry Vetter, one of their engineers, rushed by with a bleeding man on a gurney. Catherine and Mac pressed themselves against the wall. Larry caught Mac's eye as he rushed past. "Bakersfield's gone, Mac. No one left. Just got word."

Bakersfield gone.

Just like that. A city of over four hundred thousand, all dead. Or worse. Infected.

Catherine's eyes followed the gurney. Beyond the door were over a hundred patients, tested to make sure they were uninfected, but still wounded and bleeding. She needed to help the way she needed to breathe.

"Let me go, Mac." She turned and met his dark eyes. "If we all work together, maybe we can ensure there are enough people to start again. I don't want to think about what the world could become. I don't want our child to grow up in the Dark Ages."

She was still holding his hand and she could feel the emotions in him, strong and pure. He was so easy for her to read. Love. Pride. Fear.

Love won.

"Okay," he grated. He stepped away. "Go save the world, Catherine."

She smiled sadly at him. "Just our corner of it, my love."

She tugged at the front of his shirt and stood on tiptoe to kiss him. When their lips broke apart, she hooked a hand around the back of his neck and put her lips to his ear. "Thank you, darling. You are definitely getting lucky as soon as I can take a breather."

*San Francisco*
*Beach Street*

If they could tune out the sounds of violent mayhem from outside, it could almost have been a . . . a date. A romantic one, at that. Sophie had pulled her curtains and lit candles. No real way of telling if the infected had a tropism toward light, but better safe than sorry.

And it did create an atmosphere.

If it weren't the end of the world, it would be pretty cool. Jon Ryan sitting next to her at her table—he refused to let her set his place across from her. He wanted to sit right by her. As dates went, he was a ten, an impossibly handsome and attractive man. The candlelight just loved him. He was so attractive it was almost overkill. Strong, sharp features limned in the glow of the candles, which picked out the gold highlights in his long hair. Much, much more handsome than Brad Pitt had been, back in the day.

For all his looks, he didn't have an actor's softness. No, this guy was all tough male. Hard muscles that didn't look like they'd been built in a gym. They looked like they'd been won in battle. Hands not actor-soft but hard and callused and nicked. Hands that were used.

Hands that knew what they were doing.

Heat flashed through her body at the memory of him touching her as they made love. Hard and callused, yes, but his hands had also been expert and tender. She'd felt clearly the calluses on his fingertips as they circled her where she had been so slick and tender . . .

Sophie's face was probably beet red by now.

She worked with people who had special psychic gifts. She'd worked with empaths, who could read a person's emotions with a touch. Thank God Jon didn't give any signs of being gifted in that way because she would just sink to the floor and die.

"Here." She gently pushed the platter with her zucchini omelet over to him, afraid that if she held it out, he'd see that her hands were trembling. "Have some more."

He'd already eaten half of her eight-egg omelet. His manners were impeccable, but clearly he'd been hungry.

"Don't have to ask me twice." He smiled at her and cut himself another wedge.

Oh God. It was the first real smile she'd seen from him and . . . he had a dimple. It appeared, unexpectedly, in his right cheek. A dimple. Oh, this was too much. She took in a deep breath and slid the wooden cheeseboard over to him as well.

"These are all great," he said as he cut himself a slice of goat cheese.

"Yes, well, it's San Francisco," she said before she could think her words through. *"Was* San Francisco," she corrected. Who knew when the Ferry Building Farmer's Market would open again. If it could ever open again. To open, it would need the rebuilding of a subculture of farmers and cheese makers and vintners. She gave a crooked smile. "Maybe rat brains cooked over a trash fire will figure large in our future."

Jon put his hand over hers and squeezed gently. His big hand was so warm, so comforting. She looked down at her hand under his. She had a scientist's hands. Soft and pale, with only the strength necessary to pipette liquids into vials and pound the keyboard. His hand looked as if it could haul a tank.

"There won't be any rat brains in Haven. Put that image out of your mind. We're completely self-sufficient in energy and water and food. The refugees will put some strain on us but we have enormous reserves. Mac, Nick, and I are used to military planning and—well, we planned for a siege right from the start."

Oh no. Her breath blocked in her chest. Her hand slid from his and her back hit the chairback with a thud. "You *knew* this was coming?" she whispered. The words would barely come out between numb lips. "You knew and you didn't stop it?"

He grabbed her hand back. "No, God no. We didn't plan for *this*. For a massive outbreak of a deadly virus, no."

Her lungs expanded on a loud gasp. For a second there she thought—*No*. Arka had engineered the virus, not some people on a mountaintop in Northern California.

She had to wait a minute to be able to speak, though. "Okay," she said when she could keep her voice even. "Explain why you have a community that plans for sieges."

He didn't answer right away. He simply looked at her, his

bright blue eyes burning into hers. He didn't try to hide his scrutiny, didn't try to pretty it up. He just stared so intensely, it felt as if he were walking around inside her head, picking at her thoughts. Turning them over. What was he waiting for?

Finally, he spoke. "Okay." He reached out and tucked a lock of her hair behind her ear. The touch was casual, a friendly gesture, no more. But she shivered.

He noticed. Those bright ice blue eyes noticed everything.

"Two years ago I would have been shot by the U.S. government for telling you this, but I think, all things considered, that soon there might not be a U.S. military to shoot me anymore, so it's a moot point."

"If you told me, you'd have to kill me?" she teased. A thousand movies had used that line.

He wasn't smiling. "Exactly." The way he said it sobered her. "If I had talked to you about us two years ago and someone in my chain of command found out, you'd have been tracked down and disappeared. No one would ever have heard from you again. Least of all me."

This happened in the real world. She knew that. Her smile was gone. "Your chain of command is probably gone," she said softly.

His jaws clenched. "It's definitely gone," he answered. "Mac, Nick, and I belonged to a deniable military unit. Deniable means that if we were ever caught, Uncle Sam would deny our very existence. We were Ghosts. We were off the books, our pasts wiped out, our military records erased. All photographs tracked down and destroyed. We didn't exist. We deployed on missions where the U.S. government could not be seen as intervening. Posse comitatus didn't apply to us, since technically we didn't exist. Do you know what that is?"

Sophie nodded. "Sure. It's the law that stops the military from acting on American soil."

He gave a sharp nod. "Exactly. But technically we weren't military. We weren't anything. So when the military got word that a lab in Cambridge was very close to perfecting a weaponized version of *Yersinia pestis*, they called us."

She gasped. A weaponized version of Yersinia was one of the worst things she could think of. Almost as bad as what was happening outside her windows. "The plague! A genetically modified version of the bacillus that can spread quickly—maybe airborne—it would be a disaster!"

"Oh yeah." His face tightened. "Believe me when I say that the seven of us—the founders, the plankholders of Ghost Ops—were highly motivated to retrieve the material and shut the research down. We had a very short chain of command. Our team leader, Captain Lucius Ward reported to General Clancy Flynn, who reported to the President. So when we got our orders from Lucius, we were ready to go in fifteen."

"Who were the other three?"

"Three of the best teammates you can imagine. Pelton, Romero, and Lundquist."

Something about the way he said their names . . . "Did they die in the mission?"

Something dangerous flashed in his icy blue eyes. "No. It might have been better if they had. They ended up on the wrong end of a scalpel. They spent a year under the knife."

Sophie blinked.

"It was a trap, Sophie." His voice had been calm up until then. Now the heat of rage shaded through it. "It was an Arka Pharmaceuticals lab and General Flynn and Dr. Charles Lee wanted to get rid of Lucius and get rid of us. Nobody was weaponizing bubonic plague. They were actually perfecting a cancer vaccine. We were sent into battle under a lie. We were ambushed in a firefight and an explosion took out the lab. Only three of us survived, or so we thought. We thought Pelton, Romero, and Lundquist died and Lucius escaped. We thought he'd betrayed us for money." His jaws clenched and he looked away for a moment, visibly trying to control himself. "The thought that the captain would betray us for money—well, it nearly brought us to our knees. Mac particularly. He was recruited by the captain, trained by the captain to head up the Ghost Ops team. Mac would have gladly given his life for the captain. All of us would have. And here we were—betrayed, under arrest, on our way to a secret court-martial."

He looked away again, jaws clenched. The memories brought him pain, distress. Sorrow came off him in almost visible waves, though his face betrayed nothing. It didn't have to, she could see the pain.

Sophie didn't know what to do, so she did the only thing she could—she touched him. Since childhood she'd had two different types of touches. Normal touch, human skin to human skin. It could be a hug, walking arm in arm, accidental touches. But over and above that, she could also Touch. It was an entirely different thing altogether and she still didn't understand it, even after a lifetime of it.

She'd become part of the Arka research project not just to understand the science of paranormal phenomena, but to understand herself.

To understand how she could heal.

Not all the time and not always fully, because it was erratic, but when she threw a switch on inside herself, something that had no explanation in normal science happened. She was a scientist and she'd always gotten straight As in everything, including English. So she should have been able to explain to herself what happened when she threw that switch, but she couldn't. She could barely describe it.

But Sophie let it happen, this gift she barely understood.

She warmed up in a flash, heat crackling through her in a palpable wave. The heat was entirely subjective, though, because she'd taken her own temperature during a healing session and it never went above 98.6. The heat didn't feel like a fever. Fevers were a reaction to a pathology. This didn't feel like pathology, it felt . . . right. As if she were throwing a circuit of nature, and power flowed from her to the sick person.

Her first conscious use of her Touch had been at the age of twelve with Fritzi, the dumb and the beautiful. He'd been run over by a car on the street outside their house. The house had had a fence around it, but later they'd discovered that Fritzi had dug his way out. She and her parents had been having breakfast on a Saturday morning when they'd heard a loud thump and then anguished wailing.

Rushing out onto the street, they'd seen Fritzi lying on his side, whining, trying to lick his red hindquarters. Sophie's father had gathered Fritzi in his arms while Sophie clung to her father, crying as he carried the wounded animal to their porch.

While her father took out his cell to call the vet, Sophie threw her arms around Fritzi, burying her face in his soft golden fur that smelled of shampoo and dog and . . . something happened. She felt waves of heat that didn't burn. She was barely aware of the fact that Fritzi's whines had stopped and that he'd started licking her arms instead of his hindquarters. All she knew was that she loved this beautiful dog who'd been a puppy during her own puppyhood.

He stood up.

Sophie had fallen back, so weak she couldn't stand up, though Fritzi could.

They took Fritzi to the vet and a surprised Dr. Felsom told her parents that the X-rays showed bone fractures that had recently healed.

Sophie healed Nana Henderson's arthritis, her mother's breast cancer, and her father's broken femur. She'd healed an aneurysm in an old family friend, Emma Price. Aunt Emma's aneurysm had disappeared after a session with Sophie, and it was only her father's influence that had stopped Aunt Emma's cardiologist from publishing the incredible results—the clear aneurysm on the angiogram on September 12, no aneurysm on the angiogram on September 20.

No one told the cardiologist that Sophie had spent an afternoon with Aunt Emma on the seventeenth. And no one told him that Sophie spent the next week in bed, too weak to get up.

From that moment on, she was forbidden to help anyone.

Sophie had never tried to heal the spirit, but she felt that Jon had an ailment as deathly as an aneurysm. A bone-deep sorrow that in any other human would have been crippling.

The sorrow was profound and deep and old. Not linked to the suffering outside the window. That was like rain falling on an already flooded plain.

So she Touched him, and was nearly staggered by the waves of pain and sorrow.

"Go on," she urged. "Tell me."

Jon shook his head, frowning. He looked at her, opened his mouth and shut it. Something was happening to him, something he couldn't explain. She was absorbing his pain, trying to withstand the onslaught.

"Mac knew of an abandoned mine inside Mount Blue."

"Yes," she said softly. "That's the place Catherine mentioned."

He had hesitated just a second before saying the name of the location, just as no last names had been exchanged when she was talking with Elle and Catherine Young.

Jon's head was still in the Old World. In this New World, all secrets were gone. How could there be state secrets when the state had disappeared? He hadn't understood this yet, but he would.

"Right away, we had people who just . . . come to us." He raised his eyebrows, rubbed the back of his neck with his free hand. "The damnedest thing," he muttered. "It's like we became this—this magnet. For people on the run, for misfits, for people with gifts that got them into trouble. One of the first was an engineer who'd worked for a criminal construction company that got a lot of people killed and framed him for it. He just . . . showed up one evening."

His eyes slid to hers.

"You have to understand something. Mac, Nick, and I are experts in security. We're the best. The very first thing we did was surround our hideout with remote sensors so thick a fly couldn't fart without our knowing about it. And Eric—he just waltzed right in. No one should have been able to do that, but by God he did. So we knew he was either going to be a dangerous enemy or a strong ally. Turns out he's a strong ally. He built us a beautiful place that somehow just attracted people, the right kind of people." His beautiful mouth kicked up in a half smile. "Do you know who our cook is?"

Sophie shook her head. "But I'm not up on trendy chefs, so I might not recognize the name."

"Oh, you'll recognize this one, all right. Stella Cummings."

Sophie's mouth fell open. "Stella Cummings? *The* Stella Cummings? The—"

"Actress, yeah." Jon looked as if he were enjoying her astonishment.

"Wasn't she—"

"Slashed by a stalker, yeah." Jon's face turned grim again. "Took her two years and ten surgeries to get over it, and she was badly scarred. She just left Hollywood behind. Got a job slinging hash up north because she'd always loved to cook. I was with her in the diner in a small town when there was an announcement on the news that her stalker had escaped from prison. She'd barely put her life back together. Working as a cook at the diner grounded her, she said. We'd struck up a sort of friendship. We never exchanged names, though I knew who she was. She looks like Stella Cummings, only chopped up and put back together again. She was shaking so hard she could barely breathe. I told her I could take her to a place where she would be safe and she came, and now we can't do without her."

"So all these refugees streaming into . . . your headquarters are—"

"Eating like kings. Speaking of which"—he lifted a forkful of her zucchini omelet—"Fabulous."

"Thanks. So you guys set this place up. People came and found refuge with you. Did I get that right?"

"You did. And since the people who came don't want to be found, we keep it hidden. And we'd prepared for the worst case scenario—a siege. We've been working nonstop on our community, and it is almost completely self-sufficient in water, food, and energy. Now Catherine and Elle are setting up a clinic. Refugees are pouring in, but we have the space and huge food reserves, so we're going to be okay. Haven will survive this storm. We just have to make sure as many people survive as possible."

A howl came from outside. It sounded like an animal cry, but wasn't. Sophie shivered. There might be one safe space left, but it was far away and too late for this city she loved.

Now it was Jon's turn to comfort her. He put down his fork and leaned toward her, arms open. Sophie burrowed there, arms sliding around that broad back, hands pressed flat against the thick muscles of his back

"It'll be okay," he said softly and kissed her hair.

Yes. Maybe. Sophie's gift was great, but she wasn't going to be able to save the world. All she could hope for was to make it back to this safe community, snugged inside a mountain, and help produce as much vaccine as possible. If they made it. Another howl came from outside, and another. Sounds of animals snarling, fighting.

Only they weren't animals.

They were people.

She buried her head against Jon's shoulder. His arms tightened around her.

"Take me to bed, Jon," she whispered against his shoulder, eyes closed tight.

He stood so quickly his chair tipped over to the floor. He picked her up and carried her away—away from the terrible noises.


*Mount Blue*
*Haven*


His cane slammed to the floor, crossing right in front of two of the most beautiful female legs on planet Earth. The woman's eyes looked at the cane running obliquely in front of her, following it up to his hand, then going all the way up to his face.

She met his eyes and flinched. It was Stella Cummings's usual reaction to someone looking her right in the face. He was pleased to note that the reaction was less severe than it had been in the beginning, when she tried to hide, instinctively. Now she didn't avert her face much, just her eyes.

Lucius Ward reached out to hold her chin between thumb and forefinger and turned her face gently so she was looking him square in the eyes.

"Hello, beautiful," he said and bent to kiss her. Her luscious lips—with that little indent on the pillowy lower lip that millions of men had dreamed of and lusted after in her previous life—were soft against his. He could feel the scar that slashed across her mouth as a little raised ridge. He didn't care. He was covered in scars himself.

They were right in the communal kitchen's entrance. People were streaming by them like water around a boulder. Keeping one hand firmly on his cane—no point falling on his ass just because this woman took his breath away—he hooked his other around her slender neck and deepened the kiss.

Stella gave up trying to maintain discretion and kissed him back. Man, it was heaven. She opened her mouth, her tongue licking his—and right there, in their communal kitchen, right in front of just about the entire Haven population, Lucius's body woke up.

It was a miracle that perhaps only this one woman in all the world could have engineered.

Before being taken prisoner by Arka Pharmaceuticals and subjected to harsh surgical tortures for a year, Lucius wouldn't have needed a world-class beauty like Stella Cummings to get a hard-on. His dick had taken care of itself, and him, ever since he'd been twelve.

But after his rescue from the research lab-torture chamber where he and the rest of the Ghost Ops team had been held, standing upright had been almost beyond him. He'd pushed himself daily since the rescue, falling exhausted into bed each night. At first, simply standing with the help of a cane for more than five minutes at a time had been beyond him. But damned if he'd be a cripple, even though those sadistic bastards at Arka had done their best to reduce him to the level of an animal. Dr. Charles Lee, the head of Arka, the man who'd orchestrated the brutal experiments in his frenzy to find the formula for super-soldiers, had been about to discard him as human waste when Mac's wife, Catherine, led his former teammates to him.

He'd been in a coma when he arrived here at Haven, as near to death as you could be. But here he'd found his old team, he'd found superb medical care, solidarity, and . . . love. He'd found love, here in this outlaw community.

He deepened the kiss further, losing himself in her. In this beautiful, scarred, very smart woman who'd captured his heart. He would have sworn he didn't have one. All he had was loyalty—to his teammates and his country, in that order—but it turned out that, yes, he had a heart and it was hers.

Stella stepped forward, slipping one slender hand over his on the cane, the other around his waist, and the instant her torso touched his it happened. While kissing her, he'd felt a heaviness around his groin, the feeling of blood rushing around looking for a place to pool. He always felt that way around her, aroused in his head though his body was too damaged to respond.

The blood finally found its old pathways and his body woke up and smelled the roses. Or smelled *her*, Stella Cummings, once considered the most beautiful woman in the world until a slasher took a knife to her. The surgeons had done their best to put her back together again, but Stella's face looked like a jigsaw puzzle. Lucius couldn't see that. To him, she was still the most beautiful woman in the world. The most gifted actress of her generation, a woman who had enchanted millions around the world.

The woman who now held his heart in her hands.

His dick, too, apparently.

He felt the instant Stella realized what was pressing against her. Her lips smiled under his. He pulled back, pressed his forehead against hers. "Let's go lie down for a while, Stella." His voice came out thick, rough. As if it were the first time he'd spoken in years.

Stella kissed his jaw. Though she was a tall woman, she had to lift herself up to do it.

"I can't," she whispered. He could hear the regret in her voice. "And anyway, I don't know if you should—"

"Yeah. I don't know if I should either. I don't even know if I can," he said honestly. "This is the first time it's been anything but inert meat between my legs in over a year. Maybe if I used it, I'd keel over dead." He made a rumbly noise in his chest, which took him a few seconds to realize was a laugh. He'd laughed. He wasn't a laughing man, never had been. Few things about this fucked-up world amused him. This last year had been pain and helplessness and desolation. And right now they were in a crisis as a plague unlike any other had been unleashed.

But this woman—she infused him with such joy. The world was in danger, but there had to be some joy in it, otherwise why save it?

Lucius had lived with duty as his sole motivator for so long.

For most of his life. But duty was a cold and harsh mistress. Right now he had something warm and alive and magical in his arms. This was worth fighting and dying for.

Someone holding a big tin vat of tomatoes bumped them as he sped by. "Sorry," he called over his shoulder.

Stella straightened with a sigh. "I can't take time off, Lucius." She cupped his chin and tried a smile. "Much as I'd like to. Soon there will be almost three thousand of us. We're already feeding in two shifts; we're going to have to go to three soon."

"We can take the time off and we should, my darling. You've been working almost twenty-seven hours straight." He touched his finger to the dark circles under her eyes. "You're about ready to fall where you stand. General Snyder sent forty men and women to help you. He's organizing what is essentially a mess hall. The Marines know how to do this. They'll take their cues from you with regard to recipes and menus, but they don't need help in creating a mess hall."

She sighed and bowed her head. He was speaking the truth and she knew it.

"And I have gone over plans with Snyder and my men. We're bringing in refugees and Eric is overseeing a fast extension to the structure. By tonight there will be a hall large enough for everyone to sleep in, and we've set up communal showers. A platoon in ten up-armored Humvees has gone out to a ranching town fifty miles outside Bakersfield. We're in radio contact and apparently they're holding their own. The platoon won't be back before dawn. There's nothing more I can do, and there's nothing more you can do right now. I don't think I can even act on what you felt just now, but by God I'd like to lie down and hold you in my arms. I need you in my arms, Stella."

She rubbed her face against his neck and he could feel wetness. Stella wouldn't want anyone to see her crying, so he simply held her for a long moment while men and women hurried past in ordered chaos with supplies.

Finally she lifted her head and those famous eyes—a brilliant turquoise—smiled at him.

"Let's go lie down," she said huskily.

"Together," he said. Right then he made a vow to himself. For whatever time they had left—and it might be only a day—he was going to spend every night at this woman's side.

She nodded. "Together. Oh yeah."

# Chapter 6

She was so light in his arms. It surprised him.

She seemed so . . . invincible. He'd been at the Arka Pharmaceuticals headquarters building when the infection had broken out. He and Nick had barely gotten out alive, and they were highly trained warriors. She'd not only broken away from her captors, she'd taken the time to search for the original virus and the vaccine, fighting both Arka's security goons and the infected.

And then she'd made her way across a city in chaos.

Trapped in her home, she'd spent her time studying the infected and already had pointers that were going to help them evade the enemy, and were already proving useful to the Haven team out in the field.

Now, this was Ghost Ops terrain. They'd been trained, and trained hard to study and understand the enemy. When he'd been undercover in Colombia, he'd studied the *jefes* and their muscle so much, he knew everything about them, down to their diet, their bowel movements, the women they really fucked, the women they pretended to. What they bought, who they bought. He knew it all. Nothing had escaped his notice. Nothing.

And yet, flying over infected terrain, it hadn't even occurred to him to try to study patterns. Okay, he was flying over the terrain pretty fast, but he hadn't been thinking of anything but getting to Sophie Daniels before a monster ate her face. Still, he could have observed movements, migrations patterns, drawn some conclusions.

He was heartsick, but that wasn't an excuse. Sophie'd been heartsick, too, and she had pages and pages of observations.

So besides being as beautiful as a movie star, she was smart and brave. Resourceful, rational.

And, oh so delicate.

He could feel this in his arms. When they'd had frantic sex right after he fell into her apartment, he'd been too blasted with survivor's lust, guided by his combat boner, to notice much of anything besides how good she felt and how good she tasted.

But now?

Now he could feel how incredibly delicate she was, one arm around a slender torso, the other under long slender legs. Everything about her was fragile, hidden before because she was so smart and so courageous. Her soft cotton tee gaped open, showing the delicate collarbone, the narrow shoulders. Such courage, such spirit in such a fragile body.

Jon didn't have to ask where the bedroom was. Away from

the door with its potpourri and scented candles and air fresh-
ener sprays, there was another source of good smells and he
simply followed his nose.

Good soldiers have a keen sense of smell and he was one
of the best. He simply followed the scent for the room that
smelled of Sophie. There was a short corridor and he nudged
the door with his foot and . . . bingo!

The blinds were drawn, one small light on a dresser drawer,
the rest in shadow. It was a girly girl's room and he nearly
smiled. The bed was an ode to femininity—frills and flounces
and floral sheets, and a billion pillows. Most unusual for a no-
nonsense scientist.

He looked down at her, in his arms, and smiled. It was genuine, a light-hearted moment while the world burned around
them. Jon's few smiles were a cynic's smile. He had no illu-
sions about the world and the people in it. There were a lot of
things he found grimly humorous. The hypocrisy most people
tried badly to hide. The greedy, grasping nature of most people.
People were like children, with uncontrollable urges and appe-
tites. If you had a cynic's sense of humor, the world was a feast.

But right now, he had an extraordinarily beautiful, brave,
smart woman in his arms, who had shown nothing but a sense
of sacrifice. His usual cynicism somehow wouldn't kick in. His
smile reflected how good she felt in his arms, how pretty that
bed was, what they were going to do on that bed.

Sophie's hand cupped his cheek. "You smile."

He moved his head until her hand covered his mouth, then
kissed the palm of her hand. "Look carefully because it doesn't
happen often."

"No." Her own smile disappeared. "Not much to smile about
right now."

Jon placed her carefully on the bed, like depositing a jewel in its box. "Well, right, *right* now, things aren't looking so bad."

A laugh escaped her and she covered her mouth, as if laughter were forbidden. Jon gently brought her hand away from her mouth, brought it to his, kissed the palm again.

"You laugh."

She nodded. "That surprised even me."

Jon looked down at her, at this unexpected pearl that had been given to him. He lay his hand on her flat belly, absorbing the warmth of her skin through the thin tee. He shifted his hand, started pulling it up. With his other hand, he lifted her shoulders off the bed while pulling the tee up and off. She wasn't wearing a bra and she wasn't wearing panties so after he'd slipped the thin cotton pants off her hips and down her legs, she was naked and he almost closed his eyes against the picture she made on the bed.

Too much. Too much beauty. Too much sentiment in her eyes as she watched him. She didn't try to cover herself up and she didn't try to preen. She just lay there, open to him, watching him watching her.

He put his hand back on her belly, relishing the feel of her skin now that he didn't have to feel it through cloth.

"Now you," Sophie said and at first he didn't understand what she meant. The gears in his head weren't meshing too well. Then, "Oh—" She wanted him naked too.

Oh yeah.

In a second he'd stripped, as fast as he could because he didn't want to lift his hand from Sophie for anything.

"You're so beautiful," she whispered.

Jon didn't look down at himself. He knew what he looked like. Though he couldn't recall a hard-on quite as *hard* as the one he was sporting now. He didn't have to look down to know his dick was like a rock and immensely swollen. It fucking hurt.

"Am I?" he whispered back. She nodded. "That should be my line."

Sophie smiled, placed her hand over his.

Jon shut his eyes, his hand on Sophie's belly, her hand over his, the heat from her hand rising up his arm. He stood stock-still, immense tension in every muscle in his body.

And he realized: "I can't go slow, Sophie." He shook his head. "Sorry. Maybe I should—" He didn't finish the rest of the sentence because he was tempted to offer something he didn't think he could make good on. Like offering to step back, step away.

Luckily, it didn't make any difference because Sophie tugged on his forearm and he fell onto her. Just like before, only this time they were naked and he knew what to expect.

Out-of-this-world pleasure, that's what he was expecting. And that's what he got.

Warmth spread all along his body where they met.

Sophie twined her arms around his neck, opened her mouth under his and that warmth kicked up to heat. That honeyed pleasure flowing through his veins became prickling heat right under his skin, requiring immediate action.

A second later, he slid into her—into that hot secret place between her thighs—and a second after that his body slammed into action. It was completely beyond his control as he hammered into her, holding her hips with his hands.

Some very, very dim part of his mind was exerting over-watch, if not control. If he had felt anything less than welcome, anything less than desire on her part, he'd have stopped. He hoped.

As it was, Sophie was with him every step of the way, her body completely open to him, slick with juices that eased his way, holding him tightly with her arms and legs. Matching him, movement for movement.

It was so intense, so hot, it couldn't last, and it didn't. Sophie tightened around his dick, threw her head back against the pillow, and emitted a low moan that came out stuttering because he was moving in her so strongly. She dug her nails into his back, tightened around him again and again. Her orgasm pushed him right off the edge and into another world of heat and light where he had to hold his breath as his body went into overdrive. He slammed into her, moving easily now, since she was slick with juices, in a frenzy of heat so great he thought he would blow up.

And then he did.

Great shuddering convulsions so intense his eyes rolled back under his lids and his toes curled. It went on forever as every ounce of liquid in his body poured into her and at the very last moment, just as he began to still, she convulsed again, lifting her hips up against his by leveraging herself up with her legs. She rotated her hips and arched her back to take more of him, breaths coming in pants against his ear, clenching tightly around him in pulls so strong he could feel her stomach muscles working against his abdomen.

At the same moment, they blew out great gusty breaths and stilled.

Jon collapsed bonelessly on her, every cell of his body drenched in pleasure. He should move. He was heavy and he was sure he was crushing her, but damn. This felt so . . . fucking . . . *good*. He couldn't even think through the pleasure signals zapping through his body. That constant awareness he had at all times, the bit of himself he kept separate and vigilant, had taken a hike. The movie screen in his head started to blur, show static.

He made one last heroic effort and cranked an eyelid open. All he really saw was a delicate jawbone, a small pink ear and a cloud of dark shiny hair. But his hazy mind could fill in the rest. Sophie.

Everything felt so damned good exactly as he was, including his half-limp dick nestled deep within her. Oh man, that felt particularly good, like his own personal dick holster.

Mmmm.

However, good things don't last. No one knew that better than he did. Jon planted his palms on the mattress next to her head and tensed his muscles. Pulling out and rolling over wasn't going to be easy. Not because he didn't have the strength but because he didn't have the desire.

He moved his hips and instantly Sophie's arms and legs tightened around him.

"Don't," she whispered.

Oh man, no. But out of a sense of duty, he replied, "I'm heavy."

There was no refuting that and she didn't try. "I like it."

Christ. She didn't want him to pull out and roll over and he didn't want to either.

Something had messed with his soldier's brain because he knew falling asleep in this position wasn't smart, wasn't in the battle manual.

They had been taught how to sleep in battle conditions, been trained to it, sometimes with blood. They'd trained to operate at peak capacity on two hours' sleep a week. They'd been trained to come out of REM sleep fighting. In the field, Jon had never been a second away from a weapon.

Now, right now, goddammit, his weaponry was in the living room. Every single freaking piece of equipment was precious seconds away. The thought was unbearable for a professional soldier. But the thought of detaching himself from Sophie was . . . was even more unbearable. That warm softness all along his front, the silky hair tickling his face, that warm grip on his dick—he couldn't do without it. Simply couldn't.

He was being rewired.

That was his last thought before a warm perfumed blackness overcame his senses.

The noise woke him. He was instantly awake, instantly realized what it was.

Light colored the edges of Sophie's lined curtains, enough to see the time on his wrist. He'd slept until after mid-day, something he couldn't ever remember doing.

Sometime during the night he'd slipped out of and off Sophie, his subconscious being more of a gentleman than his consciousness. She was lying half on him, head in the crook of his shoulder.

He'd slept deeply, something he rarely did. That descent into deep sleep discomfited him. He sometimes had nightmares, which he hated. So he'd trained himself to go into a shallow sleep, completely unlike the semi-coma he felt he'd been in.

He'd woken up because of the noise. The noise was unlike anything he had ever heard in his life. Jagged, dissonant, feral. Growing louder.

Sophie raised her head, smiled at him, a frown between her dark eyebrows. In the faint light all he saw was pale skin and dark blue eyes.

He smoothed his hand over her hair, wishing that things were different. Wishing he were here in this absurdly frilly and comfortable bed with this amazingly beautiful and smart woman under normal circumstances.

Jon didn't do romance and he sure didn't do love. He was a love 'em and leave 'em guy, all the way. But Sophie?

Wow, with Sophie he just might have made an exception. She was absolutely fascinating, probably smarter than he was, certainly better educated. Soft, gentle, very easy to be with. And he liked the glimpses of frills, of hyperfemininity that he'd seen.

Another first. Jon's life had always been reduced to essentials. For most of his life, he could have packed all his worldly goods into one duffel bag, ready to take off in ten minutes. He owned no property outside his guns. The military had given him all the essentials and he had wanted nothing else. No ties, no belongings, and above all, no frills.

Ghost Ops had been made for him.

No emotional ties either, until Haven. He'd respected Lucius and Mac, ready to follow their orders even if it led to his death. But now he could see beneath Lucius and Mac's rough exterior, particularly with their women. It was as if they came alive in their presence. Mac was crazy about his wife, Catherine, and that child she was carrying. And Lucius—Lucius had been so beaten, so broken when he and Pelton, Romero, and Lundquist had arrived that Jon thought he could see death following Lucius around, one step behind him. Stella had yanked him right back into life.

And Nick. Man. Iceman Nick who didn't care about anything or anyone. When he'd received some secret signal from Elle that she was in danger, Jon thought Nick would go crazy. Implode from stress.

Jon didn't believe in love, of any kind. Not in love at first sight or second or even third sight. His parents had been sick fucks, incapable of loving anything except their drugs; and until Haven, until this past year, he'd never seen love at work, had never even believed it possible.

But now . . . well, suppose it was possible? Suppose you could find someone you loved and admired and who loved you right back? Something he didn't even imagine existed in the world until he saw it, firsthand, at Haven. So if you found it, what then?

"Jon?" Sophie repeated sleepily, lifting up on one elbow. He reached out and tucked a dark shiny lock of hair behind her ear. "What's that noise?"

If you found it, you protected it.

"The swarm," he said grimly. "It's coming."

They came and they came and they came. She and Jon stood by the window with the curtains open. The sky was cloudy with smoke, fire, and debris, casting a gray pall over the morning.

At first they watched on Jon's scanner fed by a couple of Haven drones. At some central control station back in Haven, they pieced together a large-scale picture from several drones. She could tell by the slight fracture marks in the hologram, which disappeared when Jon zoomed in with one drone's video feed.

It took a moment to realize what she was seeing, though she could hear it well enough. A loud, dissonant cacophony, growing louder by the minute. A noise unlike any she'd ever heard before, the very voice of utter chaos. Screams, bellows, fists against metal, glass shattering, all combined into one long rolling wall of sound that was the most frightening thing she'd ever heard.

Jon zoomed in more closely and there it was—the swarm. The main force rolling up Jones, people shoulder to shoulder, shoving each other, striking randomly, a mass so dense that for a second it looked like one single organism with an infinite number of moving parts. The front part of the wave was twenty blocks long.

Jon tapped and the focus zoomed in even more, so she could see individual faces.

Every hair on her body stood up in an archaic, primitive rush of utter terror. She couldn't imagine that so many expressions of violence and madness had ever been gathered together in the history of humanity. Even in the mass battles of the past, there must have been some human expressions among the rank and file, a few hanging back, not wanting to maim and pillage. Some who tended to the wounded. Some who simply didn't want to fight.

Here there was nothing she recognized as even vaguely human, just a boiling mass of bodies trying to kill each other.

Half the faces were covered in blood, which was almost a blessing because she couldn't see the inhumanity there. All she saw was blood on skin, sometimes dripping off the faces if the killing had been fresh. Nobody looked up, of course, because the drones were silent. Mute witnesses to mankind's degradation, flying high overhead, robotic souls unflinching, cameras emotionlessly shooting video footage that sickened her heart.

"They—" Her voice came out so faint she had to stop. She was leaning against Jon like you'd lean against a wall, to hold you up. He was absolutely solid, face without expression as he held out the monitor so she could watch. At her almost sound-less voice, his intent gaze switched from the monitor to her face.

She was a scientist. Maybe one of the few left alive. So as long as she had a beating heart and a functional brain she was going to do what was a scientist's first duty—observe reality. There could be no hypotheses without observation. She remembered one of her first biology professors laying down the law and how she had thrilled at the thought. It had been like looking into the very heart of life.

Well, now she was looking into the very heart of death, but her duty was still clear.

She coughed, gathered her strength around her like a cloak.

"They are behaving very much like a swarm," she said, proud of the fact that her voice was clear and steady, even while her heart hurt so much in her chest. She watched them boil and scramble up to the top of Jones. "There's a concept in biology known as emergence. That there can be a hierarchical form of organization not apparent at the lowest levels." She tapped the air of the hologram. "Each individual is behaving randomly, and yet in their numbers, there is a primitive form of organization there. They are following the 'nearest neighbor' rule—blindly following where the person next to them leads. If they are swarming up Jones, I can only imagine that they have an instinctive tropism for water—for the Bay. So though each individual doesn't know where he or she is going, the herd is heading for water."

Jon's jaw muscles clenched. "Can they swim?"

Could they swim? "I don't want to give a glib answer, but my instinct is to say no. Swimming requires motor control and co-ordination adjustments. I don't see any sign of that here. Many exhibit what could only be called spastic muscle movements, uncontrollable. That would be deadly in water. And I don't think they could coordinate their breathing enough to stay afloat." She looked up at him. "That's my considered opinion, but I don't know if I'd stake my life on it."

"If they are attracted to loud noises, maybe we could set up boom machines offshore. Watch them fall into the water like lemmings."

"Yes," she said slowly, turning the idea over in her mind. "That could work." She shook her head. "Do you know, that would never have occurred to me."

"No." His jaws snapped together with an audible click. "That's not the way your mind thinks. You are looking to understand their behavior. I just want to find ways to kill the fuckers." He slanted a look at her out of those ice blue eyes without turning his head. "Sorry."

Sophie closed her eyes, tried a smile. It was shaky and felt fake. "That's okay. Monsters are roaming the streets, Jon. Ripping each other to pieces. I'm not going to faint at the f-bomb."

The hologram suddenly switched from the peninsula to some kind of war room. "Jon."

It was Mac. He was sitting in a room with Catherine Young, Elle and her guy, the scarred man, Lucius Ward, and another man. He was a fireplug of a man, short—certainly next to Mac and Elle's guy and Ward—but very broad shouldered. He had a fleece plaid shirt and jeans on, but his short haircut, so extreme she could see scalp, and squared back shoulders spelled military, or at least former military, to her.

"Boss," Jon answered. "You don't need to tell us—trouble's on the way. We can see it for ourselves."

"Yeah." Mac aimed a big thumb at Catherine and Elle. "The geek squad has come up with some facts they think you should know."

Sophie felt like she was looking directly into Elle's eyes, the hologram was so lifelike. "They're swarming," she said before Elle could speak.

Elle dipped her head. "Yes, they are. Catherine and I have been observing them, with time lapses backward and forward. There's good news and bad news. Which one do you want first?"

Jon answered. "Bad news first. I can't imagine there's much good news."

"Okay." Elle hesitated. She was pale, stressed. "Soph . . ." Her voice broke and her Nick put a big arm around her. For the very first time, Sophie understood down to the bone what having a strong man at your side meant, the support it could give. She leaned back, just a little, and there Jon was. Tall, broad, solid. A pillar of strength.

She'd never believed in that whole man-woman thing. She'd always dated men who were basically her—cerebral and detached—but with a cylinder of flesh dangling between their legs that came in useful now and again. Her men had been narrow-shouldered, with pale undeveloped muscles, not too good with the physical, outside world. Bad drivers, hopeless at repairs—one boyfriend back in Chicago used to call her over to change lightbulbs, though he thanked her with food. He was a fabulous cook.

Not at any stage of her life had Sophie thought to *lean* on a man as a source of strength. She'd never had to. But now the tables were turned and Jon and everything he represented—the iron and steel world of battle, the world of sheer male physical strength—were as necessary to her as breathing. As a matter of fact, if she wanted to keep breathing, if she wanted to make it out of the trap of her flat and to safety, she was going to need Jon's qualities.

"The swarm grew through the night. It seems to be a universal phenomenon with the virus. We're seeing swarms forming in Oakland, in Sacramento. And, God, Soph. Los Angeles . . ."

Sophie gasped. The Los Angeles basin was one large catchment area, a geographical trap, with mountains to the north, east, south, and ocean to the west.

"Los Angeles is a nightmare." Elle's voice was shaky.

"San Diego's a little better," Nick picked up. "But not much. So here's what the San Francisco swarm looks like."

The hologram flickered and then there was a bird's-eye view of the Bay Area, much higher than the drones' eye view. For a moment, it looked like there had been a mudslide or a lava flow, oozing down the streets. Then the focus sharpened and it was clear that the streets were dark with infected swarming their way to the waterfront.

There was complete silence as they watched scenes that no human had ever seen before.

Elle cleared her throat. "Catherine and I have done some calculations, Soph. There's a definite tropism at work so the swarm attracts outliers. It's growing by the hour. But that also means that when the swarm has passed you, there will be a window of opportunity of, say, fifteen minutes with no infected nearby because they will all be caught up in the swarm. You can make your getaway then. We estimate that the swarm will pass by you completely by four P.M. Here—" The images tilted, the earth moving swiftly below. It followed the swarm to its edges, which could almost have been drawn. As the swarm moved, the edges were clear-cut, with no infected coming after the stragglers. "You'll have a clear shot after it passes."

Oh God, going out in broad daylight . . . Sophie looked up at Jon, whose face had tightened. Jon answered for her.

"Sophie thinks their eyesight is diminished in the dark. Wouldn't it be better to wait until after sundown?"

Mac was shaking his head. "Negative. There are apparently mini swarms forming all over the city. There's no guarantee that other swarms might not appear after dark. And you have only one set of NVGs. So make preparations to exfil around sixteen hundred hours. With luck, you'll be back in Haven before nightfall. And we can start manufacturing the vaccine."

Nick looked to his left, to the stocky ex-military man. "And so now for some good news . . ."

The man's voice was low, gruff. He dipped his head. "Jon. This is Snyder. Former General Snyder."

Sophie looked in surprise at Jon's jolt. Had that been a *growl*? His eyes shot blue ice, his entire body language that of hostility.

"Hold on, son." Snyder held up a hand with short thick fingers and a broad palm. "Before you go off the deep end, I fought the Pentagon tooth and nail over the court-martial. And I was invited to an early retirement for my pains. So don't you go growling at me, you hear?"

"Yeah? That's what Mac said. Well, it doesn't make much difference now. And what the fuck is the Pentagon doing for us now, huh?"

Snyder's mouth firmed, a flush appeared on his tanned cheeks. "We don't know. None of us can get in touch with anyone at the Pentagon. Anyone in Washington, actually."

Oh God. "Do you think—" It sounded so horrible Sophie had trouble articulating it. "Do you think they have cut California off? Can they do that?"

"They can." Snyder's jaw muscles jumped.

"We're on our own," Jon said, voice grim. "They abandoned us."

"We're on our own, son," Snyder confirmed. "But we're fighting back. Because the good news is that a lot of people have managed to circle the wagons. We can't communicate outside California but we've got a call out 24/7 to survivors and they are calling in. Unfortunately, there's not much we can do for individuals caught up on the roofs of their homes. But we've got whole communities that are bunkered down. We've managed fifteen air drops of weapons, explosives, food, and water so they can hold out until we can get the vaccine to them. We're ferrying supplies, evacuating the wounded—not infected wounded, just people who've been injured getting themselves to safety."

Sophie leaned forward. "Are you following Q-and-I protocols?" she asked urgently.

"Absolutely, we're following quarantine-and-isolation protocols." Catherine stepped into the monitor. "We're following CDC protocols, though isolation doesn't really apply here because we don't have any infected to isolate. It was deemed too dangerous."

"Yes, of course." Sophie ran through what she knew of CDC protocols. "We're looking at an engineered virus." Sophie kept her voice steady even though the thought of a scientist—a person dedicated to human knowledge—intentionally engineering this viral plague made her heartsick. "I don't have any hard data on the incubation period, but I suspect it is very short. It's important that we observe quarantine protocols."

Catherine and Elle had their heads bent over their tablets, entering data. "Got it," Catherine said, raising her head. "Anything else?"

Sophie hesitated. This didn't rise to the level of science, but they were operating in such darkness anything might be of help. "This is completely anecdotal, but from my observations, I noted several infected with light-colored eyes go from shadow to sunlight with no noticeable contraction of the pupils. I observed at least fifty cases of this through binoculars, but of course I couldn't conduct tests in controlled circumstances. Nonetheless, I feel that I can say that there is a statistically high probability that the virus fixes the pupils so that accommodation is impossible. Which of course would explain why they might have reduced vision at night. Their pupils are locked. So you might want to shine a bright light into everyone who comes into the quarantine sector and everyone you release into the general population. See if the pupils accommodate."

"We can broadcast that," said Snyder. "That would be really helpful if you can't distinguish between a normal injury and a bite. Because a lot of people are having problems putting down loved ones, even ones they know are infected."

"Particularly children," Elle added, face sad.

Oh yeah. Sophie repressed a shudder, imagining the situation . . . A mother, looking down at her stricken child. Her bitten, stricken child, who soon would become a monster. And she's the one who must decide to put the child down—before he or she turns, while it is still *her* child. Killing your child who is crying *mommy!*

*I hope you burn in hell, Charles Lee.* Dr. Charles Lee, head of Arka Pharmaceuticals. The man who had unleashed this hell on earth.

"Some of the fortified communities are gathering in refugees themselves," Snyder said, addressing Jon. "We're getting reports all the time of enclaves of uninfecteds."

"Make sure all quarantine-and-isolation protocols are followed to the letter!" Sophie said sharply.

Snyder stared directly at the camera and it was exactly as if he were staring her in the eyes. "Yes, ma'am. Doctor, sorry. I've been told in no uncertain terms that you are the expert, so we will do what you say and will continue to do so once you are back here, safe and sound. We really need that vaccine. Once we have it, we can start fighting back, reclaim some territory."

"Like we said, we should be back before nightfall," Jon added. "I hope to be airborne not long after sixteen hundred hours. I want to get out of Dodge as fast as we can."

"How long will the manufacture of the vaccine take, Doctor?" Snyder's eyes hadn't wavered from hers.

She hated being asked questions she didn't have a solid answer to. "That depends. I'm sorry to be vague but it depends. I've been told by Dr. Connolly—"

"Ross," Elle interrupted and turned bright red.

Sophie blinked. "I'm sorry?"

Elle nestled her head against the tall dark man who hadn't left her side. "I'm Elle Ross now, Soph." She looked up at the man standing next to her and simply glowed. "We got married last night. There's a nondenominational preacher here and we—we tied the knot."

Sophie brought a hand to her mouth and fought tears. A marriage. Amid all the misery and loss, a happy event. Two people swearing to love and protect each other forever in chaos and destruction. The wedding had been celebrated in what was essentially a refugee camp in the middle of a truly deadly pandemic but—two people had pledged their love to each other.

"Oh Elle . . ." Her voice broke and she took a second to steady it. "I'm so happy for you! A wedding in the middle of all this death. It's wonderful."

"Thank you, Dr. Daniels," Nick said with a solemn nod.

"Way to go, Nick," Jon said quietly.

"Yeah. This changes everything." Nick's head shifted slightly to look at Jon's image on his hologram. "Make us safe, Jon. Give us a fighting chance to turn this thing around."

Everyone froze. All of a sudden the background noise swelled, broke, like waves over rock.

Sophie looked around, spooked. Jon put a reassuring arm around her shoulders.

Mac consulted a monitor and spoke. "They're right on top of you, Jon. Boiling over Jones, it looks like there are thousands upon thousands of them. God. Report in when you're ready to leave."

"Stay safe, Soph." Elle reached a hand out. Though it looked as if she were touching air, Sophie knew that Elle had instinctively reached out to touch her. She lifted her own hand, and crazily, it felt for a moment as if they were touching. Sophie knew it was a construct of her imagination and yearning, but it made her feel better.

When she'd made that panicked phone call to Elle in the middle of the night before Arka's security got her, Sophie thought that they were both dead. A number of researchers and research subjects had gone missing and she knew she and Elle were next. She'd called Elle even though it was possible that a small delay was just long enough time for her to get caught. But Sophie desperately wanted *someone* to have a fighting chance. In the back of her mind, though, she'd believed they were doomed.

Arka recruited its security from the top levels of the military, paid them well, expected and got expert service. What hope did nerd scientists have against their quasi-military array? But even knowing it was hopeless, she'd had to try to warn her best friend.

And somehow, her best friend had managed to find the love of her life who had come roaring in to rescue her. And Sophie did manage to escape, because Arka's plans backfired disastrously.

So—you never know.

Keep fighting until you die.

The hologram winked off and it was as if an energy source had winked off as well. While they'd been talking, it was easy to imagine that they, too, were in a safe place surrounded by friends, or in Sophie's case, friend. Well, Catherine Young looked like the kind of woman who could become a friend too.

But with the hologram off, she and Jon were alone, marooned in a sea of infected, far from safety.

She shivered.

Jon put a heavy arm around her shoulders, and without thinking, without speaking, Sophie leaned into him. This was comfort at a very primitive level, but they'd been reduced to a primordial existence. Sophie rolled her head into the crook of his shoulder. Embracing a tall man could be awkward, but not with Jon. They seemed to fit together, instinctively.

He pulled her more tightly against him, arms around her back, and she felt his lips move against her hair. A kiss, perhaps.

"I'm not going to lie, Sophie, and say it will be easy, but we'll get out of here. You have my word."

Words were empty, only facts counted. That was the bedrock of Sophie's existence as a scientist. Facts came first, then the descriptive words. So she shouldn't feel comforted, but she did.

Jon clearly was a man who knew how to handle himself. If there was even the faintest hope of getting out of San Francisco alive and to this Haven, Jon could do it.

She couldn't, on her own. Not in a million years. She rested her forehead against his strong shoulder. "We have to," she murmured. "They're counting on us."

His arms tightened and she felt his chest expand to say something, but then the distant booming noise swelled, echoed around the streets. A frightening terrifying sound, so horrible she was frozen with panic for a moment. She couldn't do panic. People were counting on her.

She pushed away from him and looked up at his face. "They're here."

He nodded grimly.

Sophie pushed a panic that was primordial, instinctive, away from her. She gathered calm around her as if it were her white lab coat. She straightened her shoulders, took a deep breath. She was a scientist, and had to function as one if they were going to get out of this alive. "Does your scanner have recording functions? Voice and video?"

Jon had stepped back, too, watching her carefully, taking his cues from her. "Yes," he answered.

"Okay. When they hit Beach Street, I'm going to observe as much of the swarm as I can. So record the scene and record what I say, and we can analyze it all when we get to Haven. I don't think anyone else will have a trained eye on a swarm going by."

He nodded. "Is there anything I can do to make us safe in here?"

"Well . . ." Sophie reasoned it out. "They are obviously not organized enough to pick locks, but they are strong and have the added strength of numbers. Few make it up stairs, but in case some do, spray more perfume around the door and erect a barricade." She cocked her head, listening. "I think we have a few minutes still."

Jon moved fast. In a few moments, he'd sprayed not only perfume but squeezed lemons around the door sill and crushed cloves of garlic. Then he'd easily moved her immensely heavy Italian *madia* against the door, then shoved her steel-reinforced Poltrona Frau sofa against it. He'd just slid the sofa tightly against the *madia* when the noise rose to an unbearable crescendo.

Sophie met his eyes. "They're here," she whispered.

*Mount Blue Haven*

Elle turned away from the holographic monitor, unease in her heart. As always, Nick seemed to have a secret passageway into her thoughts. He held her shoulders in a hard grip.

"I know you're worried about your friend, and I won't bullshit you. They're in a dangerous position. But trust me when I say she's got the right guy at her side. If it can be done, Jon will get her out and bring her back to you."

She tried a smile. "Back to us. You're going to love her." She turned to everyone in the room. "Catherine, you're going to love her too. Mac . . . I guess the best I can say is that Mac won't eat her. Probably."

Mac gave a low growl.

Nick's dark face was usually sober, serious, deep lines bracketing his mouth. He rarely smiled and the lines in his face reflected that. He didn't exactly smile, but his face lightened for a moment. "Mac's not that bad. I can't say his bark is worse than his bite because . . . well it's not. If you're on his bad side, you're toast. But we're on his good side. And of course if she becomes Catherine's friend, Mac will be putty in her hands, just as he is in yours."

Elle pulled back, the idea so ludicrous it jolted her. She turned to the huge man by Catherine's side. He was by any measure a frightening-looking man. Tall, huge, badly scarred, always scowling. "Mac, are you putty in my hands?"

He gave another low growl, offset by his wife's light laugh. "Certainly." She patted her husband's huge shoulder. "He's a real pussycat."

Mac rolled his eyes, but his gaze softened when he looked down at his wife. Mac's devotion to Catherine was obvious to all, even in the short time Elle had been in Haven. She couldn't resist. "You mean if I asked him to bring me coffee, he would?"

"Now, wait a minute," Mac began, then stopped when his wife elbowed him in the ribs. They were so encased with muscle, he probably didn't even feel it. "Yes," he said through his teeth.

Nick gave a half smile. "Oh yeah. But don't get too cocky."

It wasn't a laughing moment, but Elle gave a choked laugh. "No." She shook her head. "I will definitely not get too cocky around Mac."

"Okay." Catherine clapped her hands. "Elle and I need to get back to the infirmary. Let us know when the raid team gets back with the last of the lab equipment, and we'll get set up for when Jon and Sophie make it back. General, how many more refugees will there be in the next twenty-four hours?"

"Just call me Snyder, ma'am," the General said. "We're in contact with several more communities just in the last hour. We're setting up a priority list now, based on their supplies and ammo and the number of infected they're seeing. I reckon we'll have another two hundred today and maybe four hundred to-morrow."

"General—Snyder." Elle turned to the stocky former general.

"Factor into your plans that we could ship cases of vaccine perhaps as soon as thirty-six hours from now. At some point, if we get enough of the population vaccinated and enough infected die, we might be able to turn the tide. And if we want to have some kind of basis for afterward, we need people protecting production plants and power plants and hospitals."

At her words, the men in the room visibly relaxed for a moment. Clearly none of them had thought of an afterward, they were so busy dealing with the present and dangerous emergency.

"Good thinking, Dr. Connolly—"

"Dr. Ross," Nick growled.

"Dr. Ross. Sorry." Snyder ran a broad palm over the stubble on his head. "Not thinking straight. But it's great to know that some people are planning beyond the moment. I'll pass on the word, give people some hope. Because right now, it's not looking good."

"No," Elle said softly. It wasn't looking good. Pandora's box had been opened and monsters had come out. But there had been something hidden at the bottom of Pandora's box. Something wonderful.

Hope.

# Chapter 7

*San Francisco*
*Beach Street*

They came in a flood, a bubbling madhouse tide of humanity. At first only five or six infected came running and Sophie let out a pent-up breath. She'd been bracing herself . . .

And then they came, a solid phalanx of infected, obviously down from Jones, so many they erupted right into Beach and left toward Ghirardelli Square.

With a raised eyebrow at Jon, Sophie pushed the button that cracked the window open a little, just enough to stick her head out. She pulled her head back in immediately, terrified.

It was like a river in full spate, spilling over sidewalks, down every single road, rising on the backs of the fallen, some almost reaching the second floor. When the river of infected reached Beach, she closed the window back shut. With the window open, the noise level was almost unbearable, a booming screech that the ear couldn't correlate to human noise. It was more like a huge piece of broken machinery.

Even with the triple-glazed window shut, the noise level was as high as a rock concert, only there was no backbeat. There was no beat at all, nothing rational, just loud noise emanating from once human throats.

It was almost impossible for the human eye to even distinguish individual forms. The onslaught of bodies was intertwined, limbs thrashing in such an enclosed area that fists took out eyes, legs tripped up bodies as a matter of course. They came in thousands, maybe tens of thousands, so densely packed that the bodies bent inward the closed steel garage doors and the metal barricades of the tourist shops.

Men in suits, students in T-shirts, housewives, children, of all races. They all looked alike in a horrible way, all reduced to violent mindless beings. All with the same look on their blood-streaked faces. Eyes open so wide the whites were visible all around the irises, mouths open to emit those ululating howls, heads swiveling.

Sophie surreptitiously wiped damp hands on her yoga pants and asked, voice low, "Can you take a temperature reading on the scanner?"

She didn't dare look at Jon. She didn't want him to see the horror she felt. She had to keep some kind of detachment, she had to close down her heart, that part of her that couldn't bear to watch what was happening below.

"I can't read individual temperatures," Jon answered. "But I have a general thermal reading of 102.5 degrees."

"If that's the average, some will be over 104. That's not sustainable for long. The constitution of the infected has already been severely compromised."

They both watched the violent scenes below, that dark mass of bodies swarming, killing, dying . . .

They would all die soon. It was just a question of whether they'd take the world down with them or whether something could be salvaged.

"Hand me your scanner, please."

Jon handed it over silently. Sophie reached the menu that would show heart rates, but all she saw was a flow of three-digit numbers too fast to pinpoint any one number.

"I can't tell individual rates. There are too many of them. But they are all accelerated." She handed it back. "Is the record function on?"

Jon held it up. "It is now."

Sophie wiped her mind of everything but scientific detachment and spoke clearly, for the record. "We are observing what at a conservative guess is one thousand infected currently swarming the street, with more stretching all the way to the horizon. The overall count must be in the thousands, possibly tens of thousands." She leaned a little forward to observe better. "All surface areas appear to be swarmed. They are not breaking into stores but rather the sheer number of them, pressing against both sides of the streets, is caving in the unprotected storefronts. They are pouring into every gap, every window, every open door, every alleyway. For the moment we see no signs of them making their way up to second stories, but the sheer weight of them might make that inevitable."

Sophie pressed her lips together and looked up at Jon, then at her door. He nodded reassuringly. They'd made the best barricade they could. And her door had a titanium core. They were as protected as they could be.

*Observe, Sophie!*

A strong man in a track suit wrenched the arm of a young girl out of its socket and tore it off. Sophie jolted and felt Jon's strong hand on her shoulder. "Steady," he whispered.

Yes, steady. They had to understand this to conquer it.

"There"—Sophie's mouth was completely dry and she had to lick her lips—"There is a strong tropism in action. The—ah, the infected battle violently with each other, but they are sticking close together." She tried to study the faces running past. "I see definite signs of dehydration, whether because they have been running for hours or because they are unable to procure water for themselves is an open question. Turning on a tap or opening a bottle—it is unclear whether they retain the cognitive skills to do that. Or even the fine motor skills. I see no signs of organized behavior."

The roar of the crowd was deafening. She hungered for her noise-canceling headset, but that would be merely cutting herself off from the world. That couldn't be allowed to happen, not when the world had suddenly turned so feral.

"I see—" she counted silently. "I see about one in twenty falling and disappearing in the crowd. Simply falling and being trodden over. If they were dying before, when they fall they are definitely dead. No one could survive the trampling in that crowd. I would estimate that soon more and more in the swarm will fall. When the swarm passes, the streets will be littered with the dead."

She glanced up at Jon's grim face and he nodded. She knew he would factor that into his calculations for their escape.

The noise was deafening. She had to raise her voice to be heard over the booming sounds of raw, piercing screams. The sounds of humans gone utterly mad. Their blank, vicious blood-ied faces was a sight taken from the depths of hell. No painter, not even Hieronymus Bosch, could have even imagined what she and Jon were seeing.

If there was a hell, this was it.

It was too much. A coldness descended upon her soul, as if the temperature of the world had suddenly dropped.

She was chilled down to her bones, a cold that had nothing to do with the temperature of the air but the situation of the world. It froze her mind too. She looked up at Jon, opening her mouth then closing it again. She wanted to tell him she couldn't do this, couldn't observe this massive vision of hell any longer, but her lungs wouldn't fill with enough air to form the words. She could barely breathe.

Jon somehow understood. He took her by the shoulders and pulled her to him. Oh God. Warmth. He was this huge column of warm muscle. She leaned into him, trying to absorb some of his heat, take it into herself.

"Come, Sophie. You're in shock."

Jon led her into the bedroom and made her get under the covers. She could barely walk, had to think about putting one foot in front of the other. Had to actively try not to stumble.

She didn't have to think about not falling down, though. Jon had a big arm around her waist and she felt like she couldn't fall down. He wouldn't let her.

On the way to the bed, Jon grabbed a cashmere throw that was lying across her sofa and wrapped it around her. Once she was sitting in bed, covers up to her chin, the throw around her shoulders, she knew intellectually she shouldn't be feeling any cold, but she was. It was all-pervasive, muscle and bone deep. No amount of swaddling could dissipate it.

Jon disappeared. While he was gone, it was no-Jon time. Time that didn't matter, wasn't observable. She neither thought nor felt. It was like being in suspended animation. She couldn't even register the booming, crashing noises from outside. Her bedroom looked out over an internal courtyard so the noises came over the rooftops.

A huge boom sounded, not a human noise. Some explosion somewhere. These were all thoughts that drifted through her mind without her understanding them fully.

"Here." Startled, she looked up. Jon had a steaming cup of something on one of her pretty flower-themed trays. "Drink it all down."

He put his big hand under the cup when she picked it up. He'd been right to. She seemed to have lost all muscle strength. The cup bobbled in her hand and the hot liquid would have splashed on her, burned her, if he hadn't steadied it.

His eyes were as steady as his hands. "Drink," he said quietly.

She drank. Coughed. Her vanilla tea had been laced with plenty of the aged Glenfiddich she kept on a sideboard. There was honey in there too. A drink she definitely needed.

He stood by the bedside until she drank the entire concoction, then moved to the other side of the bed, removed his boots, and got under the covers with her. With his back against the headboard, he reached for her, snuggled her against him.

The hot tea, the hot man. Warmth penetrated and with it, the numbness that had protected her dissipated.

It was all too much. She turned her face into his shoulder and wept.

Jon held Sophie as she cried. It wasn't an emotional crying jag like some women had, to get rid of stress. This was harsher, deeper, more desperate. It was a lament for the world. It was endless, bottomless grief.

He didn't even try to shush her or comfort her with words. There were no words, anyway. He simply held her. He held her at that moment not as a man held a woman he was falling for, but as a comrade held a fallen teammate. Sophie was grievously wounded, and if the wound wasn't actually bleeding, it was deadly nonetheless.

Sophie cried as if something inside her was broken, beyond healing.

Jon understood that, down to his bones. His world had been broken beyond healing in childhood.

She had one hand clutching his neck and the other holding his side. He held her tightly, one hand along her narrow back, feeling the stuttering rise and fall of her back as she sobbed and gasped for air. She was crying with her entire body, every muscle clenched in grief. In her bedroom, the sounds of the world outside were muted, her sobs audible above the shrieks and yells of the infected.

Jon held her more tightly. The world was drowning and the woman who held the key to healing was grieving in his arms. They had a perilous mission to undertake. She needed to vent her emotions now, in a safe environment, in his arms. A meltdown like this in the field would be deadly.

He couldn't fault her, though. The depth of her sorrow was a sign of the depth of her emotions. She wouldn't be what she was if she couldn't feel the horror of what was happening down to her very soul.

Something, some primordial instinct, told Jon that Sophie Daniels had never encountered the full depravity of the world. Granted, this was far worse than the depravity and heartlessness

Jon had seen in his parents and their drug-addled "friends." This was the whole world falling, not one small corner of it. But he felt as if he'd been somehow inoculated against the grief she was feeling, able to bear up under its terrible burden. If there was anyone who could understand her, and stand for her, it was him.

So he held her, giving her the warmth and the unspoken support of his body while she cried out her rage and frustration and despair. She wept hot tears, holding nothing back. It wasn't female tears of frustration but the tears of a soul in torment. She wept until she could barely breathe, breaths coming in shaking gasps. Her heart fluttered under his hand, fast and heavy, as if she were running a marathon. He tucked her more tightly against him, her tears making his T-shirt damp. He didn't care. She needed this. He almost envied her. Many times in his life he wished he could have wept out his rage, and hatred, and despair, but he never could. He just put it away somewhere deep inside where he could pretend it had dissipated.

Sophie wept a storm, and like all storms, it was too violent to last. She finally cried herself out through sheer exhaustion.

The sobs quieted, stopped. She was leaning heavily against him, as if without his support she'd collapse. That was fine. Jon would be her support for as long as she needed it. Beyond, even.

Her heart rate under his hand slowed, her breathing slowed, too, became regular. Finally she was quiet. He lifted his head and looked down at her. All he could see were absurdly long eyelashes clumped together from the tears and pale, high cheekbones. She was so still, the quiet after the storm. He hoped she'd fallen asleep. She needed to rest. Rest healed, he knew that. Just like he knew that she was going to be caught up in the lab in Haven as soon as they arrived. From what he understood, the lab was working around the clock and she seemed as dedicated as Catherine and Elle. She'd hit the ground running and would work around the clock too.

So if she could find some peace and rest in sleep, all the better.

But she wasn't asleep. She let out a long sigh. Her right hand had been tightly clutching the damp white cotton of his shirt. She opened her fist, then tried to straighten out the wrinkles where she'd clutched the material.

She sighed again, her entire narrow rib cage lifting and dropping. "I'm so sorry," she whispered.

Oh God, no. Jon dug his fingers into her thick dark hair, releasing a faint fragrance of lemon and strawberries. He massaged the back of her head, her neck. She was a knot of tension.

"Don't be sorry. You're a doctor, you know that tears release . . ." He racked his brain, trying to remember an article he'd read in the waiting room of the base doctor, there for his annual checkup. "Some kind of hormone. Don't remember which one, but one of the good ones."

"Endorphins," she said.

"There you go." He lifted his head again so he could see her face. Her lips were slightly upturned. Good. She turned her face up to his, and he saw with a sigh that she was one of those women who still looked lovely even after a crying jag. His heart gave a painful pulse in his chest. She looked beautiful and solemn. Sad, but not afraid.

She lifted a hand and cupped his jaw. Her hand was warm and soft. The coldness of shock had dissipated. "You didn't cry. We might be watching the end of the world. We have monsters running around outside, lost to us, but you didn't cry. I wish I could be like you. I can hardly breathe from the sadness. From the grief and rage."

Jon opened his mouth to say something soothing and meaningless, but something else popped out. Something dangerous, from the depths of his being. "My parents sold me when I was nine years old."

He froze. *Where the fuck had that come from? Oh fuck, oh fuck.*

He'd never told anyone, ever. Not even the military shrink they'd sent him to before allowing him to join Ghost Ops. The shrink had probed, like the proverbial blind man who senses something but cannot see it, but Jon was hard as a rock. He presented nothing but a flat granite face. The shrink knew, because it was in his files, that he'd been sent to a series of foster homes from the age of ten on, and that he'd joined the army as soon as he legally could. The shrink could pick at him and pry all he wanted, but the fucker'd got jackshit out of him.

The condition for joining Ghost Ops was that you had no family or friends. No one to care for and no one to care about you. Their pasts were wiped out and they became Ghosts, men who cast no shadow. That kind of man doesn't come from a happy, loving family. They all came from severe dysfunction.

The only person who had an inkling that there was something behind his smooth California surfer persona other than a badass warrior was Catherine McEnroe, Mac's wife. And that was only because she had this freaky . . . ability. Skill. Power. Whatever the fuck it was, it was scary shit. She'd touched him, eyes wide, and knew with that one touch that he'd been badly betrayed. She didn't have any details but she knew the heart of it.

So he had no idea why he opened his mouth and that came out. With Sophie Daniels of all people. They'd fucked, yeah. Well, it had been sex, but not like any sex he'd ever had before. He'd never had anything like that intensity, that degree of closeness, that sense of falling out of himself and into someone else.

But though he was willing to admit, in the deepest, darkest most hidden part of himself, that his heart might have been involved in the sex—either that or he had a cardiac condition—he would never have revealed anything about himself. About his secrets.

Except . . . he had.

He tried not to stiffen, not give any importance to his words but she wasn't buying it. She looked up at him, wide-eyed. Not shocked, not revulsed. Just sad. And waiting for more. Nobody could say that line and shut up afterward.

"They were drug addicts," he said, then froze again. He'd never even said the words out loud. The instant he'd joined the military, he'd felt like a page had been turned, the past wiped out. But the past was never completely wiped out. It was always there, waiting to bite you in the ass.

He wanted to continue, but something had happened to his throat. It wasn't working. He couldn't talk, he couldn't even swallow.

She broke the long silence. "That must have been hard," she said gently.

Hard. Yes, very hard. Two people who were supposed to look after him, more often than not stoned out of their minds. The money that should have gone into rent and food going into their veins. As a very little kid he'd more than once been terrified that they'd died, and in a way he'd been right. They *had* died, just not their bodies.

Sophie said nothing. Her deep blue eyes searched his, not breaking contact. Not disgusted, not frightened.

His throat eased, just a little. He found he could swallow.

"I don't remember much of my childhood. Probably better that way. I remember when I was around seven or eight finding money for the drugs became this big deal. I think they'd managed to hold down some part-time jobs to feed the habit but then they lost those. The car went. My dad or my mom would disappear for a few days. They were taken in for petty theft, then let loose. Like you'd release a fish that wasn't worth the effort of catching."

Once, in a compulsion he'd been unable to resist, he'd hacked the Sacramento police department files for the relevant years and followed his parents' decline. His mother had been arrested seven times for solicitation. She'd turned to hooking to feed the habit, with his father's blessing.

Reading the file made him feel filthy that he shared their blood. If he could have scrubbed his DNA, he would have.

He never read any files pertaining to them after that. He didn't even know if they were alive or dead, and had no desire to know. He suspected they were dead, though. Twenty-five years ago they'd been weak and emaciated. There was no way they could have survived their addiction.

Sophie had somehow snuggled closer to him, closer than when she'd been weeping. A hand lay on his chest, right over his heart. It was crazy, but it felt like her hand emanated heat, reaching deep through bone and muscle to reach the frozen bits of himself. Catherine's touch had been like that too. Warm and soothing. Sophie's touch was that, but also—though that was crazy—somehow healing.

The scenes came to him in dreams. Nightmares. He'd wake up sweating and panicked, breath coming harshly, heart pounding. For a moment after he woke up, he'd be back there, in the filthy hovel he shared with his parents, small and weak and utter prey. For a second, he was nine years old and his parents were selling him to a man who terrified him.

For the first time, he could see the scene as a man, not a terrified child. The images still disgusted him, but they didn't frighten him. The man who at the time had seemed like a powerful, malevolent giant, wasn't a giant anymore. Jon was bigger, faster, stronger. Perfectly capable of defending himself. No scumbag like the pedophile pimp who'd bought him could ever hurt him again.

He only wished he could travel back in time and kill the fucker.

"A man came to our house. I had just turned nine, though of course no one celebrated my birthday. The man who came to the house was tall, large. He"—Jon's nose wrinkled—"he smelled. He had some kind of heavy cologne. Men's colognes still nauseate me. Good thing I joined the military and didn't go into, say, advertising. I'd have spent all my time embracing the porcelain god."

To this day, he had to swallow bile if he stood next to a man wearing cologne. Women's perfumes didn't have the same effect at all.

She was watching his eyes carefully. She'd smiled a little when he mentioned barfing. Good.

For some god-awful unfathomable reason, his subconscious had started him on this trip at the wrongest possible time. He didn't want to spook her or bring her lower than she already was. But he was helpless to stop. The words were coming out, and there seemed to be no way to block them.

"But beneath the cologne was something else, something

horrifying. Some sick smell we recognize at the animal level. Something that signals there's something horribly wrong with the person."

"I've had that sensation a couple of times," Sophie said quietly. "It is a smell and it's hormonal. And it probably evolved as a biomarker for the tribe to detect and control psychopaths."

"I wish we still lived in tribes, then," he said quietly. Fuck, yeah. If he'd lived in a tribe, the members of the tribe would have looked after their young. A Harlan Popper would never have been allowed to stay in the tribe. He'd have been quietly taken away to some secluded spot and clubbed to death by the village elders.

Civilization was overrated.

"My parents had been very agitated the past few days. With hindsight, they'd run through their money, sold everything that could be sold, including my mother's sexual favors, and they were entering cold turkey. They had one more thing to sell."

"You," she said softly.

"Me."

Sophie was listening to him with every sense she had, it seemed. Through her eyes and her hand on his chest, as if she could soak up every nuance of the sorry story through her skin.

Her hand was very warm, soothing. He could feel the warmth soaking deep into his muscles.

He needed every bit of that warmth now. "It was clear who the guy was. Certainly it would have been clear to an adult. I looked him up . . . later." When he'd been far away, in time and space. "He had a rap sheet that went on forever. He was a sex predator down to his bones, but since he ran one of the largest pedophile rings in the world, he always had the money to buy the best lawyers in the business. Something like ten thousand kids passed through his hands, but he never did a day of time."

Sophie's face tightened, turned fierce. "Someone should have shot him."

Oh yeah. Someone should have shot him. Jon had thought of it himself, when he'd first looked Popper up. By that time he'd been trained in the fine art of shooting people. When scrolling through the darknet for news of Popper, he'd started making travel arrangements in his head, asking for a few days off, deciding which weapon he'd use. And then he found the last bit of news. The fucker had gone ahead and died without him. From a pointed object being skewered through his heart.

Couldn't have happened to a nicer guy.

"I was nine but I was undernourished, so I looked even younger. I was a small kid—"

She glanced up into his eyes, dropped her glance to his chest and shook her head. Yeah, he wasn't small anymore. He made sure he became strong and stayed strong. "I'm not small now. And I know how to fight. The military taught me to use every single weapon, including hands and feet, really well. But then— then I think I must have had 'prey' tattooed in invisible ink on my forehead. I think when Popper saw me he actually smacked his lips."

Though he'd never told the story to a living soul—even if he relived it often in his nightmares, waking up shaking and sweaty—he found it easy to tell her. For the first time, he felt a distance from this. Sophie was like a human buffer, providing a safe space, as if he were recounting something that had happened to someone else.

Telling Sophie felt right. Felt, even . . . healing. He would have cut his own tongue off rather than spill the sorry story to the military shrink, but Sophie? A woman he'd known for less than twenty-four hours? It felt right, crazy as that sounded.

"I even remember the amount Popper paid. Ten thousand dollars. To my parents, at that time broke and strung out, it must have seemed like Christmas and their birthdays and the Fourth of July all at once. They could stay high for a long time on that kind of money. I remember Popper handing over an envelope and my dad scrambling to open it and count the money. Popper led me away before my dad could finish counting. I was screaming at him, screaming at Popper, wriggling and kicking. My dad looked up from the money and stared straight at Popper. I remember that so clearly. He didn't even look at me. I was already gone from his head. He just said, 'Slap him and he'll shut up.' And started counting again."

"God," Sophie whispered. Her eyes were wet.

"Yeah." Jon reached up with his thumb to catch the tear that fell.

"Go on." Her hand was even hotter now, this weird warmth that sank right into his bones. The memory of this had haunted him all his life, but now . . . now it felt like he was telling a story about someone else, long ago, in a distant land.

"Popper wrestled me into the car. He must have sedated me because I woke up with a raging headache, hugely thirsty. It was almost night. We were somewhere I didn't recognize. The car had stopped, Popper was getting gas. I tried the door and it opened. He hadn't bothered switching on the child lock. He must have thought I'd stay out for much longer. I was covered with a blanket. I bunched the blanket together so that in the dark it would look like I was still under it. I made it to the back of the station. I peeked out to see his reaction, but he just got into the car and drove off. I stole a couple of bottles of water stored out back, together with some energy bars. Then I sneaked into the back of a pickup. I had no idea where the pickup was going and didn't care. I'd get off at gas stations and get onto another pickup. I ended up in Ohio. My last ride happened to be a good guy." He smiled at the memory. A fireplug of a man, short cropped gray hair, wide smile, huge heart. "Mickey Gardener. Who happened to be chief of police in Oroville, Ohio. He found me asleep in his off-duty pickup. I'd been traveling for days, had lost all sense of time. My ribs stuck out and I was sleep deprived and exhausted, and at first I couldn't talk. Didn't have the energy. He took me to the local clinic, where I was hydrated, fed, and checked for injuries. There was some kind of mixup with child services, so I stayed in the clinic longer than necessary. But after a few days in which I was fed well and slept in a bed, I realized that not talking was a really good strategy. Gardener sat down with me for half an hour, a really silent half hour, in which he asked me where I came from, how I came to be in the pickup, where my family was. And I just stonewalled him. I figured if I didn't talk they couldn't know where to send me back. And they didn't, because my parents sure as hell hadn't reported me missing. I stayed with the Gardeners for a couple of months, but I couldn't stay forever. His wife had MS and could barely get through her day. So I went through a series of foster homes. I know a lot of people complain about foster homes, but to me they were heaven. Plenty of food, clean clothes. Compared to what I grew up with, it was heaven on earth. And then I joined . . . the military."

He'd been selected immediately for Special Forces until the CIA's military arm went fishing and scooped him right up. No need to say that. No need to say that they'd recognized the killer in him immediately.

But it wasn't the killing that attracted him to the military, it was the camaraderie. Working hard together for the same thing. He'd loved every second of the team-building exercises.

"I'll bet you found comradeship and purpose in the military," Sophie said quietly.

*Bingo.* Jesus, how could she read him so clearly?

"Yeah." He swallowed. "I loved it. Loved everything about it. I loved working with a lot of smart people toward a common goal."

She smiled. "Sounds like science. I love that aspect of it too. Science isn't one lone crazy person with a microscope shouting, *Eureka!* It's a community of men and women throughout the world working together, building on each other's discoveries. It's very powerful, working with others."

Jon stopped, thought about it. "Yeah. This is the first time I looked at it that way. I guess the military life must be a lot like science." Except in the military they wore body armor and whacked people instead of watching microscope holograms in lab coats. But except for that—yeah, pretty much the same thing. "It changed my life. But then—"

"You were betrayed again. Or so you thought. By your captain," she said quietly.

He nodded.

"So we founded Haven. Everyone up there is working their ass off to save whatever can be salvaged. And the point of this long sorry story—" Jon picked up her hand where it lay on his chest, warming the area around his heart, and kissed her fingers. Damned if he couldn't swear his lips felt warmer. "The point is that even in truly awful times, when good people work together, great things can be done."

Sophie smiled, though the smile didn't touch her beautiful

eyes. "There's more you're not telling me. Lots more. But I get your message. Do you think—do you think there's much hope?"

The noise from the streets grew suddenly louder. It had been a harsh rumble all along, but the screams swelled, filling the room. She jumped when a loud boom went off. Gas mains exploding somewhere probably. Jon had been trained not to jump at unexpected noises but she hadn't been. At the boom, she took in a quick, surprised breath.

Her fingers trembled in his.

She was worried. Well, fuck, so was he. But he wasn't about to add to her worry. He kissed her hand again. "Yes, I think there's hope. Mac and Nick and the captain—and apparently General Snyder who was a great commander—are working hard to provide shelter for as many refugees as possible, and helping as many communities as they can to remain intact and fortified. They're working round the clock. They're working on it right now. Catherine and Elle are setting up a lab and, knowing them, vaccines will be rolling off the assembly line right after we get back. Those two women are amazing. I think there's a good chance we can save a whole big chunk of the state of California. We've got a lot of good, smart people on our side, and we're all working together on this. And in answer to the question you're about to ask"—he let go of her hand and rubbed his thumb over the worry lines between her eyebrows—"Yes, we're going to make it. I'll get you to Haven. I've never failed a mission yet."

Well, that wasn't quite true. He had failed one. The lab outside Cambridge, a clusterfuck of epic proportions, but only because they'd been betrayed and ambushed. That one didn't count. He wiped it from his mind and made sure that the truth of the matter—that he was going to get her and the vaccine case safely back to Haven no matter what—was in his voice, in his touch, in his gaze.

In his kiss.

Because, well, there was no resisting her. Not when chaos and death were just outside. They didn't matter right now because in here, in this bed, he had a magical woman in his arms.

Oh God. That heat he felt from her hands was magnified tenfold when he held her. Warmth penetrating him all over, so deep, so hot that he felt it even where he wasn't actually touching her.

He slid her clothes off, then his, then turned, adjusted and— *Oh yes*. Just like this. Perfect. Lying on her, feeling heat all along his front, from the top of his head to his toes, her mouth giving heat, her breasts against his chest almost glowing with heat. She slid her legs open in welcome, hugging his hips with her thighs and . . . oh man. Blazing heat like a little oven against the tip of his dick. Warm, welcoming. He slid a little inside because he'd die if he didn't. He didn't even have to think of it, his cock moved all on its own. Feeling that incredibly warm welcome, he was halfway into her when warning bells went off in his head.

Something was missing. Something he should be doing.

He released her mouth—it was damned hard to do because her mouth, all on its own, was an incredible source of pleasure—and nuzzled the side of her face, her neck. His lips were on her ear when he whispered, "Foreplay. Forgot. Again."

She'd been rubbing against him like a cat and she suddenly stilled.

"What?" The exhale of breath made a lock of his hair move, brushed against his ear, gave him goose bumps. He was half in her and wondered if she could feel his heartbeat there, inside her.

"Foreplay," he groaned. He'd forgotten all about it. The Cool Dude, forgetting foreplay. Wow, that was a first. He was good with the ladies. He knew he was never going to stick around for very long, so he made sure he got it right the first time— because chances were there wasn't going to be a second time. Certainly never a third or a fourth.

So yeah, he had foreplay down pat. Took his time, did it right. Took so long sometimes, he started thinking of other things, like the time he was reviewing a combat plan while going down on a woman. She'd had to tug on his hair to get him to stop. Foreplay was automatic for him, something he did as a matter of rote.

"Don't need it." She sighed and lifted her hips so he slid more deeply inside her. He groaned, tightened his buttocks, and pushed into her fast.

Of all the women in the world, he broke his iron-clad rule with beautiful, smart, delicate Sophie Daniels. Pure instinct took over. Foreplay was unthinkable when all he wanted was to slide as fast as possible right into that sleek, welcoming warmth. His mouth covered hers when he slid all the way in and he could feel the surprise and pleasure in her mouth, in her kiss. She groaned into his mouth. He felt the vibration more than heard the sound.

He stayed in her, keeping still. Not daring to move an inch.

Telling her his secrets had unhinged something inside him, something that had always been as tightly closed as a bank vault. It was cracking open. *He* was cracking open.

It unsettled him, rattled him. He couldn't keep his boundaries straight. He was breaking open and his self-control was oozing through the cracks.

He was in her so deeply, it was hard to tell where he stopped and she began. All the boundaries were fuzzy, fluid. Was that his heartbeat tripping wildly? How could it? His heart was always a steady sixty beats per minute, even under fire. He didn't do pounding hearts. But one of their hearts was pounding and he couldn't tell which one.

It felt like his entire body was pulsing, quaking, in the middle of a meltdown. He pressed into her more tightly, held her closer, kissed her more deeply. Because though she was the cause of the meltdown there was also some nebulous something that could be found deep within her body. Something that felt perilously close to . . . peace.

Which was absurd of course. Jon wasn't a peaceful kind of guy. And now was not a good time to be kum-bay-yaing, not with monsters raging through the streets. But somehow he was able to switch part of his eternal vigilance off and simply sink deeper into this woman, this one magical woman who made him magically feel better.

And then those tender thoughts blew away like smoke because Sophie, tired of him holding himself still deep inside her, started moving. Her hips withdrew slightly and she pulled herself up against him by pressing down on his ass with her heels. The movement made her moan and she writhed against him.

It was shockingly erotic.

He pulled back, watched her face. Their smiles were gone. He clenched his teeth against the pleasure as he moved back into her slowly. She closed her eyes, arched her back. Whispered, "More. Harder."

It was as if he'd been held back by ropes that were now cut, unleashing him.

"Open your eyes." His voice was low, hard.

Her eyes opened, but only halfway, irises glowing a deep navy blue. Slightly unfocused.

No, he wanted her attention. He wanted her focused on *him*, on the sex they were having.

He'd never had this reaction before. As long as the woman seemed to be enjoying herself, he was cool. She could be thinking anything she wanted. Hell, she could be fantasizing about some actor or singer for all he cared as long as she was having a good time. But right now, he wanted Sophie Daniels to know that she was fucking *him*. Jon Ryan.

Her eyes opened, startled. They were so gorgeous, such a deep, deep blue, like the ocean far at sea. Rimmed with dark, ridiculously long lashes.

"Look at me. Look at *us*," he said, his voice guttural. He lifted his entire torso up with his arms, away from her, so she had a good look down to where they were joined. The movement pushed him even more deeply inside her.

She looked down at them. God. His lighter pubic hair meshed with the trim triangle of dark sable between her thighs. He could see the lips of her sex clutched around his cock, pale pink on the outside, redder where the lips unfolded to accommodate him. The two of them looked like some erotic statue from the dawn of time, ancient gods fused together. He *felt* fused to her, his cock having somehow found its natural place, inside her.

He looked down at her, at all the places he hadn't visited. Her breasts—pale, with dark rose nipples. He hadn't even kissed them. What was that about? He could make a woman come by sucking on her nipples alone. His eyes dropped from her breasts down to her smooth belly, narrow waist flaring to round hips. God. Kissing her belly alone should have taken him an hour. And down, down to her sex.

Another place he hadn't visited with his mouth yet.

He didn't mind going down on women. It was fun, got them wet, sometimes made them come. A great threefer. His mouth hadn't even gone near her pussy, which was amazing. He went straight to business with Sophie, had done so the moment he'd fallen through her door, as if being inside her was this huge immense goal, whereas normally he enjoyed those little side streets.

They both had to live, just had to. He was going to get them safely out of Dodge, no question. He couldn't die before doing all the things he wanted to do to her. He hadn't touched her enough, hadn't sucked her nipples, hadn't kissed her pussy.

Just the thought of that—of his mouth closing on the lips of her sex, tongue in her, exactly as if kissing her mouth, taking his time . . .

His cock swelled in her and she gasped.

"Felt that?" He was trembling, sweating. His voice came out in gasps. "Know what that was? I just now thought of going down on you. I imagined my mouth on you, licking inside you, right where my cock is now. That's what that was about."

The words were hard, harsh. Harder than he usually used. Women liked prettier terms than that and he obliged them. Who cared? He could be a little poetic when he had to be. When it was worth his while.

He couldn't do that now. No pretty words, no poetic terms. Not with his mind blasted with lust and heat. There was no filter between what he was feeling and what came out. He was expressing himself in the crudest way possible and he couldn't backtrack and choose better words.

It was a miracle he could speak.

Her sex contracted and he hissed as if in pain. It was almost—but not quite—painful. Heat flashed through his groin, his balls pulled up tight. God.

Sophie's arms lifted, grasped his forearms, hands tight around his elbows. Her nails bit into his skin. Yes. Just a little touch of pain. Oh yeah. Felt good.

She contracted again and he swelled even further inside her.

"Jon," she panted. Her thighs started trembling. He could see her heartbeat pulsing in her left breast, making the pale silky skin shake. "I can't—I'm—"

"Coming," he growled. He set his jaw, trying to hold back on his own orgasm. At the furthest reaches of his consciousness, he was astonished at himself. He never came first, never. He could wait any woman out. He came when he wanted to, no exception to that rule. Except now, when he was on the verge of blowing up without having even started fucking yet. All he'd done was enter her and he was seeing black at the edges of his vision.

Sophie lifted herself a little, pushing him further into her and she exploded. Her sex pulled at him in wet clenches so strong he could see her belly muscles contracting. She closed her eyes as her back arched, her white neck so tempting beneath him as she pushed the back of her head against the pillow, letting out a low moan.

Oh fuck. It was just too much. *Too much.* Control was impossible here. What man could possibly control himself with beautiful Sophie Daniels contracting around him, face tight as if in pain? No one could. Sure as hell he couldn't.

With a groan, Jon lowered himself onto her and started fucking her hard, hips slamming into her, that low moan now stuttering because of his heavy thrusts. He wasn't fucking her normally with smooth and regular strokes. Oh no. That would have required some degree of control and that was beyond him. He simply made the movements necessary to give him some friction while staying as deep in her as humanly possible, more or less grinding into her with the strength of his whole body, jerking heavily and . . . he started coming.

With no warning, no idea really of what was happening to him. He was like this machine on overdrive and suddenly he slipped a gear and he was coming in huge spurts, his entire body liquefying and pouring itself into her with no holds barred, no sense of boundaries, no sense of where he ended and she began.

They were both exploding, together in an endless loop where she contracted around him again and it set him off, which set her off again, so intense it was like dying, only of pleasure not of pain.

He had no idea how long he kept moving inside her in great jerking motions. She was so wet, he was making embarrassing sounds as he moved in her. It was impossible to tell whether it was her juices or his and it didn't make any difference, the important thing was that he was able to move fast and hard in her without any impediment at all. At the beginning it would have been impossible to move like this. She had been so tight and she still was, but nature had taken care of that for them.

Jon's hips slammed against her and he came again, with no sense of how many times he'd already come. It felt like he'd been climaxing for hours, the entire world reduced to his cock moving in her, endlessly.

But finally, finally, the spurts subsided and he could feel himself soften, just a little. Or at least he wasn't painfully stone hard.

With one last cry, Sophie subsided, the soft arms and legs that had held him so tightly falling back to the bed, the tension in her thighs and groin gone.

He shouldn't, but he let his entire weight rest on Sophie because his spine had just melted. He would probably never move again, a total cripple. But a cripple that was going to lie on Sophie Daniels forever, semi-erect cock half in, half out of her.

Worked for him.

They were covered in sweat, mainly his because he recognized his smell. Overlaid by a faint smell of spring and lavender, which was her. His hair was plastered to his scalp and he could feel sweat pooling in the small of his back. They were both wet around the groin, but that wasn't sweat. He recognized that smell too.

A marking scent. His marking scent. It had never come out of him before, but he recognized it instantly. Some atavistic part of him wanted to rub himself all over Sophie so she was steeped in his scent. Parts of her weren't touching him. The soles of her feet, for instance. If some man were to take her shoes off and sniff the soles of her feet, he wouldn't smell Jon. Well, that was unthinkable.

And all over her back. They were stuck together along their fronts, but her back was Jon-less. Oh man, he had to do something about that, pronto. Just as soon as he regained the use of his spine. And limbs.

He kissed her ear lazily, because his mouth was one part of him that obeyed the command to move. "Wow," he whispered. "That was—"

And a bell sounded and the world turned upside down.

In the space of less than a second, Jon switched from exhausted, contented lover to warrior on a mission. For the merest instant he regretted interrupting what they had, though a part of him recognized that if he was going to die in the next twenty-four hours, at least he'd had the best sex of his life.

And then the instant passed and he went into full Warrior Mode.

He lifted himself up and away, standing up next to the bed.

Sophie was finally able to take a deep breath without his heavy torso on her chest. Her eyes fluttered open. "What was that?"

Jon was already assembling his gear. "I set my scanner to sound an alarm when it recognized that the trailing edge of the swarm was half an hour out. We've got thirty minutes to get ready, and then we make a break for the helicopter."

Sophie was already up. She went to the bathroom and he heard the shower go on for one minute, tops. She emerged and dressed quickly, no fumbling. Good girl.

Jon kept an eye on the time as they readied themselves. He pulled a swatch of material out of his backpack and motioned Sophie over. Her eyes held a question, but she was otherwise composed. For a second, he allowed himself a flash of pride. *What a woman.* She'd risen from a bed where they'd had the most incredible sex possible and were now on a war footing where no tender words could be spoken. In the space of a couple of minutes.

Anything that broke the mood of the deepest possible seriousness was a weakness, intolerable. She could have fumbled, pouted at the change in mood, but she didn't. She was completely ready, watching his face for cues, obedient to any gesture he made.

She was a great teammate.

She wasn't a pushover and she wasn't the kind of woman to

obey a man because he was a man. But she was supersmart and recognized that in this arena, he knew more than she did.

Once they got back to Haven, Jon would deliver her to the lab and step back while she entered a world she knew infinitely more about than he did. It was the kind of teamwork he had with his teammates, and it reassured him that he could count on her.

"Here." He stretched out the dark malleable material that seemed to absorb light. He hadn't been able to carry full-body armor, and his wouldn't fit her anyway, otherwise he'd give it to her gladly. "Hold your arms up." Her arms went immediately up. He fitted a tunic of ballistic material over her as if it were a front and back apron, making sure it fit along her sides, covering them as much as possible, Velcroing it together. It covered her arms, torso, and back and reached down to her knees.

He looked at her. She'd watched him carefully, following his murmured instructions to the letter. She looked a little like a medieval knight from space. "This is ballistic material and it's guaranteed to stop a bullet and diffuse the charge of a stunner. No one could have possibly predicted the infected. But it will save you from a bite in the areas the material covers you. It's not perfect, but it's the best I can do. Now stretch your limbs and make sure you understand your range of movement."

She stretched her arms up and to the sides. Bent forward then backward as far as she could. Exactly what he would have told her to do, only she did it before he could say it.

"Do you know how to handle a gun?"

Her eyes grew wide. "No. I'm sorry, but no."

"Stunner?"

She shook her head.

He undid his lightweight nylon belt holding his knife sheath and fitted it around her tiny waist. The knife hung low on her hip. "I can't let you out of here without some kind of weapon. If you have to, pull out the knife and try to aim for the throat. It's hard for someone untrained to aim for the heart. It's well protected inside the rib cage and you have to know what you're doing to reach the heart and not have a knife bounce off bone. That blade is sharply honed. Slash it across the throat if you can. Do you think you can do that?"

"Yes," she said firmly. "We need to get back to your base with the case and if possible me too, both intact. I won't hesitate to defend myself. And I will try to defend you, too, if necessary."

*Oh man.* Jon never had emotions before a mission. He just switched that part of himself right off. They all did. Emotions were pointless, harmful even. He never felt fear or panic or even exultation. He was all cold calculation, his mind constantly running checklists and tactics and strategy. So the wave of love and admiration that swept over him at seeing her before him, untrained, a freaking scientist of all things, but unafraid and perfectly prepared to do her very best nearly brought him to his knees. Something hot and sharp bloomed in his chest. Love. Fear. Panic. Because she could die. Most likely *would* die if they encountered more than a few infected. Jon could kill a number of them, but if they were overwhelmed . . .

*No!* He simply couldn't think that way. He had to go back to the way he'd been before Sophie. The mission. He had to be all about the mission.

"Here." Sophie handed him the scanner. "What does it say?"

He read the algorithms and switched to visual mode. "The swarm is almost past. It's tighter than I dared hope." With his finger, he dragged the visuals over a 500-meter radius. "Once the swarm passes, there are no infected in a 500-meter radius.

If we move fast, we can make it to the helo and in a couple of hours we'll be safe in Haven."

His comm unit dinged. He switched the scanner to tablet and held it so Sophie could see. "Boss, what's your news?"

Mac looked exhausted but his voice was clear, eyes focused. "We're in contact with five other communities that have assured us they can hold out until we can come get them. But if we have the vaccine and we can bring it to them, they could do mop up operations themselves with our help and stay in their homes. How are things on your end?"

"Well, you can see for yourselves, right?"

Mac nodded, held his own scanner up. He was looking at the same image of the area around Beach Street as Jon was. "You'll have yourselves a window of opportunity real soon. The lab is almost ready to start manufacturing the vaccine, or so Catherine and Elle tell me." He shrugged a massive shoulder. "When they discuss things between themselves, they don't speak English." An elbow appeared and jabbed him in the ribs. "Ouch," he said obediently. "Oh, there's someone wants to talk to Dr. Daniels."

The image cut out and Elle appeared. A big hand was around her shoulder, but Nick was off screen.

"Okay, Sophie," Elle said. "Show time. Jon will take care of you. He's the best there is . . ." There was a murmur and she shot an annoyed glance to her right, then rolled her eyes. "*One* of the best there is, Nick assures me. Don't pay any attention to him, the plague has accentuated his testosterone." She suddenly sobered and her eyes took on a glossy sheen. "Be careful out there, Soph. We need you. We need you not only because you're the best virologist I know but because we're starting to think of rebuilding and we need you for afterward as well. *I* need you. Be careful and . . . godspeed."

"Thanks, Elle," Sophie whispered and switched off the scanner herself. "Right," she said briskly. "What's the game plan?"

Jon could have hugged her right there. There was absolutely nothing in her body language or gaze that betrayed fear, though she must be terrified. What was out there wasn't anything like the usual danger. Hell, Jon would have preferred any of the hairy situations the team had been in to this. Any other situation fit in their training. They'd come up against some of the worst bad men on the planet, but Jon understood bad men, how they thought, how they acted. He'd understood since childhood, and by way of the two years spent inside the drug cartel. He'd learned about every wrinkle of a scumbag's psychology. He knew them inside out. Knew how they thought, how they planned, how they acted.

This was without precedent in the history of the world, and though he'd been thoroughly trained in escape and evasion, what was outside the confines of Sophie Daniels's pretty little apartment was like some horror from the bowels of hell. Coming in, his skin had prickled with terror and horror, an active revulsion the likes of which he'd never felt.

Sophie would be feeling that tenfold. But there she was in front of him, ready to face whatever was thrown at her, and do the very best that she could.

She was a scientist not a warrior, but she had a valiant warrior's heart.

For the very first time in his life as a soldier, Jon was terrified of dying. On missions, if he died, his teammates could carry on. Here, if he died, he would be leaving Sophie without a means of escape from the dying city. He would be condemning her to a horrible death, or, even worse than death, if she was infected but not killed, he would be condemning her to becoming a monster.

He knew that terrified her more than death, but she wasn't betraying anything other than determination on that lovely face.

He allowed himself exactly one second to be swamped with admiration, then choked it off. If they were going to survive this escape, they would need every single ounce of determination and focus in them.

"Right," he said briskly. "This is how it's going down."

She nodded, eyes locked on his. She was listening to him so intently, she was nearly vibrating.

"The helo is on the roof of the Ghirardelli Building. Are you a runner?"

She thought her response over. "Not really. I exercise, sporadically. I'm not in bad shape, but not in supergood shape either. It's pointless lying."

He nodded. Yes, it was pointless lying. He needed to know his resources and hers. He nodded to the case containing the vaccine. "Okay. Can you carry that case and run?"

She looked deeply in his eyes, opened her mouth, then closed it. "Sophie?"

She sighed. "Coming here it was hard for me to carry that thing. It's not only heavy, it's bulky. So I don't know how far I can run while lugging the case around. I wish it were otherwise, Jon, but it's not. I'm sorry."

He shook his head sharply. He didn't need her apology. She'd already been heroic in getting that case and the promise it contained away from a building in flames with crazy infected running everywhere. He remembered those first few hours; it had been a madhouse. Instead of heading for safety right away, she'd gone back for the vaccine.

He worked solutions through his mind fast. There was basically only one way to do this. "Bring it to me."

She nodded and headed for the case against the wall. She did her best but it was heavy for her. She was carrying it in her right hand and had to list left to balance the weight. She moved slowly. No way could she run with it.

Jon reached for a piece of material on a side pocket of his backpack. He knew exactly which side pocket. He was slightly OCD when it came to gear. Gear saved your life. He pulled the material out. Dynapack. Infinitely tough, infinitely stretchable, infinitely strong. He went down on one knee, bending his torso forward until his back was parallel to the ground. He handed her the stretch of Dynapack. "Put the case on my back, then wrap this around it. If you pull the corners, they will stretch into ribbons. Pull them forward and help me tie them around my chest."

He knew how weird that sounded, but Sophie didn't hesitate. The material was top secret and a miracle. In a moment, Sophie had placed the case on his back and the Dynapack on top. Each corner stretched so easily it could have been chewing gum, except this chewing gum was hyper-resistant to just about everything except maybe a 50 cal bullet. The four corners stretched around his chest and she helped him tie it in a solid knot right over his sternum.

His scanner let out a high-toned beep.

The fifteen-minute mark.

They had to hurry.

He stood and jumped to see how tightly the case was secured. It didn't budge. Bless the U.S. military for having thought up Dynapack. The case weighed about forty pounds. In training they'd marched for fifty miles humping double that. No problem.

He went down on one knee again.

"Add my backpack to that." She lifted the backpack over the case. His backpack straps were also made of Dynapack so she just lifted the straps over his shoulders. He shrugged, settling the backpack in place. He was at around sixty pounds. No problem. But he had to leave his body armor behind.

His scanner let out a high-toned beep.

The ten-minute mark.

"Okay. Pack a small backpack if you want, some personal items, girl stuff, whatever. We're heading straight for Haven and there's everything you could need there but—I have to tell you Sophie, you might never come back here again. So if there are some family mementos, whatever, you've got a minute to put it together. One. And dress warmly."

"Right," she said and disappeared into the bedroom. Exactly one minute later she came back out with a long lightweight Nomex coat over her clothes. Gloves and a watch cap. She had a smallish backpack with her.

He looked her over carefully. "Tuck your hair completely into the cap. You don't want someone to catch you by the hair." She obeyed immediately, watching him for more instructions.

She looked as ready as she'd ever be.

They were at the door and he pulled his stunner. He also had his Glock 92, which would stop a rhino in full-attack mode.

"Is there a side entrance to the building?"

"Yes," she answered. "The back stairwell exits onto an alleyway."

"Okay. This is how it's going to work. If the road ahead is clear, you go first and I'll watch your six."

"Six?"

"Your back." She nodded. "If we're attacked, I'll take point and you stay behind me, just as close as you can. Is that clear?"

She nodded again.

"Say it."

It was a principle for people who could find themselves in stressful situations. Pilots repeated verbally every single order. So did warriors going into battle.

"When there are no infected in sight, I am ahead of you. If there are infected, I stay close behind you."

He nodded. "I rappelled down from the roof. I left two ropes, both with an automatic hoist system and handholds at the bottom. I don't think the infected have the kind of intelligence that can recognize a rope."

"No, they don't," she confirmed.

"That's what I thought. Because if we're being chased there's no question of going up the central steps and climbing up until we get to the roof of the Ghirardelli Building. We'd be chased and caught. They're fast. So we'll outwit them. The two ropes are on the west wall, close to the front left corner. Repeat that."

"Two rappelling ropes, west wall, near front left corner. They have a hoist function."

"If I don't make it—" She opened her mouth and he lay his forefinger across those soft lips. "If I don't make it," he said firmly, "try to get the case off me then get to the ropes. If it's impossible to get the case, just head for the wall. You geeks are smart. The men up at Haven could try to capture an infected for you. And then you could—I don't know, isolate the virus, make the vaccine. You can do that, right?"

"In theory," she said. "But it would take weeks."

"But you could do it."

She nodded.

Okay, if something happened to him, the state of California would just continue going to hell for an extra couple of weeks.

"So make it to the wall, grab the handle of one of the ropes and activate the hoist. That's the green button you'll find to the side. Press it and it will immediately start pulling you up. Get to the helo and activate the distress signal. That's a big red button smack above the pilot's seat on the starboard side. It sets off an alarm at Haven. As soon as Haven gets an active helo going, they'll come get you. It might take a day or two or maybe more, but you should be safe up on the roof. There's a first-aid kit if you are wounded. There's also water and energy bars. Just wait, Sophie, don't move. They'll come for you. Repeat that."

She made her voice an even monotone. "If you die, I proceed to the Ghirardelli Building. If I manage to get the case off you, I carry it. If not, I abandon it. There are two ropes hanging from the building. I grab the handle of one, press the green button and rise to the roof. Press the distress button and wait."

"Okay then. So—"

"Listen!" she said urgently.

"What?"

"The noise is almost gone."

Damn. Unforgivable. He'd been so wrapped up in making Sophie realize she had to get her gorgeous ass to safety even if he was down, he hadn't kept up situational awareness. It was true. He checked the scanner. The huge swarm had passed. There were only stragglers, and behind the stragglers, nothing. He tapped the screen, zoomed out. Once the stragglers had passed, there was no thermal footprint of infected for a radius of well over 500 meters. It was their best shot.

He touched his comms. "Ryan, heading out with Dr. Daniels. See you at the homestead."

It was Nick who answered. "Bring her home, Jon, or Elle will never speak to me again."

"Roger that."

He touched Sophie, looked deeply into her eyes. "Are you ready?"

"Yes," she answered and he could tell she was.

"Let's go."

# Chapter 8

Sophie had never seen anyone move the way Jon did. Cautious, careful, each move pondered. But *fast*. He ran in small precise steps designed to keep his gun level.

First he peeked out in the corridor when he opened her apartment door. He pulled his head back, said, "Don't look around, keep focused on moving forward," and with a gentle push ushered her out the door.

It was clear what he meant. The hallway—her very nice hallway with the Italian wall sconces in her very nice building—was littered with corpses, the walls bloodstained.

She did as he said. She watched her feet, kept her focus ahead and moved as quickly and quietly as she could. They passed the elevator bay, but he'd told her elevators were traps, and anyway they didn't know if they were working or not. They headed for the staircase. Jon stopped her with a light touch to her arm. She froze.

He cracked the stairwell door open a fraction of an inch, pulled out a flexible tube from his wrist scanner, and bent it so he could look around the corner and down the stairwell without being seen.

Clear.

They made it down the stairs quietly, Jon managing to cover their backs as well.

They quietly exited the building into the alleyway and made their way along the wall toward Beach. Which was covered in bodies.

Right then, right there, Sophie resolved to survive the dash to the helicopter, to arrive in this Haven, manufacture as much vaccine as their lab could, and stop this thing. Save as many people as possible. She would not allow this abomination to continue.

Jon checked the flexible tube, checking all of Beach from the safety of the alleyway.

"All clear," he said to her in a soft, low voice that was perfectly comprehensible but wouldn't carry more than a foot. He tapped something and said in that low, calm voice, "Moving out." He listened for a second, then said, "Roger that."

He checked the street again, checked the scanner. "Okay. Now's the time. We should be at the rappelling rope in about four minutes. Go."

She went, as fast as she could. She didn't look back because Jon was there and she didn't look left or right because she trusted him to keep an eye out. To have keen situational awareness. Her job was to get herself as quickly as she could to the Ghirardelli Building, and she put everything she had into it.

Though it was late afternoon, it was dark. The many fires had cast a pall of smoke, drowning out the light of the sun. Still, there was enough light for her to see the shapes on the ground. She jumped over the bodies when she could, ran around them when she couldn't, trying as hard as possible to maintain a straight line for the Ghirardelli Building.

The air was thick with acrid smoke and something that she just knew was the smell of mass violence. Blood, burning bodies. Bodies that had voided at death. Somewhere behind them the swarm was moving away, but the noise they made was still audible. Fading inchoate screams and yells. The sound of thousands and thousands of pounding feet. The sound of madness.

Sophie couldn't run fast enough in the opposite direction.

The end of Beach Street. In the middle of the intersection, a pile of clothes stirred, a bloody head lifted, a hand reached out . . .

Jon stunned him without breaking his stride. "Look ahead, Sophie!" he yelled and she realized she'd looked back at what was now a corpse. She was flagging a bit, not used to flat out runs, but he gave no sign of that even though he carried over sixty pounds on his back. No doubt he could run faster than this but he was keeping pace with her, watching her "six" as he called it.

To the right was the grassy swathe that ran down to the water and up ahead—*Oh God!* There it was! Up ahead was the dark shadow of the Ghirardelli Building. No lights there. If there was a backup generator it was gone. No matter, the huge mass was a dark blot against the sky, unmistakable. And close, so close. She angled upward toward the left front corner and could sense Jon right behind her, though he made no sound.

How could he do that? She could hear her own boots pounding the pavement, her breath soughing in and out of her lungs from the run, but Jon was utterly silent.

The building was like some medieval castle looming up in

the sky, and she was going to scale its walls. It seemed impossible but—

A hot wind picked her up and blew her away. Lifted her straight up and back several feet, dumping her on her back. It took away sight and sound and feeling. Somehow, she was on her back, numb, deaf, hurting. The wind scoured her skin. A flash of light so bright it blinded her had erupted suddenly, like a volcano. She couldn't breathe, couldn't move. It was raining . . . bricks? Stones, hard objects. As if from a great distance, she brought her arm up to shield her face. Something grabbed her arm, pulled her sharply to the right and her back scraped across the uneven surface. It hurt.

Something huge, metallic, long and wide like a giant metal finger, hit exactly where she'd been a second before, bounced and came to rest a few feet away.

Nothing made sense. A face was over hers, mouth open. Someone shaking her arm, hard.

"-—blew up!" the person screamed. Jon. "We've got to get out of here! We're exposed!"

Her hearing was slowly coming back, but she couldn't make sense of what he was saying. She lifted her torso, something had been digging into her back, a huge brick. Her back ached. She blinked slowly. "What?"

It felt like her brain was made of molasses and her muscles had suddenly turned to water. She'd been pulled to her feet but could barely stand. Jon was beside her, screaming at her. She shook her head again, sharply, trying to clear it. Nothing made sense.

And then, suddenly, it did. Everything came back into focus. The infected, Jon, the Ghirardelli Building, which was . . . gone. Where before there had been a massive building blotting out the sky, there was now a smoking hole in the ground, flames licking up, lighting up the nightmare scene of dead bodies and destruction.

Someone was shaking her. Jon. "Are you okay?" he asked urgently.

Was she?

Sophie stiffened her knees, tested her balance. Her ears still rang, she was seeing double. "What—what happened?"

His face was tight, grim. "The Ghirardelli just blew. Probably gas mains. But it's taken out our ride. That piece of metal that almost skewered you was a rotor blade. Sophie, we've got to go. Now. That blast will attract the infected. It's possible the swarm will move back our way."

"Where?" She looked around and all she saw was streets full of dead people and crashed cars. No way out. "Where can we go?"

Jon indicated the Bay with his head. "Aim for the municipal pier, grab a boat out of here, sail up the coast. There's no way we can get out in a vehicle from here, the bridges are gone and all the roads are clogged with abandoned cars, anyway. If we go on foot we wouldn't last half an hour; and even if we could walk, we need to go north not south. We still need to cross water."

She knew that and was ashamed of herself for not remembering. Parts of her brain were still fuzzy, but she'd better unfuzz herself fast. She tried to concentrate on the waterfront, picture it in her head.

"Okay, only not the pier. There aren't always boats moored there, and the causeway would be a trap if any infected got on to it. Let's get to Fisherman's Wharf. There are always fishing boats and tour boats."

His face was grim. "You don't think the boats might be all gone? People getting out while they could?"

"Some might still be there." She tried to focus through the ringing in her ears. The infection had come so very fast. People had instinctively tried to get out of town in their cars. Most of the fishermen and tour-boat operators who owned their boats lived out of town, the real estate nearby was way too expensive for anyone to live here. There was a real chance that a few boats were still there. "Do you know how to operate one?"

"Of course," Jon said impatiently.

"Then we should try Fisherman's Wharf."

"If there's nothing there, if the boats are all gone, there's no Plan B," Jon said, voice low, face tight.

"No, there isn't. Unless we dive into the water and swim along the wharf. I don't think they can swim. That would require too much coordination."

"Okay." Jon looked around carefully, at the smoking ruins, the dead bodies, the crashed cars. "We're going to make a run for Fisherman's Wharf. Is the case waterproof?"

Sophie spared a glance at the weight and bulk of what Jon carried. If they had to dive into the ocean, he'd be weighed down by the ballast on his back. She nodded, hoping desperately it never came to that. "Waterproof, shockproof. You probably couldn't blow it up. Can you stay afloat with that thing on your back?"

He nodded, checked his scanner. "Let's go, then. Same rules. You take the lead if the way is clear and because you know the neighborhood better than I do. If there's trouble, stay behind me. So let's go steal a boat."

His face was lit by the fires still burning from the explosion, turning his face light gold and picking out the gold in his hair.

He looked like a fierce Viking god, face taut, ice blue eyes cold and aware. Suddenly, the ice in his eyes melted and he leaned down and gave her a kiss. It reassured her, warmed her. "Just you and me, babe."

That's right. They were in terrible trouble, but they were together. They'd live or die together.

Jon gave her a slight push to get her started. "I'll follow you. Go!" They took off at a run down the slight grassy slope toward Jefferson and turned right. The road paralleled the shore, at times open to the sea, at times closed because of the buildings. They ran past the historical ships, the schooners and steam tugs. One schooner had somehow become unmoored and was drifting out to sea. Ahead, Jefferson Street was dark. It wasn't a residential area but some of the restaurants and tourist shops that had their own generators were lit. The shops had all been ransacked. Not by looters but by the insane.

Hundreds of bodies littered the small narrow street, slowing them down. The row of shops ended and they had a view of open water. Water, freedom, safety.

The fishing boats were in the next open section. God, please let there be boats there! She was running flat out, breathing hard. She couldn't hear Jon behind her, but there was no doubt in her mind that he was there, keeping pace with her, watching her six.

Above the pounding of her heart was another noise rising slowly, steadily. It was too far away to make out exactly what it was but something in the noise was familiar . . .

"What's that?" she gasped.

Jon moved up to her side, running stride easy. He wasn't winded at all. He showed her the scanner, which had been attached as a wrist unit. He tapped it and the top of the scanner glowed bright orange. Her head was still too dazed by the explosion to understand it.

"Fuck. The swarm," he said. "It heard the explosion and it's headed back." He tapped again, then listened to something in his comms. "Roger that," he said.

"What?" Sophie stumbled, nearly fell. But she couldn't fall because Jon had put a strong arm around her. He lifted her off her feet and carried her at a flat-out run, a faster pace than she could possibly have kept.

"The swarm is only a few minutes away, heading straight toward us. There better be boats there, otherwise we'll just dive in and start swimming straight out and hope that you're right that they can't swim. Because if they can . . ."

He didn't have to finish that sentence. If the infected could swim, she and Jon were dead.

The sound was a roar now, that same roar that had passed by under her window for hours. Infected screaming, howling, fighting, killing, dying. And the sound of thousands of running feet. Closer and closer . . .

"Put me down," Sophie gasped. "I'll keep up." She hoped. Jon couldn't carry her, carry the case and his gear, and be ready to fight all at the same time. He put her down and she ran faster than she had ever run in her life.

If there were boats, they would be in the little commercial inlet where the next block of shops ended. They pounded the sidewalk and reached the end of the row of shops and . . . there they were! A number of boats, some ancient with flaking paint, some shiny and new, bobbing in the water. Two steel ladders led down to the small concrete dock with the boats tied to stanchions. The takeoff point for literally millions of tourists over the decades who wanted a trip around the beautiful bay.

It was no longer beautiful. The lights along the Golden Gate Bridge were dark. The bridge was barely visible as a structure against the smoky sky. A fire was raging out of control along the Marin Headlands. The city skyline was dark, as was Alcatraz.

Dark, all dark.

"Sophie!" Jon barked. "Faster!"

Oh God! The leading edge of the swarm was at Bistro Boudin, rippling down the street toward them, a solid wall of enraged humanity.

Jon grabbed the handrails of the closest vertical steel ladder and descended without touching a stair. At the bottom he looked up. "Jump. I'll catch you."

Sophie looked to her right, at the crazed line of infected running full tilt, their screams echoing in her ears and didn't think twice. She jumped.

Jon caught her deftly, swung with her in his arms, and deposited her on the deck of the nearest fishing boat. It was old, dilapidated. *The Summer of Love* painted on her side.

"Checking fuel," Jon shouted. "Get ready to jump to the next one."

He did something to the engine and it sputtered to life, but he took one look at the fuel gauge, grabbed her hand, and jumped to the next one, their boots thudding loudly on the deck.

Jon disappeared into the pilot's cabin and a few seconds later there was the powerful roar of an engine; she could feel the shudder beneath her feet. "Fuel tank full!" Jon shouted from within the cabin. "Can you cast off?"

Yes, she could. She'd had a boyfriend who was a sailor, and though she couldn't sail herself, she'd learned to make herself useful. Sophie hurried to the bow, reaching over to grab the rope and screamed as a grimy hand caught hers. She barely had time to hear the angry snarl of a nonhuman voice when the man's head exploded.

"Sophie! Get back!" Jon screamed.

She jumped back and tripped over a bucket. Horribly, another man fell to the dock level from above. And another. And suddenly the narrow ledge was full of infected, hands outstretched. Up on the street level, crazed, maddened faces were snarling down at her, writhing to try to get down. None of the infected could handle the ladder so they were simply throwing themselves over the railing down to the dock. Some died in the fall, but the dead bodies cushioned the next who threw themselves over. A writhing snarling mass of violence. The noise level was deafening.

She couldn't get to the rope, the infected were scrambling to get to her, growling and grasping. If she went for the rope, they'd grab her. but they couldn't leave without unmooring the boat. The boat rocked as an infected tried to jump on, lost his footing and fell into the sea. He sank like a rock.

Jon revved the engine, ready to take off like a rocket if she could just get to where that damned rope anchored the boat. But there was no way. The stanchion was now hidden in the boiling mass of the infected, the rope disappearing between the legs of a blood-covered man in a once-elegant suit howling and snarling at her.

She was paralyzed, looked around for something, anything, that would allow her to cut the rope. It couldn't be a knife because she couldn't saw through the rope. It would take too long, they'd grab her. It had to be something like a hatchet . . .

The rope parted suddenly, as if an invisible hand had swung that hatchet, severing it in one blow. What happened? Then one monster's head exploded, then another. She glanced back to see Jon aiming and shooting precisely with one hand, while starting to back the boat out of the tiny harbor.

A thud to her right and she screamed. An infected. A lithe young man, hands out in claws, inhuman sounds coming from his throat.

Jon blew the young man away, then another who'd jumped aboard. A stream of infected jumped on the other boat then tried to jump to theirs, clearly unable to judge distances. It was like a waterfall, a waterfall of humans pouring into the ocean. But another young man, an athlete by his build, made a spectacular leap, catching onto the gunwale, starting to haul himself in, screaming all the while.

One well-aimed bullet, the screaming stopped, and the man fell back, sinking into a pool of red.

They backed away quickly, beginning the turnaround to head out to the open sea, when Jon took careful aim at the boat next to them. "Cover your head!" he screamed and shot into the boat. Immediately it exploded, fuel spilling over the infected, lighting the dark afternoon sky with a nightmarish view of burning infected, those right behind the columns of burning, living flesh pushing them into the water to get a chance at killing her and Jon and catching fire themselves.

Then Jon got the boat turned around completely and throttled the engine wide open. The prow lifted, they skirted the tourist boardwalk behind them and then headed toward the open sea.

Sophie sat on the deck, exhausted, trembling, and watched the burning creatures until Jon turned a corner around a pier and they disappeared from sight.

The screams could still be heard, though, becoming fainter and fainter as they headed northwest.

When she felt her legs could carry her, Sophie went into the pilot's cabin and watched Jon pilot the boat. His movements were fast, precise, the boat steady. He clearly knew what he was doing. It was as if he sensed her presence by a change in the air molecules. He turned, one hand on the wheel, one arm outstretched.

With a sob, Sophie stumbled to him, burying her face against his shoulder. He'd somehow had time to divest himself of the vaccine case and his backpack. They were stowed neatly in a corner.

Jon was headed for the Golden Gate Bridge and then the wide Pacific beyond it. To their left, the city burned. Columns of fire had merged and entire city blocks were aflame. Every once in a while a distant boom sounded.

A great city, brought to its knees.

Finally, finally, the huge empty horizon stretched in front of them. The ocean. Jon steered them north.

Neither spoke until the sounds of the dying city could no longer be heard.

"We made it," Sophie whispered.

He kissed the top of her head, hugged her more tightly to him, steering one-handed.

"We made it."

# Chapter 9

Jon cast a worried glance at Sophie, huddled shivering in a corner. Her head was on her knees, hands tucked under her arms in a vain attempt to hide from him the fact that they were trembling.

Hell. There was nothing to be ashamed of. They'd just come out of something worse than a firefight.

For all the tight situations he'd been in, outnumbered and outgunned, Jon had never faced a battle like that before. In every other firefight, he'd been combating humans and he could understand even the worst scumbag. These infected— they had no sense of self-preservation. It was terrifying to see them throw themselves into the water, hungry to attack, and then sink to the bottom. To see them throwing themselves over the parapet, landing as a heap of broken bones on the small pier, had unnerved him. It went against the human grain. They couldn't think, couldn't reason, so you couldn't outwit them in any way. They were absolutely terrifying.

He was fucking spooked too.

Sophie had been as brave as any warrior. She was un-trained—a scientist for fuck's sake—and yet she'd outshone many a fellow soldier, never losing her nerve under hair-raising circumstances.

They'd done it, but now Sophie needed a little care, which he was more than happy to provide. They'd lucked out with this boat. It was a working fishing boat, but its owner had tricked it out with every modern enhancement. It had excellent radar, so he had no fear of running into other boats, and it had the latest type of autopilot. He could leave the helm and tend to Sophie, and know they wouldn't be running aground or ramming an-other boat. The system was very sophisticated and would move around any obstacles.

He was going to travel up the coast until he was more or less at the same latitude as Mount Blue. It was going to be hard to make their way overland. The infected were everywhere, even if not as concentrated as in San Francisco. They needed to find a vehicle and try to make their way on roads that were clogged with stalled cars.

On the way down in the helo, he'd found very few roads with clear stretches and without abandoned cars, so it would have to be a vehicle with off the road capabilities. God, he wished he had one of their hovercars, little miracle cars that could be driven either in wheeled vehicle mode or hovercraft mode. But he didn't.

He'd have to try to find an undamaged four-wheel drive with a full tank of gas and/or a fully charged engine. Not easy, be-cause there weren't going to be functioning charging stations, and there weren't going to be gas stations anywhere on the route to Haven.

But that was for after they landed. First things first.

The galley was well equipped. It had all the fixings for a traumatized young woman. He hunkered down next to Sophie with a steaming cup of tea, a good finger of excellent whiskey in it. She looked at it then at him, deep blue eyes sad and lost. She made no move to reach for the tea, though she obviously wanted it.

Very gently, Jon pulled one of her hands away, put the cup in her hand, then placed his hand under hers. It was trembling. No way would he allow that hot tea to spill on her. He had her hand. He watched as she sipped, coughed.

"This is the second time you've done this. I like whiskey," she said. "Too bad you put tea in it."

"Drink," he said.

She did. By the time she finished the cup, color had come back into her face and her hands no longer trembled in his.

He searched her eyes. "You okay?"

She didn't even try to misunderstand. "That was so scary," she whispered. "I thought we weren't going to make it. If you hadn't been so fast with that gun, we wouldn't have. It was so close!"

She was spooked. He had to help her with this, otherwise she'd play those scenes over and over again in her head. He knew hardened warriors who suffered from PTSD from less harrowing experiences. Jon took her chin in his hand, keeping her focused on him. He had to convince her now and it had to stick. "We made it. It's in the past. Over. The infected can't touch you now and that's what counts. Wipe it from your mind. Close only counts in horseshoes—"

"And hand grenades," she added with a faint smile.

Jon looked at her carefully. What he wanted to do was grab her up and hold her tight, for her and for himself. He'd been scared shitless that he'd lose her back at the pier. If he grabbed her and held her she'd understand that he'd been scared and that wouldn't do. So he merely bent to touch his lips to hers. Soft lips that opened under his . . . Oh yeah.

The comms unit beeped. He pulled back, looked at Sophie with a raised brow, and she nodded. He set it to hologram and speakerphone so communicating wouldn't be just over his ear unit. She had every right to hear the intel. They were lovers, but they were also teammates on a dangerous mission. You don't hide intel from a teammate.

Mac and Nick were in the foreground. Jon could see Catherine and Elle working in the background with people he didn't recognize.

"Helo's down," Jon said.

"Yeah." Mac's basso profundo voice was grim. "We saw the whole thing. That was quick thinking, making for the waterfront. We're glad you got out. Elle nearly had a heart attack."

Nick nodded. "Yeah, we had some tense moments there, bro. Luckily, you paid attention to my sterling soldiering advice."

It was a running joke, to the extent that Nick was able to joke. They were of equal abilities. Nick was a slightly better shooter and Jon was sneakier, better at lying, better at strategizing. But they were both more than mission capable.

Jon let the snark slide. "Well, we could use some advice right about now. Do you have us up on screen?"

"Oh yeah," Mac said. "And we've got your waypoints mapped out. And something else." Mac turned behind him and beckoned. A middle-aged guy stepped forward. Plaid shirt, chinos. Balding. Thin intelligent face. Unusually, he wore glasses. Most people had their eyes corrected with surgery. Wearing glasses was definitely a retro statement. "Jon, meet Jason Robb. Jason's one of our refugees and he's got some intel for you."

Robb's face filled the hologram. "I watched on screen as your helicopter blew up and you guys escaped. Really impressive, man. It's my understanding that Dr. Daniels and you are carrying a vaccine. Everyone's rooting for you, son."

Jon nodded. It was nice that people were rooting for him, but he needed a little more than that. They were streaming north, but once they made landfall they were going to be in a shitload of trouble.

"We've been looking at the maps," Mac said. "The best place to make landfall is around Eureka, where there's a straight line over to us here at Haven."

Jon kept quiet. Robb might be a newbie at this but Mac and Nick weren't. They knew damn well how difficult making landfall and making their way east to Haven was going to be. It was almost a suicide mission.

"That's where I come in," Robb said, pushing his glasses back up to the bridge of his nose. "I run—I ran a sort of fancy B & B about twenty miles south of Eureka, near the Humbolt Bay Refuge. Right now, the drones show no infected in the entire Refuge itself. My B & B has a wall around it and is open only to the sea. We have a pier you can dock at. Let me show you. These are stored images because Google went down about two hours ago." He tapped on a tablet and aerial views came up of a stucco compound, landscaped gardens around it, a bright blue oval that was a swimming pool, surrounded by adobe walls. Sure enough, a small wooden finger jutted out from the beach. A pier.

"So we were thinking of you and Sophie holing up there

during daylight. The Redwood Highway is free of obstacles nearly back up to Eureka and you can head east here." Nick's finger traced up the Redwood Highway to a point two miles south of the city. "There's a pileup here, so you'll have to leave the road."

"I have a four-wheel drive in the garage," Robb said. "It's a hybrid. A Lynx. I don't know whether the charger is working or not, but even if the electricity is down, it should have had time to charge before it went offline. And the LPG tank is full. I don't know if it can carry you all the way over, that depends on how many detours you have to take, but with some luck you can siphon some LPG from abandoned hybrids if you have to. I think all the charging stations are down. The Lynx's real hardy. You can go off road. The only problem is that they tell me you should drive after sundown, without headlights. I don't know how you can do that."

"You still night vision capable?" Mac asked.

"Yeah." His NV goggles were still fully charged. It would have been a nightmare driving off road for 250 miles in the dark. Even with NV it was going to be almost impossible.

But impossible was what Ghost Ops used to do for breakfast. And the stakes were higher than any mission he'd ever been on. He had a beautiful woman to keep safe and a vaccine that could save millions to deliver. He was going to get them safely to Haven. No question.

"So, Mr. Ryan," Robb began.

"Jon."

"Jon. The main house is open on the beach side. You'll move past the pool and pool house, then there are steps up to a patio. There's a security system. The code is montecarlo2015." He glanced sideways, his face softening. "Montecarlo is where I met my wife. Once you've punched in the code, go inside and then punch in *mylove* to set the security system again." Even in the hologram, Jon could see the man's cheeks turn pink. Mac looked away, lips tight against a smile, and Nick rolled his eyes behind the man's back.

"If the electricity has gone, what then?"

"We have a generator guaranteed to run for ninety-six hours if the mains go off; we never went full solar. But if something has happened, if you can climb, get up to the second story and go in through a window. The second story is where the four guest bedrooms are, and we switched the security off. Damned things went crazy every time a guest opened the window for some air. Even if the fridge and freezer are no longer working, there's food that should still be good. We get our water from an artesian well, run by a very small solar generator, so you'll have plenty of running water, hot and cold. Use anything you want in the house, take anything you need. The welcome and safety we've received here—well, I couldn't thank you and your friends in a thousand lifetimes. Everything in the house is yours."

Jon dipped his head. "Thank you. The vehicle?"

Robb grinned in pride. "Brand-new. Top of the line. I keep it fully serviced. To open the garage door, press the remote in the tray between the seats. It opens the gate in the outer wall too. These guys here seem to be really well organized, but if you can, bring some of the food we've got stocked. Flour, bags of dried fruit, things that won't spoil. Oh, and if it's not too much trouble, my wife, uh, she'd really like a big pink cashmere shawl that's draped over a chair in our bedroom. She's really attached to that shawl. I gave it to her for our fifth wedding anniversary. You guys seem to have the only intact communication system in California, so if you have any problems, just get me back online. No problem."

"You're very generous, sir—" Jon began.

"God, no!" Robb lifted his hands in horror. His eyes were suddenly glassy with unshed tears. "Don't thank me! This place has saved our lives. Everyone has shared generously. I couldn't possibly pay back what I owe you. So consider that house yours for the duration."

Responding to a touch on his shoulder, Robb moved away, the camera automatically adjusting its focus to Mac and Nick.

"So," Jon said. "Sitrep."

Mac and Nick separated and there he was, Captain Lucius Ward. The man Jon had loved like a father. The man who'd put together the Ghost Ops team and made them tighter than brothers. The man who'd nearly broken him when Jon thought the captain had betrayed them. He hadn't. How could they have ever thought that? That the captain could betray them? He'd have died first and he almost did die. When the intel Catherine had brought them—that the captain and three of their teammates were being held in one of Arka's research facilities, and they'd gone down to rescue them—the four men they'd rescued had been as close to death as Jon ever wanted to see.

If not for the intensive care Catherine and later Elle provided, his captain and teammates would never have made it.

Jon straightened and Sophie looked at him in surprise. "Sir."

The last time Jon had seen the captain, he needed two sticks to walk. Now he only needed one. Probably the reason for that was behind him, the once famous actress Stella Cummings, now their chef and head of the communal kitchens. Though her beautiful face had been slashed to ribbons, she was still beautiful in everyone's eyes. Not to mention the fact that they ate better than any community on earth.

"Jon," the captain replied. "We have some news. Good news."

Jon blinked. Good news. Christ. "That's—that's good," he said lamely. He hardly knew where to put good news in his head. No place for it.

"The U.S. government has started getting its finger out of its butt." Someone slapped him lightly on the back and he turned his head and mouthed *sorry*. "They're not ready to cross the quarantine zone, though, the fuckers. *Sorry*," he said before the hand could slap him again. "There's a lot of confusion in the military going right up to the Joint Chiefs level, and in government, going right to the top. The fact that a former general, that dickhead Clancy Flynn—"

He braced himself, but clearly Stella had given up on cleaning his language up. And Flynn *was* a dickhead. Had been a dickhead. A murderous son of a bitch dickhead. Luckily, he was now dead.

"Flynn was part of the creation of this virus, so there's been a lot of finger-pointing. I begged them in Washington—*begged* them—for a helo to pick you guys up, but there have been outbreaks of infection in Idaho, Oregon, Nevada, and Texas and they are busy trying to contain them together with setting up a reporting system in every community in the U.S. I simply haven't been able to get through to anyone who has an airborne command. Actually, we can't get through to anyone. That helo manufacturer I told you about, his fuel tanks blew. Nobody can use them until we can scavenge more fuel, but that won't be soon."

Fuck. Jon had been hoping for a helo pickup. Not going to happen. "So what's the situation between us and you?"

The captain's bald head was cruelly crisscrossed with surgical scars. When his jaw muscles tightened, the scars danced on his head. "Not good. We've got pockets, strongholds really, of uninfected but they are holed up, and if you make a beeline, they're not close enough to come out and help. You're just going to have to make a run for it at night."

"Over uneven terrain. In the dark, with night vision." Yeah, that was going to be fun.

Lucius shrugged. "All you can do is hope the Lynx is up to it. We can't clear the way for you with bombs. The noise and maybe the light would attract them."

"Yeah, we saw that in San Francisco."

"Get that case to us, son, but don't get here without Dr. Daniels, or I won't answer for your safety. And Elle would have my head. But once we have vaccines, we're going to save us a lot of souls. Couple people here are already starting planning for after. Rebuilding. We save enough people, we can start society all over again. Which is better than what we thought we'd be facing when this clusterfuck started."

Fuck yeah. They had been looking at a future in which they might have been the only people alive in California. Maybe the world. If people were already thinking of rebuilding, someone was feeling hope.

"Okay, son, that's about it. We'll be with you every step of the way but we can't help. Get here safely with the vaccine and Dr. Daniels and we'll start saving the world. Before I sign off there's someone who wants to talk with Dr. Daniels."

He shuffled slowly aside and Elle took his place. Her face was pinched and anxious, but cleared when she saw Sophie. Her hand went to her throat. "Oh God, Soph! You're okay! When the helicopter blew up, we thought—we thought you wouldn't make it. We watched you guys get out of Dodge. I don't think I've ever been as scared as that in my life."

Sophie took Jon's hand, held it tightly. "Jon got us out safely. I knew he would." She turned her head, kissed his cheek. Jon looked at her, at her mouth, and was tempted. Really, really tempted.

Silence.

Elle's eyes opened and everything but a lightbulb went up over her head. She looked at a faintly smiling Sophie, to him, then back to Sophie, and her mouth opened as wide as her eyes. A big hand reached over and gently closed her mouth.

Sophie wasn't helping her, and damned if Jon was going to. He didn't care who knew he and Sophie were together. He'd found her and he was damned well going to keep her.

"Oh, um. Okay." Elle was having trouble shifting gears.

Catherine joined her, tilted her head toward Elle and murmured, "The lab. Tell her about the lab."

"Yes." Elle shook herself out of her stupor and bounced straight into nerd scientist mode. "Okay. The lab. We've got a good cell line going, so incubation time will be a matter of minutes. There's a refugee here who worked at the Stanford research lab and we're putting together an application via patch instead of injection. With that delivery system, we can double the inoculations."

"Do we have an estimate of survivors?" Sophie asked.

Elle turned her head, spoke with Catherine, who spoke to someone else off screen. Elle checked a mini tablet then looked up. "Anywhere between one and two million people. As of now. That number will go down."

Everyone was silent.

At the last census, California's population stood at a little

under sixty million. Jon glanced to his right, to the silent land-
mass of the coastline, dark except for a few fires. The whole state
was the graveyard of about fifty-eight million people, dead or
dying over the course of the past forty-eight hours. More than
a million people an hour. Possibly the largest and fastest death
event in the history of the world. Dead bodies piled up like a
vast slaughterhouse. Men and women and children . . . Nothing
they could ever do would bring them back to life. Teachers and
firemen and grade-schoolers and musicians and doctors. The list
went on and on. Humankind in California was reduced to a few
strongholds fighting for survival, hunkering down like cavemen,
shot back in time to ten thousand years ago.

Warmth on his hand. He glanced down to see Sophie's small
hand over his. Her hand was unusually warm, it seemed that
heat spread up his arm, into his chest. He realized he'd been
breathing shallowly, chest tight. Now his lungs expanded as he
drew in the soft night sea air. That touch somehow steadied
him. He opened his hand, catching her fingers between his, enjoying the glow of heat that came from her as steady as a flame.

"Sophie was right," Elle said. "The infected are dying fast.
They have no instinct of self-preservation. I have been unable
to observe any signs of infected being able to feed themselves or
even drink water. That swarm in San Francisco? Judging from
the thermal scans about one-third of that swarm is already
dead. The infected are in effect the walking dead, only they
still have the power to inflict great harm."

"What's the lab's capacity?" Sophie asked.

Catherine answered, checking her tablet. "About fifty thousand doses in a twenty-four-hour period."

Sophie frowned. "Any hope of another lab somewhere
coming online?"

"Yes. Two people here know of labs that can be converted and brought online as soon as we have the staffing and can create secure conditions. Right now, nobody can be spared, but we have forty Marines arriving tomorrow with their families. They've already volunteered for anything we might need them to do."

Mac looked up from his tablet. "Jon, we've just sent you the GPS coordinates of Robb's compound. Check the perimeter when you arrive and contact us when you're secure. We're going to have to start pulling our drones, fuel is getting low. I can't keep twenty-four-hour oversight for you when we also have to check for survivors. When you're secure for the day, we'll call back the two drones watching you, and hope to send them out again when you exfil. We'll do our best, anyway."

"Roger that," Jon said. "Hooah."

"Hooah." Mac hesitated, then said something no military commander ever said before a mission. An op was all about getting the mission accomplished. All about grabbing what had to be grabbed. Killing whoever needed killing. The mission was first and last. If someone died, that was simply the way it rolled. No one ever talked about safety in the pre-mission briefing. It was never about safety, it was all about doing the job. But now it was a new ball game. "Stay safe," he said.

Jon's despair had been almost palpable as his people in Haven were putting together scenarios for the future. It had hung like a dark cloud around him. Just as despair had hung around him when he talked of his past, his parents. He'd suffered and survived so much.

Her touch was instinctive, as instinctive as if he had been grievously wounded and she'd moved to stanch the flow of blood. As instinctive as when they'd talked about his past, back at her apartment. He'd been wounded then, too, though, with that tough-guy exterior he'd probably rather be shot in the face than admit it. His voice had been laconic, emotionless. And underneath the skin, his emotions were boiling—a mixture of rage and sorrow and despair.

Then she'd touched him and felt a form of healing begin. That had never happened to her before, her gift used for spiritual illness. It had never even occurred to her that she could do such a thing. Maybe she could only do that with Jon. Maybe the sexual connection was so strong, they were linked in some way. She'd had sex before, but never such intensely intimate sex.

For long moments, she'd lost the separation between them, the separation that exists between all human beings, closed up in their skins. For long moments, she'd felt part of him, beneath the skin, inside his heart.

That wasn't a good thing. There was a reason people were separate, apart. Such close links would be dangerous if they were common. She'd been inside him, he'd been inside her, in the most intimate kind of way. Not the connection of the flesh, which is easy, superficial. But a connection of the spirit.

It was dangerous. Someone who was *inside* you could rip you to pieces.

She shivered.

"Here." Jon did something to the display panel and left the wheel. He rummaged in the cabin until he found a blanket, dragged a bench over, and placed it behind the wheel. He sat her down on it, draped the blanket around her, and put his arm around her with an audible grunt of satisfaction.

Sophie knew exactly how he felt. Sitting next to him on the speeding boat, so close she could feel his body heat, his arm around her, felt good, felt . . . *right*. She tipped her head against his shoulder and felt his lips kiss her hair.

"Rest now. We've still got a long journey ahead of us."

"Don't you need to, um . . ." What was the word? *Drive* felt wrong. "Pilot the boat?" She could hear the quaver in her voice and hated it. The adrenaline of their escape was still coursing through her body. The blanket was a lightweight thermal blanket and she was warm underneath it, but the trembling wasn't from cold.

Jon tightened his arm around her. "It's on autopilot. See this?" He tapped a dial. She nodded. "Radar and IR and thermal scanner. We're not going to run into any boats, even those adrift. We've got another nine or ten hours to go, so I want you to relax, if you can."

*Relax?* "How can I relax when—"

He kissed her. He turned, took her in both arms and kissed her and kissed her. One big hand held the back of her head, as if she might want to turn away when nothing on this earth would make her turn away. His mouth was so delicious! Heat came off him like steam off an iron. She'd been so cold up until a few moments ago. The cold of fear, of adrenaline rushing through her system. The cold even of despair, because there was no guarantee that they'd make it. No guarantee that she could get the vaccine up to Haven. She and Jon were willing to die to complete this mission and they might end up doing just that.

But she couldn't think that as Jon kissed her. Kissed her as if his life depended on it. In a very real sense, her life certainly did. He pulled back, ran his thumb under her eyes. "You're tired," he said gently. "Rest."

Sophie thought she could never rest again, but she was wrong. Leaning against Jon's broad shoulder, she watched as the dark mainland drifted by. With no light pollution the stars were bright, constellations she hadn't seen in years decorating the sky. The light from some of those stars was a million years old, before mankind had begun its journey. And even if mankind ceased to exist, those same cold, bright stars would send their light across the vast expanse of the universe, forever. Uncaring about men.

The boat was steady, the sea calm. They arrowed their way silently through the water, hardly any spray lifting. Twice a boom came from the mainland. Other than that, silence.

Everyone was so used to the sounds of civilization. Cars, generators, TVs. She wasn't a camper, didn't go trekking over the weekends. She was a city girl, used to city noises. This was the still silence not of peace but of a world breaking down.

Jon's hand lifted from where it cupped her shoulder to run a long, callused finger down her cheek.

And yet, and yet. The world was breaking down, yes, but there were some smart, strong people working hard to hold it together. Like the man holding her. She looked straight ahead into the blackness, feeling his solid, warm strength along her side, feeling his strong hand caressing her cheek, playing with her hair.

A man she barely knew, and yet she knew him down to his core. Knew the strength and honor in him. Knew that he was fearless, that he worked for the good. She'd *felt* his pain when he spoke of the betrayal of his parents and what he thought had been the betrayal of the man he'd chosen to follow. It had been as painful and as deep as any wound, any organic illness. Most people, when grievously wounded, curled up and withdrew from the world. It was the body's natural reflex, to curl in on itself. But not Jon. Jon had turned himself into a man of strength and he stepped forward, not backward.

There was so much she didn't know about him. His tastes in music and movies. What kind of food he liked. How strong a sense of humor he had. How well read he was.

None of that really mattered, though, when measured against her understanding of his character.

Not to mention he was a god in bed.

That took her by surprise because Sophie didn't really judge men by their prowess in the bedroom. It was a nice extra if it was there, that was all. But sex with Jon was . . . was overwhelming. Almost an extrasensory event. Beyond the five senses, moving into a world beyond her ken. The sheer power of the experience swept her away. When he kissed her, caressed her, entered her, the world disappeared and there was only the two of them, an explosion of heat and light.

Life.

When they were surrounded by death.

Here on the vast dark ocean it was almost easy to forget for a few moments that the world was ripping itself apart. Here, right now, under the vast star-filled sky, arrowing their way north, they could simply be a normal couple going on vacation, with no deeper concerns than the quality of the food at their destination.

She rolled that in her head for a moment. She and Jon, a normal couple in a normal world. How could that have worked out? Where would they have met? They could have met at—oh, a movie theater? Or perhaps at an outdoor café? Or at a concert? Met, flirted, liked each other. Dated a few times, gone to bed, had sex, found themselves compatible.

The usual, like normal people did.

But no, that scenario didn't work. Their regular lives held no points of intersection. He was a warrior, constantly on mission, and then he'd had to go into hiding. She was absorbed in her job. She didn't go to the movies or linger at outdoor cafés or go to concerts. She had a nice home entertainment system and saw all her films and listened to her music at home. Her life was home and work and home again.

Particularly this past year working on the Arka project with Elle, that electric feeling of being on the cutting edge of science, of discovering something completely new. That had kept her so absorbed, there hadn't been time for anything else. This past year she and Elle had been married to the lab.

No, she'd never have met Jon under other circumstances.

How strange to think that it took the end of the world to bring them together.

Her thoughts were lazy now, lulled by the sound of the boat skimming over the flat dark sea. People were dying, society was dying all across the land to her right. She hadn't seen anything outside San Francisco, but it was easy to imagine. Towns and cities devastated. Homes abandoned, front doors open, wrecked furniture inside. Cars left where they were, blocking roads. Smashed windows everywhere, shattered little shards of light on the streets. Whole sections of towns burned to the ground.

And bodies. Bodies everywhere, both the infected and the healthy, locked in a death struggle. Most of the population, dead.

She closed her eyes and leaned more heavily against Jon. Against his solid strength. She took enormous consolation in feeling him against her, breathing slowly and easily, moving a little at times to check on gauges and do whatever one did when piloting a boat. There was a palpable sense of vast strength, enormous reserves, as if he could keep going forever.

On the mainland was tragedy on a vast scale, a death toll in the millions. But right here, right now, on this silent boat cutting through the sea, she felt safe with Jon. He'd see them to the B & B compound, get them overland to this place, this Haven. Where Elle was, with her man. Where Catherine Young was, a woman she knew by reputation. With Jon's teammates and a whole community of people surviving, thinking beyond this almost-extinction event to a possible future. Planning for it, even.

There was fear in her, cold slimy fear penetrating down to the bone. And yet, and yet . . . there was also a sense of safety with Jon. It was partly his godlike physique, of course. She'd never touched a man as strong as Jon. He gave the impression of leanness, but his muscles were thick, the strength going deep. And he was so brave. Every second of their mad dash from her apartment to the marina, Jon had clearly been willing to sacrifice himself for her.

Partly, it was his training as a soldier. The infected hordes had been unnerving in a primordial way. Terrifying beyond words. But through it all, Jon had been absolutely steady, never faltering, always thinking several steps ahead, even when all this was totally unprecedented. There was no way he could have trained for this nightmare scenario, and yet it was as if he'd trained for it all his life.

What she'd seen of him in action made her think she would follow him straight into the jaws of hell itself because he'd lead them right back out.

They had a long trek in front of them, one they might not survive. But right now, she gave herself over completely to the boat ride, breathing in the cold salty night air. Every once in a while, a gust brought the chemical stink of something burning, but it dissipated the further north they went. They had long stretches on the calm flat sea from which the only smell was of the sea itself, and the only light that of the stars overhead, the Milky Way looping its bright way across the sky.

"Seems almost peaceful, doesn't it?" Jon's deep voice was quiet.

"Mm-hm." She sighed. "It would be nice to think we're on a—a boating trip, going north to go camping or something."

He slanted a glance down at her, his ice blue eyes bright in the starlight. "You go camping?"

Sophie laughed. "Nope. Not a chance. Bears and mosquitoes and squatting to take a poop." She gave a theatrical shudder. "Not for me. I imagine you're the camping sort of guy, am I right?"

"No way." It was his turn to laugh. "We do what you'd call camping in the rough for a living. We once slept outdoors for three months in—in a place that was equatorial jungle. Mosquitoes the size of birds, spiders the size of dinner plates, I kid you not. We had to smother ourselves in enough Deet to cause liver damage. Part of those three months was the monsoon season, so we got toe and crotch rot. We couldn't use heat for cooking so we ate MREs—Meals Ready to Eat, though 'Meal' is stretching it. They're like lightly flavored sludge, and gum you up. We couldn't talk and we couldn't move. So pitching a tent somewhere and using oak leaves for toilet paper is not my favorite leisure activity, no."

Sophie laughed. She could see it, see how uncomfortable he and his teammates had been. She'd seen his captain and two of his teammates. They looked just as hard and driven as Jon. They'd lived in those appalling conditions for three months and—

"Did you accomplish what you set out to do? In those three months?"

His eyes narrowed to a light blue slit, firm beautiful mouth curved up in a smile. God. He was devastating when he smiled. "Oh yeah," he said softly. "We did."

"Whacked a bad guy, eh?" she said and he recoiled.

"Who told—" then he bit his lips.

Sophie laughed. "I can't imagine any other reason for camping out under those conditions for three months. If it was intelligence you were after, there are easier ways. A listening drone at a high altitude would have done it."

He smiled again and mimed zipping his mouth shut. Oh God. Now a *dimple.* Not fair. A dimple was overkill.

She sighed.

So he'd camped out for three months to kill someone. Someone who undoubtedly needed killing. If you'd asked her even a week ago if she could become the lover of a man who killed for a living, she'd have said no. Unequivocally no.

But that was then and this was now. She'd known, theoretically, as a purely abstract concept, that evil existed in the world. She'd been five years old when the Twin Towers fell. She remembered watching it with her parents, both of them silent and dismayed. She hadn't quite understood what had happened, but she had understood that evil had come into the world. She'd felt it quite distinctly. The first time in her young life that she'd understood even the concept of evil.

What had been unleashed now was evil on an unimaginable scale. She'd been able to piece together some of the story from Dr. Charles Lee's computer. He'd been working on a secret program of human enhancement via a new drug. Genetic material delivered in a viral vector. Only it had backfired. It had, yes, enhanced the infected's performance. The infected were indeed stronger and faster and utterly unafraid. They were also insane. And doomed to die in a few days like some monstrous insect that was born, lived, and died in the space of a week.

And she knew the reason the virus was so virulent. It was because Dr. Lee had been in such a hurry. For some reason, he'd been under massive time pressure. If she'd had access to all his files, she could have pieced it together, though now it was ancient history.

And because Dr. Charles Lee had been in a hurry, he'd created an abomination that had the potential to wipe human life off the face of the earth. If they couldn't contain it, only a few strongholds on the planet would survive. On the vast steppes of Central Asia, perhaps. In Antarctica, maybe. Some isolated tribes in Amazonia. The poor souls on the Space Station wouldn't survive because there would be no one left on earth with the technical expertise to bring them back down.

All of this was evil. And combating this required not only her skills and Elle's skills and Catherine's skills, but it also required the skills of Jon Ryan and his fellow warriors. And she could only be happy that he was a trained killer because he was the right man in the right place.

She would never have escaped San Francisco with the vaccine without him. She'd have died in her apartment when the water and food ran out. And anyway, before that happened, the vaccine would have been rendered inert.

Jon had saved her life, saved the vaccine, and was still doing it.

He was also teaching her about love. The tough, trained killer had opened an unimagined world to her. While chaos ruled in the streets outside her windows, he'd given her pleasure she'd never even known existed. It wasn't casual, what they shared.

They were two people who would never have gotten together under any other possible circumstances, but what they had, forged in fire and death, was real. She believed that with all her heart.

She breathed in, no burning smells at all, only the salt spray and diesel from the engine. A very old-fashioned smell. Nothing ran on diesel anymore except boats and the few heavy trucks left on the road.

His finger caressed her cheek. "Beautiful night for the end of the world." She felt his deep voice vibrate in his chest.

"It is."

His large hand slid into her hair, holding her still as he leaned over and kissed her brow. "But if we do our jobs right and our guys up in Haven do their jobs right, it might not be the end of the world, after all."

"What do you think it might be like?"

"What?"

"The aftermath. What do you think might happen? Best-case scenario."

"Well." He took a deep sigh. "Best-case scenario. I'm the wrong guy to ask about a best-case scenario; soldiers tend to look at worst-case scenarios and plan accordingly. But okay. So . . . everything goes well in the next week. We stabilize the uninfected in their homes. Make sure they can protect themselves and have ample food and water. Once we get some air support, we drop in supplies. It looks like by next week most of the infected might be dead, if they can't fend for themselves. But we don't know if pockets of the virus can survive—you and your brainiac girlfriends will be able to tell us about that. So we need to make sure that vaccine gets to every able-bodied and able-minded man, woman, and child in the continental USA. And strict protocols on who gets in and out of the country. So international commerce is going to stop for a while. There's going to be an international economic crisis. The U.S. government is going to be very, very sorry it behaved like it did with us in California. It behaved badly, but there was a lot of panic. But if I know my captain and Mac, and I do, and if Snyder is as tough as his reputation, our guys are going to milk that regret for all it's worth. Any reconstruction work and money going on is going to happen here first."

She was listening and not listening. The words made sense and sounded nice. Underneath the words, his tone was level, the sound of a man who was already thinking ahead, part of a team of very smart people. Survivors.

Survivors. They were going to survive this. She felt that suddenly, in her bones. Strength of purpose, comradeship with a team of people, growing by the day. It was what was going to let them survive this terrible ordeal.

And who knew? Someday, maybe, this night rush up the coast of California, a brave warrior and a scientist, carrying a vaccine that could inoculate millions, would become part of history. Like Paul Revere's ride, only bigger, with something more important than victory in a war of independence at stake.

Someday perhaps schoolkids would read about this. Their mad dash upcountry, Haven's gathering in of thousands of uninfected, helping pockets of uninfected survive, then the pushback—she could see it. Fanning out in armored convoys, bearing the vaccine. Shoring up defenses, bringing supplies, moving on. The fortified communities reaching out to each other. Clearing bodies, clearing transport lines. The government lifting the quarantine, reconstruction workers pouring in . . .

God. It felt so good just to think in these terms. Not cowering, hoping to survive another night but fighting back. Helping others survive, rebuilding.

This nighttime trip would be an integral part of all that. The narrow boat spearing through the water, Jon watchful at the helm. The indifferent star-filled sky overhead watching over them.

Hope, which had fled her, crept back into her heart. Carefully. For hope was a fragile thing. But once hope takes root, it grows strong.

The sliver of moon traced a silver path through the calm ocean. Little ripples sometimes flashed over the ocean's surface, like twinkling stars. The quiet of the night, the low hum of the engine, the slight rocking of the boat lulled her, calmed her, and she drifted gently to sleep.

*Mount Blue*

Someone was tapping on her cheek. Elle instinctively tried to move her head away from the annoying tapping, but it was no use. Her eyes popped open and it took just a second to get oriented.

White room. White walls, white floor, lots of people in white lab coats. Smell of Formalin and reagents and electrical equipment. A lab. *The* lab, at Haven.

"That's it, Sleeping Beauty," her husband said, pulling gently at her shoulders until she sat up straight in her chair instead of slumping. "It's bedtime for you."

She blinked, shook her head. "No." The protest was automatic. So much to do, so little time. "We're behind in our schedule—"

"There will be no schedule if you work yourself to death," he said, touching the skin beneath her eyes. "You're exhausted. You've got bags under your eyes, Dr. Ross."

"Way to go, Mr. Ross. Convince your wife to do something by complaining about her looks."

He gave his slow smile. The one that never failed to turn her heart over. She'd been told that smile had been nonexistent until she came back into his life. "You're the most beautiful woman in the world, Dr. Ross. A few sleepless nights aren't going to change that. So stop fishing for compliments and trying to change the subject. The subject is you. You've been working the best part of three days. Mac hauled Catherine off to bed, against her objections." He shook his head. "You two just don't know when to quit."

Elle was bone tired. But there was so *much* to do before the vaccine arrived. When it did, they had to hit the ground running. "We've still got to stabilize the accelerated cell line, check the reagents, test the equipment."

"Well, if you two make a mistake because you're exhausted, you'll just have to waste time correcting that mistake. Honey, part of our training is knowing when to find a way to rest because no one can go flat-out for days at a time."

She gave him her own smile. "Oh. I thought you, Mac, Jon, and the captain were Supermen. Able to leap tall buildings in a single bound. Able to do your warrior thing for weeks, months."

"Uh-uh." Nick lifted her out of her chair, put a firm hand to the small of her back, started walking her out of the lab. "You're not going to distract me. You're going to our quarters, you're going to eat something warm, and then you're going to bed. You'll thank me later." He tapped his comms, said something quiet about food to someone on the other end while they walked down the corridor to the elevator that would take them to their quarters.

Quarters. That's what he called it. It sounded Spartan, but it wasn't. In any other place, it would be considered a very elegant small apartment with every modern con known to man, and some unknown. Like walls that could be turned into windows looking out over a mountain and the valley beyond.

She had a brand-new husband. It still surprised her. The spiritual counselor who'd officiated at their wedding ceremony had also married Mac and Catherine and was busy marrying couples who realized, in the midst of extreme danger, how much they loved each other. Nothing like the end of the world to get your priorities straight.

Haven worked. If there was one thing that had been brought home to her in the short time she'd been here at Haven, it was that Nick, Jon, and Mac, their captain, Lucius Ward, the three other Ghost Ops men who'd been rescued and, though half dead on their feet, capable of accomplishing a great deal and last, but certainly not least, the scary-looking but punctiliously polite former General Snyder, all of them were superbly capable men.

She, Catherine, and Sophie were good at what they did; they'd be able to produce the vaccine in industrial quantities, no question. But for what came next, delivering the doses to besieged communities, protecting the convoys as they made their slow laborious way around the state, coordinating air drops, ensuring that the growing number of refugees here at Haven had sufficient shelter, food, and water—that was something the men had to do. She knew nothing of security or logistics.

They'd created this amazing place while undercover as outlaws. They could do this too.

Nick was hurrying her to their place so she could rest, but he was as tired as she was. He had to be. She couldn't remember the last time he rested.

If she rested then he had to too.

Nick ushered her into their quarters. The nearly invisible door whooshed open at exactly the right time, just before Nick and she would have bumped noses against what looked like a wall. It had been coded to their bodies. Their morphology was the key that opened the door.

Nick rushed her in, then stopped, sniffing.

Elle lifted her head too, breathing in the deeply delicious smells. "Bless Stella," she said at the sight of the big steel industrial cart with covered dishes on it.

"Yeah, bless her," Nick said fervently. "Now you—" He touched the tip of a callused finger to her nose. "You are going to take a nice warm shower while I get this all set out. You're going to eat and then you're going to bed."

"Yes, Dad." Elle rolled her eyes but it was lost on Nick, who was busy uncovering dishes, setting out plates. God, the smells! Her stomach growled and she remembered she hadn't eaten in almost twenty-four hours. Now that Nick had forced her to pay attention to herself, she realized how hungry and tired she was. He'd been right and she was wrong. Fainting from hunger and exhaustion wasn't going to help anyone.

By the time Elle came out from the bathroom, where she'd had a blissfully long and hot shower, Nick had arranged everything on the dining table. Done right too. Mats and plates and cutlery and two glasses, because there was also some wine decanting.

She could afford one glass of wine. It would probably help her sleep.

"Madame," Nick intoned, a huge snowy napkin over one brawny forearm, the other hand pulling out her chair for her. He was trying to keep a straight face because Nick Ross did not look like a butler. Not in the slightest. He did look like a tough, very sexy man pretending for a second or two to be a butler.

Elle sat with a sigh, her first moment of relaxation since the plague began.

Nick was piling her plate high with food.

"Nick," she murmured. Her stomach started closing up. He looked up with a sharp gaze and stopped immediately. He set her plate in front of her.

"Eat," he ordered. "You're not hungry, I get that. You're too tired and stressed to be hungry. But trust me when I say you need some hot food in you. Once you start, you'll feel better. Start with one bite."

Okay. She tried a bite of risotto. Mushroom risotto, creamy, with cheese and butter. *Too rich*, she thought, until it settled warmly in her stomach.

"Another," Nick said and she put another bite in her mouth. Instead of a blocked system, gullet and stomach closed tighter than a fist, her system opened up and accepted another bite. And she found she was ravenous.

"That's my girl," Nick said as she started tasting the other dishes. Besides the risotto, which was of course delicious, Stella had sent a ragout of vegetables, baked goat cheese, an orange and fennel salad, fresh focaccia, and homemade raspberry ice cream.

She ate half of what was on her plate and sat back to watch Nick demolish everything else, fast and neat.

She sipped at her wine. "So. Sophie and Jon." She cleared her throat delicately. "That was a surprise."

Nick stopped, fork in midair. "Why?"

"I don't know." Elle turned her glass in her hands. "It just feels . . . weird."

She'd been utterly taken aback at seeing Sophie take Jon's hand, smile up at him in that unmistakable way women had when looking at their man. The way she looked at Nick, the way Catherine looked at Mac. Though it took a lot of courage on Catherine's part to look at Mac that way. Mac looked like he ate fragile young scientists for breakfast and spat out the bones.

Still, Catherine was very, very happy. And Mac was visibly completely in love with her. So that was working out okay.

"Weird how?" Nick spooned up the last of the raspberry ice cream and held it in front of her mouth. It was divine but she was stuffed. She shook her head.

"Well, for one thing, Jon doesn't seem her type."

"Sophie has a type?"

"Hmm. She's very picky." And detached when it came to men. They both were. Well, Elle wasn't anymore. She couldn't be detached about Nick. She'd loved him practically her whole life. He was in her blood and he made that blood boil. Sophie wasn't like that, she didn't do passion. Elle had seen her date dozens of men and Sophie shrugged them off. Perfectly acceptable men in suits, with retirement accounts, good jobs, advanced degrees. Sophie would go out once or twice then get bored.

So, a guy like Jon would be off Sophie's radar. Wouldn't he?

"What's Jon like?" Suddenly, Elle needed to know about the man with her friend. Sophie was out there all alone in incredible danger, becoming emotionally involved with the man sent to protect her. "He seems so—so cold. And controlled."

"You don't know him," Nick said, eyes steady on hers.

She ducked her head. No, no she didn't know Jon. She'd only met him days ago and those days had been stressful. And then the plague struck. She lifted her eyes to Nick's. "My best friend in the world is with him, right now. Her life in his hands."

"I can reassure you there, honey," Nick said briskly. "Jon is as good as they come. If anyone can keep your friend safe, that's Jon. He's fast and he's tough. And cool. Always thinking five steps ahead. Man's a machine."

"Saying he's a machine isn't helping," she whispered. This was insane. All she needed to care about was Jon bringing Sophie safely to Haven. What difference did it make if he was going to break Sophie's heart afterward? And yet—and yet . . . Sophie's *face* when she looked at Jon. Elle had never seen that expression before. Open, completely vulnerable. In the midst of all that chaos and death.

"Stop that." Nick looked at a spot over her head, then kissed her. "Stop overthinking this. I can practically see all the thoughts buzzing around in your head. You're just exhausting yourself and you're not doing your friend any good at all."

"I know." Elle shook her head. "I just can't help worrying about her."

"Stop it," Nick said again.

"Make me," Elle said. It came upon her like a burst of electricity. Her man, her husband, sitting there with all that coiled energy that seemed like such a part of him, like a panther or a lion. Some primal animal. Her man. The man she knew could kiss her and love her into a stupor. That was *exactly* what she needed, right this minute. To be loved into a stupor, to shove these thoughts circling endlessly right out of her head. "Make me forget all of this."

She was astounded at the voice coming out of her mouth.

Sultry, husky, daring. Pure sex. She'd never had that voice before in her life.

It had a magic effect on Nick. That tough, handsome face had been puckered with worry for her, tender and gentle. Suddenly, his features tightened, eyes glittering. The skin over his cheeks suffused with blood, as did his full lips. That was what he looked like during sex, though he wasn't even touching her.

But he was thinking about it . . . Oh yeah. Worried, tender Nick was gone, and Nick the conquering warrior was here, right in front of her. Predator looking at his prey.

The air around them suddenly bloomed with pheromones. The air was hot and heavy, and she could barely pull in a breath.

"You want me to make you stop thinking?" he asked. Nick's voice was a deep low growl. Oh God. Just hearing that tone made her skin prickle. He moved forward. "I can do that."

Nick kissed her, one of those kisses that went straight to pure sex. Some of his kisses were light and tender, tentative, like a question. This wasn't one of them. It was immediately openmouthed, carnal. A statement.

In a moment, they were on the bed, Nick lying heavily on top of her. Though Nick had been in her mind and heart since she was girl, they'd had sex one night—he'd been her first and last—and then had been separated for ten years. A week ago they'd found each other again, in the midst of terror and danger. Everything about being with Nick was unsettled and unsettling except for the fact that she loved him.

Every time they made love it seemed like something different from the last time. There was no routine, as she had always assumed other couples had. At times the sex was fast and furious, at times soft and languid. Never twice the same thing in a row.

This time, too, seemed different. He was urgent—his muscles tense, mouth demanding, hands quickly removing her clothes. And yet at the same time there was a vast tenderness there as his hard hands touched her, rolling her this way and that as he unbuttoned, unzipped, unclasped, shimmied down various items. And even when she was naked, he didn't move heavily on her, spreading her legs with his thighs, ready to enter her quickly. No, she was naked but Nick wasn't in her, something that would have given her cognitive dissonance if it weren't for the fact that his hands were so busy. His hands gave her almost as much pleasure as his sex. Cupping her shoulders, down over her breasts, thumbs brushing against her nipples giving her pleasure that shot straight to her womb, then skimming her sides, reaching her thighs, pulling them apart . . .

She waited in hot anticipation to feel his heavy weight shifting on top of her, because like any lab rat that had been fed pellets as a reward she knew, like she knew that the sun would rise in the east the next day, that amazing pleasure would follow. So she held her breath a little, eyes closed so she could concentrate on the feel of his body on hers, and waited.

But instead of rolling on top of her and entering her, he shifted lower. He opened her legs so his wide torso could fit between them, lifting them high and bending her thighs back so she was completely open to him.

And then his mouth was on her breasts and Oh! . . . Hot honey flowed through her veins.

Foreplay was rare with Nick and she cherished it. He was always apologetic about the lack after they had sex, but, well, Nick was Nick. And he knew what he wanted and what he wanted was to be inside her as deep and as hard as he could get, as fast as he could. His words, not hers.

Every single time he vowed to go slowly and every single time he failed.

So it was astonishing to feel him tense and hard as usual but making no move to enter her. It was hard to complain, though, while he was kissing one breast then another, taking a nipple in his mouth and tugging so hard a line shot straight to her sex and throbbed in time with his mouth.

She found herself relaxing, falling back into the arms of pleasure as if into a warm ocean, letting the current sweep her away. Nick's dark head moved over her breasts and she lifted a lazy hand to run it through his thick dark-brown hair. For such a hard man, his hair was so soft. She loved to touch it.

Looking down, all she could see was the top of his head, dark lashes, slashes of cheekbone and his mouth on her breast, suckling like a baby. Only this was no infant. Nick was a fully-grown male and he didn't make her feel motherly. Without looking up he whispered against her skin, "Close your eyes."

"What?"

"Close your eyes, you'll feel more."

Her eyes closed, and . . . Yes . . . Every single nerve ending was reporting back to headquarters. She could feel it all, everything, so intensely it was as if a wind had come to scour away several layers of skin. She could feel his mouth moving over her delicate skin, the rough day-old beard biting a little. His callused hands down her sides were warm and hard. He slid them to her hips then, unexpectedly, his entire body slid down. Her breasts, wet from his mouth, felt cold.

Her eyes fluttered open.

"Eyes. Closed," Nick whispered and she closed them again.

Nick kissed his way down her stomach, licking and taking tiny love bites, his face so close to her belly his eyelashes gave her butterfly kisses. Lower still, chin nuzzling against her pubic hair, then he opened her with his thumbs and, Oh God! Her back arched and Nick reached out with one big hand splayed on her chest and gently pushed her down. Her neck tilted back into the pillow, shaking with the intensity of the sensations. There was no question now of opening her eyes because she didn't have any strength to do anything but lie there, stunned by lavish pleasure.

He was kissing her there, kissing her sex, exactly as he kissed her mouth, his tongue creating electric pleasure. Pleasure so intense she forgot to breathe, couldn't think, was lost. And as he pleasured her with soft, deep kisses, pressure rising like the ocean rising to break upon the shore and she lost herself in the sharp, pulsing delight of an orgasm, the world fell away. All of it, forgotten. The grief, the danger, the knowledge that a deadly plague had been unleashed from *her* lab, a virus so deadly it could wipe humanity from the face of the earth, was wiped from her mind. She'd felt the weight of responsibility in every fiber of her being, sorrowful duty driving her on beyond her strength, unable to sleep or to rest.

That was what Nick had given her. A moment's pleasure beyond her ability to resist and as necessary as air.

She wanted to thank Nick but the words wouldn't form before she drifted away into sleep.

# Chapter 10

*Near Eureka*

The compound was exactly where the GPS said it would be, exactly as it had appeared in satellite photos. Two adobe walls that became concrete where they plunged into the ocean to create a private section of beach. Beyond, the shimmer of a pool and several light-colored structures set among lush vegetation. It was that moment when dawn was breaking, when vision was limited, but night vision no longer worked. That moment when professional soldiers never attacked.

Pros needed the night.

He'd been watching the shore carefully through NV goggles while Sophie slept. She needed to sleep. She'd been white as ice, dark bruises under haunted eyes. She'd never have admitted it, but she was shaking for an hour after they'd made it onto the boat.

Fuck, it had been close. Thank God he'd packed his Glock together with the stunner. They'd never have been able to cut the rope from the pier with a hatchet while all the infected were throwing themselves forward, hoping to make it onto the boat.

He'd never seen anything like that. He'd known they were fearless, but that had been something else. It had felt as if they were *eager* to die, just as long as someone, somehow got to them. Every single instinct he had as a warrior was wrong, didn't help. A warrior assumed his enemies didn't want to die and didn't want maiming wounds. You used that in soldiering, counted on it. Not even suicide bombers—and he'd had the immense pleasure of taking out a few—had behaved like that.

The infected had thrown themselves with abandon from the street level down onto the pier even though most of them fell in a useless heap, bones too broken to stand. But at the end, when fifty, a hundred people were lying there, broken, the next ones to fall fell on the broken bodies, not the concrete pier, and survived. They'd unhesitatingly leaped into the water, without any thought of water as a medium that could kill. Jon had watched in horror as dozens died after stepping off the pier, falling straight down, arms still flailing, still trying to grab him and Sophie.

This was the kind of danger no training could prepare you for, because it was, in the most literal sense of the term, alien. It couldn't have been more different if green monsters had stepped off a spaceship to attack. Aliens who did not share reflexes or instincts with humans.

So if he was terrified, so shocked it was only his training that kept him going, how could Sophie have felt less? And yet, terrified and shocked herself, she hadn't broken stride, hadn't faltered.

And she was brilliant. And a fucking beauty.

A woman like no other.

Man, he hadn't known women like this existed. He was way more experienced at fucking than relating. He'd spent his entire adult life in the military. And a lot of that time had been spent undercover, when having an affair could be lethal if you chose the wrong woman. Or deadly for her. For long stretches of time, fucking a woman meant painting a huge bull's-eye on her back. So no, relating, having an affair, hadn't been a good idea.

Undercover, his entire existence was a lie. He had no problems with lying and could keep it all straight in his head, no question. At various times he'd told women he was the son of an optometrist and lawyer, the son of a banker and a homemaker, the son of a professor of history and a bookstore owner. He had entire legends he could unspool instantly and be completely consistent and believable. Tales of his childhood, quirks of aunts and uncles, favorite pets. Oh yes, Jon could be convincing.

And at no time, ever, had he told any woman what he'd told Sophie. Even now he was astonished at himself. Not that he regretted it, no, but he was surprised. It hadn't been part of the mission in any way to bond with Sophie and yet . . . there it was. He'd told her who he really was, what he really came from.

Shit. That's what he came from. Misery and degradation

Every single story he'd ever told a woman had been rehearsed over and over until the genuine tones of sincerity could be heard. No one had ever questioned his cover story. Stories. There'd been so many of them.

He couldn't imagine ever telling anyone the truth, not even his teammates in Ghost Ops. He'd catch a bullet for them, every single man, but he'd never tell them the truth of his childhood. And here he'd told Sophie everything, without any hesitation. In fact, it had come geysering out of him, unstoppable, like blood out of a slashed artery.

He shook his head, barely understanding himself. Maybe it was this end-of-the-world thing. He could tell Sophie anything—even the truth—because they were going to die. But no. He knew he was going to do everything in his power—and his powers were considerable—to survive and to make sure Sophie survived. So that wasn't it.

For some crazy reason, he wanted Sophie to *understand* him, to *see* him as he really was. Tainted blood and everything. Yeah, how nuts was that? An exfil with a civilian was all about trust. Not the soldier's trust but the civilian's trust. Civilians had to instinctively trust that the soldier was going to get them the hell away, because when the soldier said jump, one second later the target's shoes had to be off the ground. Total blind trust was what would get them out. And so what did he do? Tell Sophie where he came from, not guaranteed to inspire a whole lot of trust, no.

What the fuck?

For the first time ever since he'd become a soldier, Jon was of two minds, had two conflicting desires.

Get Sophie out safely.

Let her know who he really was.

It was a form of insanity, maybe a reaction to the craziness and chaos he'd seen out on the streets. That was it. Except . . . he felt better after he'd told her. Cleaner, lighter.

Jon put down his binocs, checked his scanner. No infected. That made sense. It was a pretty empty part of the world, with the Humboldt State Park not far away. The infected could only go as far as their feet could take them. There hadn't been any people here before, and there weren't any infected now.

He looked around at the long flat beach stretching far into the distance north and south and at the vast flat expanse of the ocean.

Safe. They were safe. It seemed almost impossible after the scenes in San Francisco but they'd been granted this little oasis of calm. He had to make the most of it because they were going to have to cross the state through populated areas without being able to use the roads. In the dark.

"Honey." Jon nudged Sophie's shoulder with his own and watched her come out of the stages of sleep. Her breathing, slow and deep, became shallow, her eyes cycling rapidly behind her eyelids, hands opening and closing.

Suddenly her eyes opened and he was the first thing she saw.

Coming out of sleep can be a fearsome thing, that transition from the dream world to the real world. Particularly *this* world, breaking down before their eyes. So he was prepared for her to wake up plunged into despair because whatever she'd dreamed about, her worst possible nightmare, couldn't be worse than what was happening now.

She astonished him. Her eyes opened, focused on him like a deep blue beam, and she smiled when she saw him. "Hey." Her voice was husky with sleep. Face soft with emotion.

Goddamn. His throat was tight, his chest was tight. That soft look, lips slightly upturned . . . He cleared his throat. "Hey, yourself."

She turned her head, taking everything in. To the east, past the compound, the sky was lighter than the color of her eyes, and over the ocean it was a deep blue, darker than her eyes. It was chilly, but there wasn't a cloud in the sky. She studied the compound, silent and welcoming in the dawn. "We're here. We made it."

"We did. Up you go." He gave her his hand and she stood, still clutching the thermal blanket. "Let's get the boat squared away and go explore our new temporary home."

She nodded. He wanted to make sure the boat would be available to them at all times. They were safe here, but that could change in a heartbeat.

They tied the boat to the pier and walked down it, feet loud on the uneven planks. They carried everything with them—Sophie, her backpack, and Jon his combat pack and the vaccine case. If they had to make a run for it, they had to have everything to hand.

Sandstone steps led from the beach to the lowest level of the compound and . . .

"Wow," Sophie breathed.

"Yeah." It was spectacular, much more than a B & B. It was a mansion, spreading out over several stories but somehow intimate at the same time. "But we don't have time to sightsee. I want to get inside."

Jon hustled them along. They skirted an infinity pool, huge enameled planters with flowering plants, up cobblestoned pathways, across a terracotta-tiled terrace that could have doubled as a tennis court until they came to the entrance—a double-wide set of armored glass doors that were mirrored so he couldn't see inside. Jon checked his scanner compulsively. They were fucked if there were any infected inside. But the screen was blank. He checked the side of the huge glass entrance and found a screen. One swipe and the screen turned into a keypad. He had once memorized one hundred complex banking passwords of the Cortez cartel. One password was child's play. He entered the code, and with a slight pneumatic hiss, the huge glass door—as wide as his living room wall back in Haven—slid left.

Jon held Sophie back with an arm and entered silently, stunner up, eye on his scanner. There was the faintest possibility that the armored glass doors had a shield coating that provided a barrier so he couldn't read the presence of infected. But even past the glass doors, inside the huge foyer, the scanner was blank. He holstered the stunner and held his hand out to Sophie, who crossed the threshold wide-eyed.

There was another screen to the side of the door. He disengaged the alarm and relocked the door, punching in *mylove* with a secret smile.

He looked at Sophie.

She'd slept some in the boat, sitting up. She was far from rested. Her body had pumped itself full of norepinephrine—adrenaline—to use her body's resources to the fullest. She'd run as fast as she could, suppressed fear reactions as much as she could, and the trembling afterward had been the price. He was surprised at how well she was doing. Most civilians would be a wreck for days afterward as the chemicals of terror washed out of their systems.

He himself, like his teammates, had been inoculated against that during training, and they had a different biochemical reaction to stress, anyway. They'd been tested for it. His brain, like that of Mac and Nick and the captain, like that of all Special Forces soldiers, released a chemical called neuropeptide Y that automatically counteracted stress hormones and kept the frontal lobe ticking while that of other people subjected to the same stress simply shut down.

In other words, he was wired to keep calm under intense pressure.

It was a trick of his body and he'd been born that way, just like every other special forces soldier.

He wished he could give Sophie the gift of time to come down from the stress of their flight out of San Francisco, but he couldn't. So maybe he could pamper her instead.

"It's beautiful." Sophie smiled, tilted her head back to look at the ceiling of the atrium, two stories high. A huge chandelier, big flowering plants . . . even empty it had a feeling of warm welcome.

Jon nodded. "It is. What do you want first—shower or food? The way Robb described it there should be running hot water."

"Shower, definitely."

"Okay." Jon tugged at her hand. "Master bedroom and bath on the first floor, that's what Robb said. Let's explore."

They walked through a tall arch right into the Robb living area. Man, it was nice. Jon had never had a home of his own, military all the way since he was seventeen. His quarters at Haven were the closest thing to a personal space he'd ever had. But if he were ever to have a home of his own—and he couldn't imagine how—this would be what he'd want.

They walked through large rooms that somehow were both beautiful and cozy. Man, Robb had more rooms than Jon had guns.

Finally they opened a door onto a huge bedroom that had two sitting areas and a door on the other side of the room. Far, far away.

"Looks like we're here." Jon checked the scanner once more, then started dumping their gear onto a sofa, the case on the hardwood floor next to the sofa. It felt good to shed the weight.

Sophie dropped her backpack and stretched her shoulders.

The windows faced east and the room was suddenly flooded with light as the sun rose up over the walls. Everything in the room gleamed. The light picked out the bright colors of the sofas and the multicolored bedspread. Small pots of still-fresh flowers were everywhere, thriving plants everywhere, making the air smell fresh.

Sophie roamed around the room, touching the furniture lightly. She stopped at a chair and picked something up.

"Look, Jon." It was a large pale pink shawl, scarf . . . thing. She held it up, stroked it, then carefully folded it and tucked it into her backpack. "It's so beautiful. Pure cashmere. No wonder Robb's wife wants it. It's a wonderful gift."

It was. Jon stood in the middle of the luxurious beautiful room, filled with light in all senses of the term.

No one had ever accused Jon of being a sensitive man. As far as he knew, he didn't have a sensitive bone in his body. And yet—he was picking up on the vibes of this room. A room that had been carefully decorated to please all the senses, a room that somehow still held the echoes of a man who loved his wife.

He stopped at an oil portrait of Robb hanging over a simple yet elegant cabinet. The man was bending slightly forward, as if ready to come right out of the painting. He was dressed casually in a sweatshirt, solid, middle-aged. A little more handsome than in real life. Jon peered at the signature in the lower right-hand corner. Anna Robb. So the wife was an artist, and loved her husband right back.

Jon rubbed absently at a place on his chest, then shepherded Sophie to the far wall. He'd been right. The door opened onto an opulent bathroom with more showerheads than he'd had hot meals. Acres of tile and light green marble, accessories catering to every single bodily function, including . . . Jon looked at that shower with the built-in bench, his body automatically responding to the idea of him there with Sophie on his lap, hot water streaming down over them . . . Then he looked at Sophie's bruised eyes.

No, he thought with a sigh. No way.

"We're free to use anything in the house. I'm sure you can find something clean to wear. You'll feel better after a shower and a change. I'll check for another shower. I think I saw the kitchen and dining room on the way here, so we can meet there in, say, ten minutes." Sophie's eyebrows rose. "Okay, fifteen." They rose even higher and he sighed and said, "Meet you in the kitchen whenever you're ready."

Jon had time to shower, shave, find the kitchen, set the table, and start studying the fully stocked fridge, freezer, and pantry before Sophie showed up. He smelled her before he saw her. It was Anna Robb's perfume—or shampoo or shower junk or whatever—but it suited Sophie. Fresh and springlike and it mixed well with the smell of her own skin, which was imprinted deeply into Jon's lizard brain.

His dick sprang to attention.

Fuck.

He'd put his lightweight cotton sweatpants on and his woodie would be visible from the moon. Certainly from the drone overhead if it hadn't already left.

What *was* this? His dick did what it was told, always. In the Cortez stronghold, he'd had Joaquin's sister constantly rubbing against him like a cat in heat. And since fucking Cortez's sister while fucking with their business was a guaranteed one-way ticket to a grave, he'd kept it in his pants. Even hinted he might be gay.

He didn't care, because Carmela hadn't turned him on in any way. He'd watched as, stoned out of her mind, she'd fucked her way through the entire security team in the compound, and there'd been practically an army there.

So, no, Carmela hadn't been a temptation, but Sophie sure as hell was.

"Jon?" God, even her *voice* nearly brought him to his knees. It certainly brought him fully, painfully erect. "What are you cooking?"

Luckily, Jon was a highly trained warrior with lightning-fast reflexes that had got him out of many a tight spot.

He grabbed an apron that was hanging next to the stove. It was one of those fancy full-frontal heavy cotton things, deep burgundy with the name of some winery stitched on it in gold letters. Right across the chest. Perfect—kept the eye on chest level and not lower. He was tying it around his waist as he turned, and was able to keep his voice light.

"I don't need to cook anything. Look." With a dramatic flourish, he opened the huge stainless steel refrigerator door, covering himself. Not for nothing had they been taught to multitask. Shoot and roll. Run and reconnoiter. Talk and hide a woodie.

Man, he was good.

Sophie buried her pretty head in the freezer compartment, and while she was running through the ample selection, Jon thought truly terrible thoughts, like they could be dead this time tomorrow. Brought his boner right down, it did.

Sophie stood up with her arms full. "Okay, I've made my choices. Do you want to go through them?"

"Nah, I'm happy to eat whatever you choose."

She smiled. "Well then, take that apron off and join me at the table."

Oh shit. "No, I, uh—" It was really hard to think when the blood that was supposed to be in your head was lower down. "I'm going to nuke the nukeable ones, so that officially makes me cook, right? Chef, I mean."

She tilted her head and examined him. The god of horny soldiers was with him because her eyes never went below his neck. "Okay. I saw a salad in the fridge too. Do you want me to dress it?"

"Ah—" For just a second Jon pulled a blank, imagining a salad in a frilly dress. His hands were full so he couldn't thunk himself in the forehead. "Yeah. Sure. I like balsamic."

There was an MP6 player in a docking station and he switched it on. The room instantly filled with music. It was like being in the middle of a jazz ensemble, right smack in the middle, next to the bass. The Robbs sure had top-notch stuff. Jon had priced a system like that and it cost upward of ten thousand dollars.

Sophie was boogeying to the table with a big salad bowl, bare-foot, humming the tune she apparently knew. Some jazzed-up rock ballad.

Jon stared at her back as she fiddled with various condiments, pretty feet moving in some kind of complicated dance moves.

"Geeks dance?" he called as the microwave dinged and he took something out, put something else in. He couldn't be bothered to look at what he was doing because Sophie dancing was just . . . magic.

She looked over her shoulder and smiled at him, did another little complicated dance move and bowed. "Ten years at Mrs. Purcell's Dance Academy. Did classical ballet, jazz, ballroom. If you ask nicely, and if I can find a pair of tap shoes, I can tap dance for you."

God. Sophie tap dancing. He'd pay good money to see that.

Wait. They'd stolen millions from the cartel. He had lots of money. "I'd pay a million dollars to see you tap dance for me."

Sophie laughed, then looked at his face. Her pretty jaw dropped. "You're serious."

"As a heart attack. The very first chance I get to find tap dancing shoes, you're on." He stacked the hot plates on a tray and walked over.

"Do warriors dance?"

Fuck, no. "Two left feet, sorry."

"I'll bet I could get you to do a mean salsa."

Jon stared. "You mean those complicated Latin American steps? No way." He shuddered at the thought.

"You spent time in South America. You told me you spent two years."

He shook his head, breathing in the luscious smells coming from the food. He dug in. It tasted as good as it smelled.

"Colombia, which is like a country from another galaxy. And I was undercover, trying to stay alive. Not much dancing going on." Shooting and torturing and whoring and coke-sniffing, yeah. Dancing? Not so much.

"Come out dancing with me and you'll be Fred Astaire in no time." She'd found a blue tracksuit in Anna Robb's closet that looked great on her. She was more slender than Anna Robb so it hung loosely, but the color brought out the deep blue of her eyes and accentuated her pale, perfect skin.

He laughed. "I find that hard to believe, but you're on."

They smiled at each other, then suddenly their smiles faded. For just a moment, they'd lived in a little bubble of alternate reality, the world as it once was. But outside this beautiful home was the world as it was now. Millions dead, entire cities burned to the ground, monsters ravaging the streets.

It would be a long, long time before anyone danced again.

Sophie hung her head, a stricken look on her face. A single tear welled over, tracked down her pale cheek.

Tears. Fuck no. Jon would do anything to make her feel better. Anything.

He wiped away the tear with his thumb. "What would have happened if we hadn't met right now?"

Sophie's face lifted. "What?"

"If we hadn't met now but, say, a year ago. What would have happened? Because, you know, we've got something going here." He waved a finger between them, then heaped her plate with slow-cooked peppers, roast lamb, and warm corn bread. "So given that there's . . . chemistry"—which was a mild word for what he was feeling—"given that, how do you think it would have played out? You'd take me dancing, okay. Maybe I'd take you target shooting. And then?"

She sniffed, gave a soggy half laugh. "You'd take me *target shooting*? Is that your idea of showing a girl a good time?"

He had no idea. He'd never had a real relationship, never courted a woman, never even thought of it. He had fuck buddies and even they were occasional. He tended to disappear in and out of women's lives. Nobody missed him when he was gone and it was mutual. Easier that way. Safer.

"Well, since it's a mind exercise, let's suppose I wasn't in black ops, I was in something else. Something like—"

His mind pulled a blank.

Sophie cocked her head, looked at him carefully. "What were you good at in college?"

This was *exactly* the point where Jon started lying. He'd invent some bullshit about what a great time he'd had in college, how he'd played football and scraped by with gentleman's

Cs. He'd spin funny stories about what he'd done, and he'd be perfectly plausible and he'd remember every single word he told her, just as he remembered every single word of every single bullshit story he'd told every woman.

But Sophie was different. Those beautiful eyes were sharp, intelligent, and kind. It was the fucking end of the fucking world. He didn't have to keep anyone's secrets anymore. Not Uncle Sam's, not Ghost Ops', not even his own.

He could—and he felt a sharp thump of shock in his heart—he could tell her the truth. Be himself.

"I didn't go to college," he said, looking her straight in the eyes. "I went straight into the military, where it was discovered that I have an aptitude for combat and for undercover work. By that I mean I have an aptitude for lying. I don't like saying this, but it's true. But I swear to you, right here, Sophie, that I will never lie to you. And you are the first person since I was nine years old I have been able to say that to."

She reached over, held his hand tightly.

"Going into the military made a lot of sense for you. It became your surrogate family."

Jon nodded, throat tight.

"But . . . besides shooting and fighting and lying, what else were you good at?"

"Computers. I have an affinity for computers." In virtual reality, you could be anyone you wanted to be. And computers were cool and logical. Unlike people, you could always figure them out. People didn't operate on binary code.

"Okay. Let's work with that. Because clearly if you were constantly on mission we wouldn't have been able to date in any meaningful way. So . . . let's suppose you worked for some computer firm in Silicon Valley and we met at, let's say, a party. In San Francisco. Does that work for you?"

"No." Jon shook his head. "Absolutely not. Because if I were a civilian, I wouldn't work for anyone. I'd own the company."

"Oh!" Sophie's face lit with amusement. "So you're *rich*?"

"Damn straight."

"Okay, then. This gets better and better. So I go to a party, which I normally do rarely and reluctantly, and lo and behold here's this handsome blond guy, very rich, owns his own company. I'm not particularly in the market, but he's got these incredible ice blue eyes and he's ripped—and let's remember he's rich, and I go, *Whoa!*"

"And me?" Jon helped himself to seconds of everything. "I meet this stunning geek. A scientist who looks like a movie star only better, and I get turned on by the thought of her in a white lab coat."

Sophie laughed. "There is nothing sexy about lab coats, Jon. Trust me on this."

He waggled his eyebrows. "A lab coat and nothing else?"

She thought about it, grinned. "Okay. That would work. So—we meet. We're both attracted. What happens? And I warn you, I'm not tremendously smooth in social situations."

"Well." Jon took her hand. "I take your hand and look deeply in your eyes and ask you some incredibly intelligent questions about viruses."

"And am I expected to ask you some incredibly intelligent questions about computer code?"

"No. Just standing there and breathing would do the trick. That would've worked for me. And I would've asked you out to dinner the next evening. And the evening after that, and the one after that."

"No coy games?"

"Man, no. Coy's not my thing. I want something, I go after it." Jon couldn't think of something he'd wanted and hadn't made a beeline for. It had just never been a woman before.

"Well, frankly, I don't think I would have said no. A year ago, though, I was working pretty long hours. I don't know if I would have been free for dinner all the time."

"I'd have come down and invited you out to lunch. You have a lunch place?"

"You'd drive down from Palo Alto every day to take me out to lunch?" At Jon's decisive nod, she shook her head at his looniness. "Okay, yes. I do have a lunch place, around the corner from the Arka building. This really nice Asian fusion fast-food eatery. Buffet-style. Not chic but good."

"I don't need chic and even marginally good is fine. Considering how much crap I've eaten in the field. So—I'd drive down to have lunch with you. As often as I could."

"That would have been so nice," Sophie said softly, curling her hand around his.

Would have, could have . . . all of this belonged to a world long gone. A world that actually never was, because Jon wasn't a successful entrepreneur, a man with a good job and a bright future. Before the shit came down, he'd been a warrior turned outlaw with no ability to offer any woman, let alone a woman as bright and desirable as Sophie, any kind of future. So this little fantasy was doubly impossible.

But . . . shit. It was enticing. He could see it, feel it, he could almost taste it, this alternate universe. The one where he got to meet Sophie, woo her, wed her even, because—why the fuck not? Why should he be the only one incapable of having a wife, a family? The Ghost Ops team had been chosen precisely because they didn't have families, and were very unlikely to create any. If you'd held his feet to the fire, he'd have sworn Mac and Nick were like him—completely incapable of love and bonding. And just look at them now. They were head over heels in love with their mates, and Mac was going to become a father, as weird as that sounded. So why should he be different?

His drive to become a soldier just as soon as humanly possible came straight from the horrors of his childhood. From his visceral understanding, learned well before he had the words to express it, of how dangerous and violent the world was. Particularly to the small and weak.

He hadn't even formulated to himself his desire to sign up. It had seemed as natural a next step as breathing. The military, with its emphasis on teamwork and structure, had seemed God-given at the time. Not to mention the fact that he *relished* the training. The harder, the tougher he became, the better.

His every waking thought had been to make himself strong and never be a helpless victim again. And to make sure there were as few people like his parents and Popper as possible in the world.

But—just supposing that hadn't been his obsession because he'd been safe and loved as a child. It was hard to fathom, but just suppose. It might very well be that without all that darkness in his childhood he'd have gone to MIT or Stanford, become a computer expert, founded a company. Met a lovely woman like Sophie, marry her, even. Why not? Have kids. Other people had kids. Just because he panicked at the thought of children of his in this world didn't mean the other Jon, AltJon, would panic.

He'd love and protect his wife and their children, who would grow up in turn happy and healthy. Maybe in a house just like this one, which emanated love and happiness in every corner.

The images bloomed bright for a moment, then faded. Because the real Jon, and the real world, were right there in front of his eyes. There was no rosy future for him with Sophie as his wife. He'd been cut off from that practically at birth. How the fuck was he supposed to know anything about creating a happy marriage, a happy family?

His parents had been so damaged, they could barely stand upright. Their blood flowed in his veins. No, he was genetically unsuited for a happy family life. This was a brief moment in time in which he indulged in a flash fantasy, but the truth was, Jon wasn't mate material. He was damaged inside, broken. It wasn't his fault, but there it was. He lacked everything, every instinct, that would allow him to marry and stay married. He was too used to lying, to being undercover, to knowing he was moving on. To the next op, the next mission.

And what the hell was he thinking anyway?

Monsters were running around the streets. Civilization had fallen. Mac and Catherine were going to bring a child into a world that might be reverting right back to the Stone Age at the speed of light.

The future was dark, as bleak as it had ever been in the history of humanity . . .

His hand in Sophie's was suddenly warm, the warmth creeping up his arm. He lost his train of thought, trying to put it all back together again, but he couldn't. All he could think about was how warm his hand in Sophie's was and—

"That's a fabulous song!" Sophie exclaimed and stood up, pulling him up with her. "Let's dance."

The song was familiar. He couldn't have named it, though his cell phone could. But his cell was in his backpack next to one of the sofas. Never mind, what difference did it make that he didn't know the name of the song? He never paid attention to music, knew nothing about it, but you couldn't avoid it. It was everywhere—in restaurants and shops, elevators and airports. He'd never paid the slightest attention to the song, but he could actually hum along if he had a voice, which he didn't.

"I warned you, didn't I, that I can't dance?" He looked uneasily down at their feet. Her pretty feet were bare. He'd put his boots back on. "I really don't want to step on your toes, so maybe this isn't such a good idea."

She was humming the tune, moving smoothly into his arms. "Tut-tut, Jon. Big bad warrior, scared of a woman's feet. Scared of a little music." She shook her head sorrowfully. "I can't believe this. You, a coward."

He opened his mouth to answer her, a little shocked. No one had ever called him a coward before. He was just about to shoot off a response when he realized . . . he was dancing! She'd just moved them into the rhythm while he wasn't paying attention. He was *dancing!* The real thing, too, not the miserable two-step that was basically shifting his weight from one foot to the other, which was the best he'd ever achieved before. He was moving, doing real steps. And it was all Sophie. She wasn't exactly leading, but every move she made was so natural, fit the music so well, and left a little opening where his body naturally fit, that they were dancing with some real moves.

"I'm dancing," he said. He sounded as stunned as he felt.

"Good going, slick. Now let's kick it up a notch and make a turn." And by God they did, together. Totally naturally and gracefully. They turned again. It felt like flying. Her legs moved easily against his and they were thigh to thigh, hip to hip, breast to chest. She had to feel his hard-on, but she just kept on dancing and he kept on following her.

It was magic. Unlike anything he'd ever felt or done before. He and Sophie were like one person, led by the music. Moving together, breathing together. He'd swear their heartbeats were synchronized. She moved closer because the closer they were, the better they danced. It was one of the very few moments in his life in which Jon simply let go and let someone else take over. But it was okay because this was Sophie.

The beat was seductive, fast enough to be lively, slow enough to allow him to keep the beat, the music so familiar it was in his head already before it reached his ears. Sophie's entire body was alive under his hands. She danced with her shoulders and her breasts and—oh God!—with her hips against his, brushing against his hard-on in a natural way, without being provocative, though of course she was. This was Sophie. All she had to do was breathe and he was there.

Normally a woodie that wasn't going anywhere hurt. Was ridiculous, a waste of energy. But this one was okay. They'd be on that big bed soon enough and, in the meantime, crazy as it sounded, they were basically making love. Okay, technically his dick wasn't inside her but now they were so close that if they weren't both dressed, it would take just a second. Lift her up, position her legs around his waist, and there he'd be—balls deep in Sophie.

But as a second best, this wasn't bad. Wasn't bad at all. His hand had drifted down from the small of her back to her luscious bottom, and he was holding her tightly against him. Each movement opened up the lips of her sex against him.

The sweat suit pants were cotton and she wasn't wearing any

underwear. His cock had surged upward when he realized that. Against him, beneath the top and the sweatpants, there was no barrier, nothing but warm woman. So with each sway and whirl, her soft breasts moved against his chest and his cock was more firmly lodged against the lips of her sex. Each movement made him swell, but it wasn't just his cock.

Every bit of him grew, became supersensitive. Every cell of his body felt attuned to the woman in his arms, to the music, to the very air. The room glowed with early morning sun, but the woman in his arms glowed even more. She was like sunlight in his arms, light in every sense of the word.

The music rose, the soft undertones of the beat now prevailing, heavy and insistent, echoing his heartbeat—rising, rising, then stopped. Somehow Sophie had coaxed him with her body into a series of twirls, stopping exactly with the music, up on tiptoe at the end of the last twirl, fully against him, breathing hard.

He was breathing hard, too, but not from the exercise. The entire dance had been a form of foreplay, the best in his life. Foreplay to a beat. Shit, he was going to have to remember this moment, because it was never going to get better.

The morning light caught her face and it was glowing, radiant, eyes bright, cheeks flushed, full mouth open, lips slightly pouting. God. Irresistible. He didn't even try to resist.

Her mouth tasted of fruit and honey, the most incredible delicacy that had ever touched his. No light kisses, not after that dance, which had been pure sex, everything but penetration. He plunged into her mouth, starving for that taste and even after they stopped moving, his heart continued that fast beat of the music, as if he were running. It felt like they were moving only they weren't, it's just that the world spun around them.

Sophie went even further up on tiptoe, arms tight around his neck, breasts arching against his chest. Her hips moved, sex rubbing hard against his dick and he swelled even more. She felt it, moved against him harder, moaned into his mouth.

The temptation to drop to the floor, pulling down her pants and his, sliding into her fast and start fucking her hard, was enormous. She wanted it, he wanted it, the floor was right there. But . . . this was Sophie.

"Bed," he gasped when he lifted his mouth slightly.

"Bed," she repeated and kissed him hard. She was lifting herself slightly so that she was riding his cock instead of rubbing it back and forth.

Jon gasped for air. He was on fire.

Bed. Right now. The fastest way there was to carry her because the bedroom was about a mile from the kitchen, and carrying her was more romantic than dragging her by the hand at a dead run. He picked her up and the moment her head was cradled against him, she kissed him, mouth hot and sweet.

His knees buckled. He managed to stiffen them at the last second before falling in a heap right onto the light-colored hardwood floor. All of a sudden the distance from here to the bedroom seemed like a chasm, an impossible distance. Sophie was kissing him and kissing him and he felt weak and rubbery, completely different, right down to his core.

Jon never felt weak. He'd once taken a bullet. It had gone right through him without hitting major organs or a bone or an artery, and he'd been patched up. He'd been mostly angry and a little sheepish because he hadn't zagged fast enough. But weak? Fuck no. He could run as long as he had to, he could march with a hundred-pound pack for as long as he had to, but right now, carrying Sophie into Robb's bedroom just seemed impossible. He wanted to get there as fast as possible, but someone had nailed his boots to the ground.

"Bed," Sophie whispered against his mouth again, and it was as if someone had released him from bonds. He took off at a sprint, carrying her.

Special Ops soldiers are taught to run in a special way, so they can run and shoot straight at the same time. It came in really useful right now because he wanted to run and carry and kiss Sophie at the same time. It was a funny, short-stepped gait that looked weird to outsiders, but it got the job done. And Sophie wasn't looking at his feet, her eyes were closed.

And damned if his eyes didn't close too. Which was crazy, of course. He was running with a woman in his arms through unfamiliar territory *with his eyes closed*. Any drill instructor he'd ever come across would have screamed in his face and ordered him to drop and give him five hundred push-ups.

But Jon had really good spatial awareness and a really good memory. He knew where everything was. He wasn't going to fall down with Sophie in his arms. Not now, not ever.

In seconds they were in the master bedroom that looked east, the sun halfway up the sky filling the room with light. It blossomed under his eyelids because his eyes were still closed, kissing Sophie. All he saw behind his closed eyes was gold.

She slid down his body to her feet. He was holding her still for his kiss with one hand behind her head, the other feverishly pulling down the sweat suit pants, unzipping the hoodie, and then Sophie was naked in his arms. He held her so tightly she gasped and he loosened his hold a little. It was amazingly hard to do.

"You now." Jon opened his eyes to see Sophie half smiling up at him. She was aroused. Her high cheekbones were flushed, her eyes wide and sparkling, her mouth full and red from his kisses, dark hair tousled from his hands.

She'd said something but he hadn't understood. He was beyond understanding words—all he understood now was body language and his body was telling him, *Get into Sophie as fast as you can.* And her body must have been telling her more or less the same thing. Her nipples were hard, deep pink, the left breast trembling with her heartbeat. She was flushed down to her breasts as if she'd already had an orgasm.

Maybe she had? Maybe she'd climaxed while they were dancing. Man, what a turn-on that idea was. There was one way to find out. His hand moved from her back down the delicate curve, over her luscious ass, all the way down. He waggled his hand and her legs obediently opened and he touched her there, right there, where he wanted to put his cock.

Soon.

He ran his fingers down her slick opening from behind. He all but sighed. Her lips there were puffy and wet, like pouty lips waiting for his kiss.

"Take your clothes off, Jon."

Sophie was talking. He heard the noise and could even feel the puff of her breath against his neck, but the words made no sense. No words made sense just now. The only thing that made any sense at all was the feel of Sophie against him, his fingers sliding in and out of her soft wetness. He slid a finger in and she clenched around him, like the beginning of an orgasm. Oh yeah . . .

And then she was moving away from him, sliding out of his arms, his hand sliding out of her. He felt cold and bereft. Why was she moving?

"Jon!" She slapped his chest.

Jon rubbed it. Not because she'd hurt him—she couldn't hurt him if she tried unless she had a firearm—but because something inside his chest felt inflamed, almost painful.

She'd called his name. He made a sound. If you were charitable it could be considered a *huh?* But really, it was a grunt.

Sophie rolled her eyes, then tugged on his shoulder, pulling him down. He went willingly. He was more than willing to do whatever Sophie wanted. She wanted him to bend over? Hell yeah! He bent over, waiting for whatever she wanted.

What she wanted was to pull off his long-sleeved tee. And when he straightened, pull down his pants. His dick sproinged out. He toed off his boots, stepped away from his pants, and they both looked down at his dick, flushed with eagerness, shiny with pre-come at the tip, so hard it was practically flat against his stomach.

She looked up at him. "That's quite something."

He had no air in his lungs to answer her and even if he did have some air, he had no words. He just looked at her dumbly, like an animal hoping for a treat.

Sophie smiled at him. Her face was beautiful in repose, but when she smiled, it was like the sun coming out, brighter than what was shining down through the windows.

Her fingers curled up in a *come to me* gesture.

Oh yeah.

For a second, it had been as if he were under a spell. Her looking at him, staring at his dick, had somehow paralyzed him. He was waiting for whatever she wanted, only she hadn't let him know what it was. Now, with that curl of her long, slender fingers, she made it explicit. She wanted him.

*Now* he knew what to do.

He was nearly shaking with excitement, as if he'd never had

sex before in his life. And really he hadn't. Not like this, anyway.

If he'd had some blood in his head, he'd have been ashamed of himself. He was super cool in bed. He had a strategic mind that extended itself to sex. He could catch the smallest clue, like broken breathing, a slight flush. Give him ten minutes, and he'd become the world's greatest expert on what kind of sex that woman wanted and he'd oblige. Fast, slow, hard, soft. He could do it all.

His entire repertory had simply fled from him now. There was only one kind of sex he was capable of with Sophie and that was the desperate kind. But she deserved better than that.

So he took a deep breath, and with superhuman discipline he calmed himself down a little. Tensed his muscles to make them go slow. There wasn't anything in the world he could do about his dick, though. Nothing could make it go down just a little so it looked more like a human organ and less like a caveman's club. It felt like it would never go down again in his lifetime. Like an erection was a permanent state.

"Make me go slow," he pleaded. He reached his hand out, slowly, pushing it through the air as if through a hard barrier. He touched her shoulder, palm completely open. He had strong hands and he was unsure he'd be able to regulate his strength if he cupped her shoulder. "I don't have too much control now, so make sure I don't overdo it." He closed his eyes, swallowed. "Don't . . . hurt you." That last came out of a scratchy throat. He felt scratchy, all over, buzzed with anxiety. Not a good feeling. Man, the idea of hurting Sophie . . .

He opened his eyes again. He'd been half expecting a look of triumph or at least pleasure, because he'd just put all the power in Sophie's hands. He'd told her how excited he was, that he didn't have much control. In any other woman he'd expect coy smugness. But Sophie's look was sober, tender. It was as if she could see that he was suffering and couldn't bear it. She touched his cheek and again there was that weird warmth, that feeling of well-being.

"I won't let you hurt me, Jon. You think you might hurt me, but you couldn't. Trust me on this." Keeping her hand on his cheek, she lifted herself on tiptoe to kiss his cheek.

A kiss on the cheek. Considering the image that had been buzzing around in his head—holding her still with his hands while he hammered into her—a kiss on the cheek was nothing. Not even scratching the itch.

But—it worked, somehow. The buzzing in his head and the almost-violent sexual images floating around inside it slowed, disappeared. What was left was a soft humming and images of gentle kisses and slow, tender movements.

Yeah, that was it.

Before that nasty buzzing could get going again, Jon moved forward and she shuffled backward until her knees touched the edge of the bed. "Lie down, honey."

She obeyed. Robb and his Anna hadn't made the bed before fleeing, so Sophie settled down on rumpled sheets. They were flowery and made a nest around her so she looked like a pearl on a bed of roses. Her skin glowed, pale and perfect, her dark hair tousled around her head. Long, slender, graceful limbs. Soft eyes looking at him, waiting for him.

His limbs moved jerkily as he lay down next to her. He wanted inside her like he wanted his next breath, but she was just too beautiful. He wanted to feast on her for just a little while more.

Stretched out at her side, Jon touched an eyebrow with the tip of his forefinger. Just the lightest touch. Everything about her sent him into sensory overload. Every inch of her body called out to be looked at, touched, kissed. He'd start slow, just like he promised.

He followed the dark graceful eyebrows. His finger traced the perfect oval of her face, lingering on the dimple in her slightly pointed chin. Next, her lips, velvety soft. They opened at his touch and she breathed in deeply. She followed his eyes as he looked at her, finger tracing her jawline, then down, across the delicate collarbones. She was flushed, light rose over pearl.

Jon's eyes dropped as did his finger, down over the center line of her body, between her breasts. Up again, to lightly circle her nipples, now a deep rose color. When he stroked her breast, his thumb ran over the velvety skin of her nipple and she shivered.

"You like that?" Jon whispered, unable to take his eyes from her breasts.

"I like it all, Jon." Her voice was low, too, though there was probably no one within a radius of fifty miles. No one human, anyway.

He bent quickly, licked her nipple, keeping his hand on her belly. When he licked it again, her belly muscles contracted. He let out his breath in a long, slow release.

He liked that he was engaging in a little foreplay, but this was more about him, really. Him trying to gain some control. These slow movements, step by step, were helping him.

The tip of his forefinger ran along her side, where she narrowed to a ridiculously small waist then flared out again. She was as perfect a woman as he'd ever seen in his life. Then over her belly to the belly button, the cutest little innie ever. It made him smile just looking at it.

His big, tanned, scarred hand looked like a blunt instrument on her velvety skin. It was the most erotic contrast possible.

His eyes rose to hers now because he was going exploring in a place where he couldn't see so he wanted to watch her face. The finger went down, down. She didn't need for him to tell her to open her legs. They opened automatically, her heels making a swishing sound on the sheets. Jon kept watching her eyes, but he had excellent peripheral vision and she made this luscious picture on the rose-patterned sheets, skin flushed all over, cherry red nipples, the lips of her sex shiny and open.

For him.

He touched her there, as delicately as he could. Such tender, tender flesh and his hands were so calloused. But there was no abrasion because she was so slick, so ready for him. His forefinger slid into her and she just closed around his finger like a little mouth. He pulled out a little, pressed in, and she gave a little sigh.

Again, and again. Then her sex clamped around his finger in one convulsive pull that showed again in her belly muscles.

If he were a gentleman, he'd let her climax around his fingers, then he'd go down on her and make her come again and then and only then he would mount her.

But he wasn't a gentleman. Not in any way. He slid his hand out from her and pulled her thighs even further apart, moved over her and slid into her, all in one smooth hard motion.

They both stilled. He was fully on top of her, trying to keep some of the weight of his torso on his forearms. He tilted his head forward until his forehead met hers.

"That feels so good." Her voice was low, warm and rich.

He nodded, his head against hers.

"It would feel even better if you moved, though." Her lips curved in one of those mysterious Mona Lisa smiles only beautiful women knew how to produce.

He exhaled slowly. Pulled out. Pushed back in. It felt like heaven. He was finding it hard to pull out because it felt so good just being buried deep inside Sophie, where it was warm and tight and welcoming. But he tried it again. It was awful pulling back, fantastic sliding back in.

Again.

His movements weren't smooth and steady as they usually were. They were jerky, rough. He was barely in control of himself, moving on instinct alone.

Sophie lay her hand on his butt and directed his movements, guiding him until he was able to control himself enough to smooth out his thrusts. Oh yeah. It was better this way, much, much better. He'd lost himself for a moment there, but he came back into himself. Just enough.

He took over, thrusting slowly, steadily, head bowed over hers. A drop of sweat fell from him onto her temple. He wanted to lift his hand and wipe it away but any movements at all besides what he was doing seemed impossible. She didn't even seem to notice, thank God.

Sophie arched suddenly, lifted her legs around his hips, drew in a shocked breath. Her sex contracted once, twice, and then suddenly she gave a sharp cry and started rocking against him, soft tissues pulling at his cock tightly, milking him . . .

Control shattered. Jon's hips hammered into her, hard, fast, rough. If she'd given any sign of distress it might have penetrated the heat in his head. Maybe. He hoped. As it was, Sophie was crying out but not with pain. She was clinging to him tightly with her arms and legs. He lowered his entire weight onto her so he could hold her hips while fucking her just as hard as he could. The bed rocked, swayed, the tall wood and leather headboard beat a hard tattoo against the wall.

It was fast, violent, hot. Hot-hot-hot. Their bodies were plastered together with sweat. It came pouring out of him and his lungs were on fire.

Sophie's head was buried in his neck and she licked him, then bit him. That kicked him up another gear. He was pistoning wildly inside her, panting, sweating . . . it was too much. Just as Sophie gave another wild cry, he plunged deeply inside her and held himself there as every single drop of moisture in his body poured into her.

He was digging his toes in the mattress to stay as deeply inside her as he could while he exploded in waves, shuddering and shaking.

He'd never had an experience as intense as that. It was entirely possible that he blacked out for a second or two. When it was all over, he was sprawled on her with his entire weight, plastered to her with his sweat, their groins wet with his come.

He was ashamed of himself. Sort of. The thing was it had all felt so goddamned *good*. He should assess the damage, right away. Find out how she was, see if he'd hurt her or even disgusted her because for a while there he'd definitely behaved like an animal in rut.

But every muscle in his body was lax, not responding to orders from central command. All he could do was lie on her and pant, trying to get oxygen back into his lungs, blood back to his head.

It took forever.

But finally, finally, a little control came back. Not much. Just enough to raise his head to see if she was smiling or snarling. If she was mad at him for losing control. He'd have to explain to her as carefully as he could that that wasn't the way he usually operated and that he'd try to be more gentle the next time, if there was a next time. Maybe she was disgusted with him. All that sweating and groaning and, well, he didn't smell like springtime either.

So he lifted his head, prepared for just about anything— happiness, anger, anything in between, and instead what he got was Sophie's head turned to the side, eyes closed and what was that? He turned his ear to her mouth and grinned.

Sophie Daniels, virologist, sexy, classy woman, was snoring. Light delicate little exhalations that barely qualified, totally unlike the rhinoceros snorts of his teammates in the field, but definitely snores. Delighted with her, delighted with what was happening to him, he slowly turned with her in his arms, so gently he managed to stay inside her, and adjusted her on top of him. Sophie made a wonderful blanket. Soft and light.

He took in one deep happy breath and let it out, and fell asleep.

# Chapter 11

Sophie was dreaming. She and Jon were dancing on a rickety wooden pier far out over the ocean. The wind was still, the water calm, bright sun picking out diamond-like reflections in the water. Each step they took made the pier rock and sway, made the wood creak. Jon was kissing her cheek, over and over, a tender look on his face . . .

"Sophie, wake up. It's nearly sundown. Time to go."

Not kissing, tapping at her cheek.

She woke in a swoop, disoriented. She wasn't on a pier out over the ocean. She was in a bed and the room was filled with shadows. Outside the windows, the sky was the dark pink of sunset.

She sat up, still groggy, and pushed her hair out of her eyes. Sitting up, she felt the muscles between her thighs, the tissues of her sex, complain. She was sore and she blushed a bright red when she remembered just how those muscles and tissues had become sore.

Jon was standing several feet away from the bed, face grim

and tight. He looked like he'd been up for hours and he looked like a completely different man from the one who'd been in bed with her.

"We'll go just as soon as it becomes dark enough to use night vision." His voice was tight, clipped, impersonal. Team leader to teammate. "I made you sandwiches. Eat as much as you can; you're going to need fuel. I don't want to stop unless we absolutely have to—it's going to be a trek. There's time for you to take a shower if you want. I've already taken mine. But I'd like to leave in half an hour."

Sophie watched his face more than listened to his words. He'd carefully erased any emotion from his face and looked and sounded like a robot. An incredibly good-looking robot whose manufacturer had given it ripped muscles.

"Okay." She carefully matched her tone to his. Impersonal, matter of fact. "I'll be ready in half an hour."

He nodded and marched rather than walked out of the room. Mission-ready.

Sophie showered, rummaged in Mrs. Robb's amazingly well-stocked closets, and came up with a silk undershirt, a thick cashmere turtle-necked sweater, jeans. Her own Nomex coat and winter boots completed the outfit—Apocalypse Chic. In the kitchen she found the food Jon had set up: two ham-and-cheese sandwiches and fruit juice. The Robbs believed in living right—the bread was whole wheat, the cooked ham and Swiss cheese delicious. Jon had even peeled two apples for her and quartered them.

Jon showed up exactly half an hour after he'd woken her up. He was dressed for battle, exactly as he was when he showed up at her door, the Nordic god who seemingly fell from the sky on top of her. She remembered clearly the huge emotions of the moment—terror and hope in equal measure.

And then, they'd made love. As if those emotions had cut right through the usual getting-to-know-you phase. Strong enough to blast right through all the walls people put up.

She'd known who he was at that instant—a man who'd walked through hell to find her. Not much else was necessary to know. It had been enough, more than enough, to get past her defenses.

It was sunset now; the sky outside the windows a darkening blue.

"I've checked the vehicle," Jon said. "She's good to go, fully charged and with a full tank of LPG. With luck, she'll last till we get to Haven. I loaded her up with food. The Robbs have a full stock of staples and I stacked as much inside as the vehicle can carry. I know Haven has ample stores, but I checked with HQ and refugees are pouring in. The food will come in handy."

"Did you track our route?"

Jon pulled a face. "Sort of."

He showed her an expanded map with GPS waypoints. "The satellites took photographs of the roads from here to Haven." He traced a path with his finger from where they were on the coast eastward to Mount Blue, a desolate part of the state. She'd never been there. "The Lynx has off-the-road capabilities and she's strong, but going off road will also mean increased fuel consumption. We've got a map of where we can travel on highways and roads and where they are blocked by vehicles. The thing is, the photographs were taken the day before yesterday and the satellites are down now. Our drones are being used to scan for pockets of survivors, and they don't know when they can assign some to us. So, we're operating essentially on old intel in a hostile environment."

He looked at her narrow-eyed, as if expecting something from her. She showed him her determined face. She was not going to slow him down in any way; she was going to do everything in her power to help.

"The scanner works, right?" she asked. "We'll know where the infected are."

"Oh yeah, it works all right. And as long as we keep moving, we won't have anything to fear from the infected. They sure can't outrun us. We just have to make sure we don't run into trouble off road."

Sophie looked out the window at the rising darkness. "I'm ready when you are, Jon."

"Okay," he answered, but he didn't move. He kept his face neutral but there was something, some strong emotion, quivering just beneath the surface. He looked tense, like the string of a bow before release. He looked like he needed something badly, but Sophie had no clue what that might be.

"Jon?"

He suddenly lunged and wrapped his arms around her. His grip was so tight she could barely breathe, and beneath his clothes Jon was trembling, his breath quick and rough.

"I'm not going to let anything happen to you," he said, voice low, husky, strained. As if it was hard for him to get the words out. "That's my promise to you. I'll get you to Haven safely." He swallowed hard. She could feel it and hear it. "Trust me. Trust me to get you to safety."

Though his words were reassuring, somehow Sophie felt that *he* needed reassurance, as if he would fall apart if she weren't holding on to him.

"I trust you, Jon," she said softly.

He jolted, then settled down onto her so heavily, she was bearing his weight. Just for a moment. Then he straightened, stepped back, holding her by the shoulders. "Good. We're going to do this. You'll get to Haven, you have my word."

He dropped his hands and took another step backward, all elite soldier now. He all but saluted, face completely neutral, expressionless.

The robot was back.

Except he didn't fool her. Jon was no robot. That tight hold he had on his emotions was because he felt them too keenly.

He wanted her to trust him? God, yes. At that moment Sophie knew, beyond a shadow of a doubt, that he would sacrifice his life for her if it could get her to safety. This went beyond getting the case back to the labs. This was about *her*, Sophie Daniels. But she couldn't let on that she understood that, not now, not when he had to show her he was all supersoldier, utterly emotionless.

Her only possible response was to stay neutral herself. "Okay." She dipped her head. "So I guess we're heading on out."

The Lynx was a surprising vehicle. She'd never seen one in real life, only in ads. Nobody needed a private vehicle in San Francisco. She just rented a CityCar from the city when she needed transportation, so she wasn't up on the latest models. This thing looked like a beast, like something she'd laugh at if she encountered it on city streets. Huge, high and broad, a complete waste of material. Except right now they were going to trust their lives to this beast, and it looked like it was up for it. Its size and toughness were welcome if they were going to have to go off road.

"Bless you, Jason Robb," she said as she ran her hand along the beast's flank.

Jon looked up briefly from fitting her backpack into the rear compartment. "Yeah, we're really lucky. I don't think a normal vehicle could make this trip. We have something back at Haven that would be even better than this, but it's there and we're here."

Sophie looked the Beast over, realizing it was something she couldn't drive, not even on freeways, let alone in the wild. "Can I help you in any way, Jon? Can I navigate for you?"

Jon had come around to the passenger side and opened the door. The floor of the vehicle was higher than her breasts. The small step that appeared from the flank of the vehicle was absolutely necessary. Jon gave her a quick boost and she settled into the seat. Inside, it was enormous, like a small room. Jon had packed the back tightly, covering the windows to midpoint. But the car would have sensors and video cameras for rear view vision.

"No. We're going to have to travel with the lights off because the light would attract the infected. I have night vision goggles and the waypoints are on the GPS. But we're going to have to be ready to change the itinerary at any moment."

Jon's comms unit crackled and she saw movement. He pressed a button and the hologram was projected. His teammates, Mac, and Nick. And Elle.

"We're ready to roll out," Jon said. "Anything we need to know?"

Mac looked tired and drawn. "The infection has spread to the rest of the country. There are now severe outbreaks in Houston, Dallas, Seattle, Denver, Chicago, and Boston. Plus a number of smaller cities. Martial law has been declared in half the country. We know this because our comms system is picking up sporadic signals, but we are completely unable to establish any kind of radio contact with anyone in the military. There is no priority higher than getting that case to a safe place; there is nothing more important that the U.S. military could achieve, and we can't communicate with them, not in any way. Snyder tried, and he connected with a lieutenant somewhere for half a minute, then they were cut off." His jaw flexed. "But we're trying 24/7 to get through. The instant we do, we'll get a bird to you, no matter where you are. But you're not getting help any time soon, Jon. Neither are we. We're on our own. The good news is that we still have people pouring in and we've located more strongholds. People are dug in and most of those communities are going to make it. The countryside is littered with the bodies of the infected. They are dying fast."

Sophie snapped to attention. "Do you have any hazmat suits, sir?"

"Mac."

"Okay, Mac. Do you?"

Mac turned to Elle.

"Yes," Elle said. "Three. Nick picked them up when he went to a research lab to liberate some equipment for us. Why?"

"We need dead bodies. We need to know how long the virus can survive in corpses. I think we should be okay. The most virulent viruses known to us—the hemorrhagic fever viruses like Ebola—cannot last more than three days in corpses. Smallpox can't survive more than twenty-four hours. And most viruses deteriorate when exposed to ultraviolet rays. A lot of the dead infected will be outdoors. This is my best assessment. But . . .

we need to be sure. So have two men in hazmat suits find a dead infected, put him in another hazmat suit and we'll try to replicate a Level-4 containment lab to the best of our ability."

Nick stirred, looked at Elle, then back at her. "Sounds dangerous for you guys."

"It's all dangerous, Nick," Sophie said before Elle could talk. "But we're going to beat this thing, and when we start reconstruction we will also have to know whether a coyote who slinks away with an infected's arm will become infected and infect a human being in turn. I don't think the virus is transmissible to animals because it was tailored for humans, but we must know for certain. We have to know whether we need to undertake a massive program of burying in mass graves dug very deep and lined and covered with cement or if we can simply bury the dead normally, because the virus is dead. Any mass graves that would have to be dug under containment conditions would take months and months. And in the meantime, men, women, and children will starve to death. If we know that the virus can't survive outside a live body, we can bury the dead quickly even as we care for the living."

Nick nodded, a brusque up and down movement. "On it. I'll grab one of the ex-Marines not on guard duty and go out." He disappeared from the screen.

Elle's eyes followed him, then turned back to the vid. "And I'll set up a separate lab with Catherine, trying to make it as much a containment lab as we can."

"How are you doing for supplies?" Jon asked.

Mac sighed, a huge heave of his massive chest. "Up until yesterday I'd have said we're doing fine, but we just got another influx of three hundred refugees. We've got people sleeping in the corridors in shifts. We're down to about four days' reserves."

"Well, we're bringing in as much as we can in the Lynx. And if ever a helo can be spared, Robb's got enormous stocks of food here."

"Yeah. He said. So we've done as much on our end as we can for you. We lost satellite contact about twelve hours ago, so we can't give you any more details on the terrain you're going to have to cross. ETA?"

"The way I mapped it, if we get a straight run, we should be at Haven at around 0700 hours tomorrow morning. That's if we don't run into problems. If the Herrington Bridge is still intact. If we don't run into more infected than we can deal with. If Robb's Lynx holds up. Lots of variables."

Mac gave a two-fingered salute off his forehead. "We'll be at the road entrance to Haven from 0600 hours on. Good luck, soldier." Mac's gaze turned to Sophie, then back to Jon. "Bring her home."

"Yessir. See you at 0700 hours tomorrow." Jon's jaw was tight as he switched off the comms unit and turned to her. He was less wild-eyed than before, steadier. Mission-ready. "You ready, honey? It's going to be a long, hard trip."

Dangerous too. He hadn't mentioned that part. He didn't need to. "Ready" was all she said.

Jon pushed a button and the engine lit up. There was barely any noise, just a low controlled purr, which was lucky since noise attracted the infected. He didn't switch the headlights on. With a great deal of luck, they would be able to find their way home silently and invisibly.

Sophie hardly dared hope for such luck, but since their ride back to Haven—the helicopter—had blown up back in San Francisco, she figured the scales needed balancing and that would do nicely. A long, hard, safe trek across the state. Yes, she was up for that.

"Heading out," Jon said and the Lynx moved forward. He pressed a button on the panel. The gate behind the house started slowly rolling open. It was set in the high walls cutting the compound off from the rest of the world. Jon went slowly over the gate tracks set in the ground, pushed the button again, and the gates closed.

Sophie turned her head to look at the compound one last time, already almost invisible in the darkness. A massive dark shape in the general darkness.

"I'm very grateful to that place," she said. "In more ways than one." She smiled and put her hand on Jon's arm. Just for a second, just to let him know the deeper meaning of her words. His hard profile didn't change, but he placed his hand over hers briefly, then removed it.

Sophie missed that hand. Jon had a way of inspiring trust with the merest touch, but now he needed to concentrate on the task in front of him, getting them and the case to Haven, safe and sound. She was scared, but she was also determined to help, not hinder him. Though he hadn't asked her to, she resolved to keep an eye on the scanner set on the dashboard signaling the existence of infected within a 500-meter radius.

The monitor with the waypoints was above the scanner so Jon could reference them both easily at a glance. "It looks like we have safe, clear passage right across the Humboldt State Park," he said. "It must have been fairly deserted before the infection hit. As of yesterday there were no pileups. The pileups begin right after we leave the park and we'll have to go off road." He shot her a look. "It won't be comfortable."

Sophie looked at him and sighed. "I'm not a cream puff, Jon. I can take a little jostling."

His face transformed suddenly. In a flash his cheekbones flushed and his eyes narrowed, and she realized that there could be sexual innuendos inferred in her words. Of course, when she and Jon were in the same room, sex was in the room too. And they were in an enclosed space here in the Lynx, which was suddenly suffused with pheromones.

"You are most definitely a cream puff, honey. *My* cream puff and I love gobbling you up. Jostling you too."

Heat flashed and oxygen fled the cabin of the vehicle. There was some snappy sexy comeback, and if she had access to her brain, she'd have said it. Definitely. As it was, she didn't have access to her brain, only to her sex organs. Her thighs clenched hard as her vagina contracted. Oh God. Had he noticed?

Yes, he definitely had.

But they were rolling out onto a road now and he didn't say anything. He put on his night vision gear, which looked like unusually thick sunglasses, and turned to the road ahead.

Sophie couldn't see anything in the total darkness. She had never been in a moving vehicle before without any lights at all, not even headlights. It was unnerving.

Her time in California had been spent studying and working, she'd never made it up this far north before. She knew about the park, of course. It had the tallest trees in the world, that was all she knew.

Soon they were deep in the forest, but she could only tell by negative input. The black sky's blackness became even more absolute with the tall canopy blotting out the night sky. She could infer trees by an abstract structure, maybe some kind of electric charge of living things, but not by sight. They were almost visible out of the corner of her eye but disappeared when she looked straight at them, like ghosts or goblins.

Jon wasn't having any problems, though. He was seeing everything, clearly in control. For just a moment, Sophie was tempted to ask to peer through the night vision glasses but resisted. It would be folly for him to take them off, even for a second. They weren't on a sightseeing trip, they were running for their lives.

So on they drove, through darkness for her, through a flat green-tinted dayscape for Jon. The only thing that told her they were on a road was the smooth feel of the asphalt beneath the wheels. Soon, she knew, that would stop and the truly dangerous part would begin.

There was silence in the vehicle. Sophie didn't feel like breaking it, though she knew Jon would answer if she made a comment. But really, what was there to say? She wanted to know more about this beautiful warrior, much more. She wanted to find out how he could have remained sane under constant stress while undercover. She wanted to understand how he felt about his teammates. She wanted to find out what his love life had been.

But—it could go either one of two ways. Either they were ambushed or the vehicle crashed and they died and she'd meet her maker together with one of the bravest men she'd ever met. Or—they'd make it to Haven and work hard, hand in hand, to put the world back together. If they were lucky enough to walk through door number two, there'd be plenty of time to explore fascinating Jon World.

There was something almost soothing about this journey in darkness and silence. The world was insane outside the vehicle, but inside, she and Jon were two people working hard together to achieve something difficult under dangerous circumstances. Not much more had to be said. They both understood the danger, they were both ready for it. Maybe this was what it was like for warriors on a mission? No talking, the time for talking was done. Just action. And a strong sense of common purpose.

After an hour of smooth rolling, Jon spoke. He glanced at the map and back at the road and said, "Going off road, Sophie. There's a pileup about a hundred yards ahead and beyond that, the road is littered with crashed cars and trucks for the next fifty miles. It would take us days to get past them. I don't have much depth perception, so it might be a bumpy ride."

"Okay," she said quietly. "You concentrate on the road, and I'll watch the scanner."

He nodded and maneuvered them off the road.

They were well out of the state park or at least on the edges of it. Without being able to see much, Sophie could sense fewer tall trees, the canopy overhead disappearing as under the wheels they transitioned from smooth asphalt to rocky surface. The wheels slid and Jon cursed, regaining control. Jon was leaning forward a little now, because there was no road to follow anymore, just badlands.

One wheel dipped into a deep hole and Jon fought to keep the vehicle upright. Sophie knocked her head badly against the window but didn't make a sound. Jon couldn't be distracted now. She braced herself against the door so the next time the Lynx rocked, she was able to keep herself upright, though the seat belt pulled so tight against her chest it hurt.

The vehicle rocked as if in a strong wind as it climbed out of the hole.

The really hard part had begun.

Later, Jon would barely understand how he did it. Adrenaline, terror—they helped. What didn't help was having Sophie with him. Every time he fought the wheel to keep the vehicle upright, he had to fight the temptation to hold her back against her seat with his arm. It was pure instinct and it wasn't helping. Like himself, she was strapped in via a five-point belt and his arm was much less effective a barrier than the belt. But every single goddamned time, he was distracted from the driving by wanting to protect Sophie.

The only thing he could do to protect Sophie was getting her to Haven safely as fast as possible and the constant distraction of her next to him was putting both their lives at risk. He tried not to look at her but he couldn't stop smelling her, some mixture of Anna Robb's soap and shampoo and Sophie's skin. He remembered the smell of Sophie's skin in the deepest recesses of his brain. She was a distraction and he had to wrestle with himself just as much as he wrestled with the wheel to keep them moving.

It wasn't as if she was deliberately distracting him, God no. Even when the vehicle slid out of control for a few seconds, teetered for an instant on two wheels, even when he had to wrench the car to avoid an almost invisible hole, she didn't make a sound. He could feel her anxiety like waves beating up against the shore, but she didn't say a word and she didn't make any movements that could have distracted him.

But she did distract him. She didn't want to, that was clear, but she did. He couldn't fucking keep her out of his mind.

Swerving, testing out the depth of craters because he couldn't see for shit—all he saw was vague contours but not the size of hillocks and vales—gunning the engine when he saw he had a clear shot, slowing down to a walking pace where the land was strewn with boulders and brush. And all the time he was thinking of her, trying to keep the ride as smooth as possible, terrified the night vision wouldn't show him where the ground sheared off into a cliff until it was too late and they were rolling down the sheer face to the bottom of the cliff.

He'd always had a very good imagination. It helped, as a soldier. He could think ahead and see the scenarios for each decision on a decision tree. But now that gift turned on him and bit him on the ass. Because his mind created two really good images to deal with. One: the car slides down a steep hill, hits the bottom and explodes or, even better, two: he and Sophie trapped in the vehicle until some infected comes along and tears Sophie's heart out of her chest.

That last one was rendered in full living color, with sound effects.

Shit! He wanted to pound the wheel but didn't, because he needed to control the wheel and he needed to control his reactions. How crazy was that? He was nothing but cool and calm under pressure, even extreme pressure. Except apparently now, when it would be really useful to switch to Cool Surfer Dude instead of sweaty desperate Totally Uncool Dude.

The vehicle lurched heavily to the right, tilting slightly, the left wheels lifting off the ground—Jon wrenched the car back to where at least the four wheels were touching the ground at the same time.

He had to stop thinking of her, stop trying to keep her safe. Because if he kept having divided attention, he'd kill them both. Or worse—kill himself and maybe leave her alive in the middle of the badlands.

That image—of him crushed in an accident, Sophie alive and staked out like a goat for the monsters to find her—got his head straight. He had to focus. Focus was what he did, focus was what Jon was all about. So he narrowed his attention to the vehicle and the road, nothing else existed in the whole wide world. There was only the feel of the vehicle and the terrain in front of them.

The GPS waypoints Mac and the others at Haven had mapped out for him were twenty-four hours old and worse than useless. What was miles and miles of empty roadway on their map turned out to be cluttered with pileups, articulated trucks jacked sideways, one huge tractor trailer upside down like an enormous black cockroach, wheels in the air instead of legs.

Every single inch of this nightmare journey was one he had to feel his way through. In the end it was easier to just stay off road since it was so hard to get on and get off at irregular intervals. The Lynx could smash its way through the guardrails easily enough, but after ten or twelve times Jon thought he might be undermining the structural integrity of the fenders, so he just abandoned highways. There were some state roads he could follow for a while. When he came across tangles of wrecked cars, if the road wasn't on a raised grade, it was easy enough to simply drive off road, skirt the wreck, then drive back on.

What wasn't so easy was ignoring the bodies around the pileups. He was glad Sophie didn't have night vision. Driving by an endless succession of broken human beings was hard to take for him. She would be heartsick.

He had to keep to under twenty miles an hour so he could correct if the car slid or threatened to overturn, but he'd counted on thirty miles an hour, making it to Mount Blue by around sunrise. At this rate, they'd arrive several hours after dawn.

No matter. He gripped the wheel harder, fighting the temptation to speed up. That could get them killed. They'd get to Haven when they got there. Not before and not later.

After six hours of driving, Jon's muscles were aching. If this were any other situation he'd stop and stretch. But it was what it was, and he didn't want to endanger Sophie by stopping, not even if the scanner was clear.

He was trying to negotiate a sudden dip in the land that turned out to be almost a pit when Sophie said, very quietly, "Jon."

He couldn't look at her until he'd gunned the engine to work the vehicle up and over the other side of the deep depression. Then he spared her a quick glance.

"What?"

"Infected." She tilted the scanner so he could see clearly. Yep, a pack of them. About twenty, milling aimlessly about 500 meters west.

"Car's very quiet," he said. "Maybe we can slip by without them noticing."

He concentrated fiercely on the road, speeding up. They would be safe in the cabin, but he didn't want to engage with infected at all. He pushed the car's speed up even more, carefully threading around trees and humps in the ground.

Finally, Sophie spoke again. "We've cleared them."

"Good." Jon eased up on the accelerator. They'd been traveling dangerously fast, at a clip he couldn't maintain without risking an accident. "Are you hungry? Thirsty? There's some food and water in the cooler right behind my seat."

"I'll eat and drink at Haven." Sophie reached out, caressed his cheek lightly. Her hand was warm, soft. Comforting. "Until then I think we need to pay attention to the road."

Jon grunted. It was exactly what a fellow soldier would say. Top priority—the mission. Creature comforts can come when the op is done. In the meantime, do what you have to do to come back safely.

Sophie looked around. The darkness was absolute, but the quality of the darkness changed. "What's the landscape like now?"

"More open," Jon replied. "We're coming now into open ground. If the clouds break, you'll see starlight."

She craned her neck to look out the side window but the cloud cover was thick. "The darkness is oppressive," she said quietly. "I'm glad you have night vision."

Jon grunted. He was glad too. Otherwise, this nighttime journey across California would have been impossible.

To the north was a source of light, showing up in night vision as a diffuse glare. They turned a corner and even Sophie could see it. "What is it?" she asked.

Jon checked that they had a relatively flat surface for the next kilometer, then tapped the side of his night vision goggles, turning them into high magnification binoculars. "A fire." He exhaled a breath. "Looks like either a school or hospital."

They were both silent. Schools. Hospitals. Universities. All the things that helped humans live human lives. Without them people lived short, stunted lives, ignorant and bestial.

Sophie's voice was quiet but determined. "We're going to re-build. As soon as we can get the vaccine into production, we'll do our best to inoculate as many people as possible and we'll get the vaccine to the military as soon as they are capable of doing more than defending against the infected. But we'll do it and we'll rebuild. All of us will have a difficult five or ten years, but our children will live normal lives. We'll make sure of it."

*Our children.* Jon's heart gave a huge thump in his chest. Children. He knew that she was speaking generally and that she didn't mean that she and Jon would have kids together, but somehow the idea, the image, zinged straight to some up-to-now dormant part of his brain and lodged there. He couldn't shake it out of his head.

His and Sophie's children. A little girl, maybe two, looking just like Sophie. Pretty and solemn and smart. Loving him, looking to him for protection. *Oh God.*

*What the fuck was this?* He had *never* wanted kids, ever. And had taken great precautions against fatherhood because the idea of a kid of his alone in the world, without protection . . .

His heart gave another huge thump in his chest. Good thing he knew, without a doubt, that no kid of his was out there.

His parents had been great at giving a big example of how not to be parents. Feckless and cruel in their indifference to anything but the next high, he'd had an example up close and personal of what not to do.

He knew what not to do. He had that down pat.

But being a good father? No frigging clue. He'd never seen it. He'd found structure and discipline in the military and then in Ghost Ops, but there wasn't any touchy-feely nurturing going on there. Military life was really binary. Do. Obey. And *not do* and *not obey* hadn't been options. You aren't gently persuaded to do something in the military, explaining the reasons why. No moral lessons drawn, no rules for living. Just—get this done or you'll be sorry.

That was how he had intended to live out his entire life. Under the iron discipline of a military existence.

Jon wasn't a naturally philosophical person, but the few times he ever thought about his future, maybe life after Ghost Ops, he'd drawn a blank. He was going to die young so what was the use of planning for life after Ghost Ops. What could possibly fill his life? He'd had plenty of sex partners but never a girlfriend, so the question of a long-term relationship or—*God!*—kids had never come up.

Marriage and children, a family, had never filled that blank space in his head. Being a husband and father wasn't anything he could ever see for himself. Or, really, for any of his teammates, though Mac and Nick seemed happy now that they were settled.

Really happy, in fact. Really, really happy. Mac, in particular, was going to be a father, and before the shit came down he'd been ecstatic.

His heart gave another big thump and he rubbed his chest, because it freaking *hurt*.

"Maybe—" Sophie said hesitantly, then stopped.

Jon waited but she didn't finish the thought. "Maybe?" he prodded.

The surface had turned smoother. This was a stretch of plateau that seemed fairly flat so he could pay attention to what she was saying.

"Maybe what, Sophie?"

She sighed, a little exhalation of breath in the silence of the cabin. "I know it sounds crazy, considering that we're risking our lives just driving a couple of hundred miles and we can't even drive on roads because there are too many crashed cars and"—she swallowed, that long white throat working—"too many dead bodies. I know what we left behind in San Francisco and I can't even think about L.A. or San Diego or Sacramento. So much death and destruction, it's hard to even think of after . . . But the thing is . . ." She turned in her seat and looked at him. The night vision goggles covered his entire range of sight, but he had excellent peripheral vision. He could see her clearly, slightly green-tinged, beautiful and earnest, eyes wide in the darkness. "The thing is—what if we can rebuild *better*? There was so much wrong with the world, Jon. So much needless cruelty and materialism and crassness and exploitation. Suppose we can learn from the past and particularly from this tragedy? From what I could tell from Dr. Lee's computer, the virus was designed to make huge amounts of money. Dr. Lee was a gifted scientist. He knew perfectly well that there were enormous risks involved and yet he continued the research. He and that idiot Flynn were willing to blow up the world if it made them money. But maybe—I don't know. Maybe if there are just a few of us left and we have to band together to survive, we can build something better. Better than what was."

Silence. Jon mulled the idea over. *Better*. Something better.

Like Haven.

Haven was a community of misfits and geniuses and people on the run. They could only rely on themselves and they did. Everyone pitched in, everyone gave, no one complained. It was what drove Mac, Nick, and Jon to protect Haven with every ounce of their being.

"But maybe that's just a crazy idea. Wishful thinking." She sighed.

"Not so crazy," Jon said softly.

A world like Haven. He found himself smiling. *Oh yeah. A world like Haven was worth fighting for.*

It was an endless ride, uncomfortable, rocky, dangerous. And yet Sophie was happy in the dark cabin with Jon. He was doing a magnificent job of steering them through the badlands even though they were rarely on an actual asphalted road. She knew beyond a shadow of a doubt that as fast as any vehicle and any driver could take her to safety, that was as fast as Jon was going.

She was almost completely blind. A low cloud cover blocked off the stars and the sliver of moon, and there were no lights anywhere except occasionally a column of flame where something burned. She saw nothing. When driving through the redwood forest there had been faint shadows, more an idea of shapes than actual shapes, the canopy darker than the night. When they reached the middle of the state and open land, she could discern nothing other than blackness. Jon stopped calling out when the car would lurch. They often dove into holes, climbing out a minute later, rocking over fallen trees and boulders. It was pointless for Jon to warn her, he'd spend all his time calling out instead of paying attention to the landscape in front of him.

Sophie simply strapped her belt more tightly, hung on to the handle above the door, and endured the teeth-rattling ride.

Still, she'd rather this horrible bone-crunching ride over rough terrain with Jon than the smoothest ride in the latest Mercedes model with anyone else. He sat next to her, grappling with the steering wheel, concentrated on the terrain ahead and keeping them upright—and yet she felt closer to him than she'd ever felt to another human being.

He was a warrior and she felt like a warrior too. They were in a war, together, fighting the odds. Teammates and lovers.

There was a very faint light from the scanners lighting Jon's face from below. Not quite enough to make out features but enough to highlight the strong jawline and high cheekbones. When he said that maybe, just maybe the idea of building something better in the aftermath of the infection was not so crazy, the corners of his hard mouth turned up because it made sense to him, too, and at that precise moment . . . she fell in love.

Hard.

She'd more or less written love off. How to negotiate telling her lover that she could heal but that it was an uncertain gift? That she could, but maybe she couldn't? That it was a poisoned chalice? He'd either believe her or run for the hills away from the lunatic, and she had no idea which would be worse. It would completely skew the relationship, make it off kilter, make it about something other than two people. Her "gift" would lie between them like an unwanted lover.

No, love was off the table. Sex, too, apparently, since she rarely found herself attracted enough to sleep with a man. Casual affairs were sad. Dangerous. Better to just take sex and relationships off the table.

Jon had broadsided her. They'd had sex before she even knew him, and it had been so intense she thought her heart would blow. And the man was even better than the sex. Her body had told her what to do before her mind could boycott it.

She and Jon were a couple in the most primitive sense of the term—running for their lives, depending on each other completely, in total harmony. He was irrevocably a part of her. She studied his face in the faint light.

Handsome, yes. But there were a lot of good-looking guys around. Buff too. But again, a lot of men went to the gym religiously, though Jon's muscles were of an entirely different order. Muscles for work, not for show.

She had no idea what his tastes in music and movies and books were.

Didn't matter. Because those were details, like clothes covering a man. The real man underneath the trappings, the essence of him, was brave beyond compare. Honorable and true. Even when he'd told her his great gift was lying, he was telling the truth. He'd completely glided over how dangerous undercover work was. How one misstep could betray you. She was fiercely happy he was a brilliant liar because it meant he'd survived where other men would have been killed.

"You're looking at me," Jon said, eyes straight ahead. "What?"

That was another thing. No games with Jon.

"I love you," she said quietly.

The vehicle swerved, then righted itself. *"What?"*

"You heard me." Sophie had never felt more sure of herself.

It was insane to tell a man you'd just met that you loved him. In the mating game, *don't show your hand* was rule number one. But that was in the old world. Now they were in a new world and the old rules didn't apply here.

"I love you. I could beat around the bush and say I'm attracted to you—because I am—or that I like you—because I do—but it's more than that. And on the off chance that we don't make it, I wanted you to know. Because it's important."

He was silent. Something was going on inside of him. Though she could barely make out his face, she could see his jaw muscles working, bunching and releasing as if he were chewing on words.

Sophie wasn't expecting much in the way of an answer. It didn't make any difference. The world had become raw and violent, stripped down to bedrock. No time for games or ploys, no sense to them either. She'd said what she had to say and was happy with that. They could be dead in the next hour.

"Sophie." Jon's voice was a low growl.

Sophie kept her face forward. "It's okay, Jon. You don't have to say anything. Whatever you feel is okay."

His hands opened then closed tightly around the wheel, face tight with concentration. He took in a deep breath then let it out in a whoosh. "Well, all I can say is that it's a lucky thing you love me because . . . I love you right back. And I have never said that to another human being in my life." In the deep gloom she saw him shake his head. "I can barely believe I'm saying it now."

He reached out with one big hand and took hers, curling his fingers in hers. He brought the back of her hand to his mouth and kissed it. Her hand turned warm, as if his lips transferred fire.

After that, there wasn't much else to say. All the usual things Sophie supposed a man and a woman said to each other after declarations of love were perfectly pointless. There was no talking of where to go from here. The future for the moment didn't exist. All that existed was right now, trekking slowly across California, hoping to make it to Haven.

And anyway, everything that needed to be said had been said. Jon had risked death for her when he didn't know her. Sophie had no doubt that he would fight to the death for her now. In their escape from San Francisco, she'd have died for him.

That was it. That was what was important.

Everything else was noise.

Hour after hour rolled by. Though the cabin was warm,

Sophie wasn't even tempted to sleep. The ride was rough but beyond that, Jon was doing something almost impossible, ferrying them across the state off road, and in the dark. She knew how hard depth perception was with night vision. That they were still intact and hadn't rolled over into a ditch or crashed into a boulder was entirely thanks to his driving skills. She couldn't help him, but she could keep vigil with him, every step of the way.

There was the faintest change in the sky ahead, to the east. Not so much light as the promise of light. Dawn was about an hour away.

The land tilted upward. They were beginning the long climb to Mount Blue.

Red light flashed from the scanners. "Infected?" Jon asked. His posture was tense, raked slightly forward. The faint dawn light was beginning to interfere with the night vision.

Sophie studied the monitor carefully. "No. Two deer. I can't tell the sex because antlers won't show up in IR."

"Why are they showing up at all?" Jon asked. "Are they infected?"

"I don't think so. Animals have a higher base temperature than humans, that's all. Dogs have a base temperature of about 101. They are sick if their temperature is 99 degrees and below. Deer typically have a base temperature of about 104 degrees." She observed the monitor for several minutes, then sighed in relief. "They're not infected," she said decidedly. "Their movements are normal and they can stand still. Human infected can't be still. Their nervous systems are too compromised."

She looked at Jon. She could see him a little more clearly

now in the dawn light. To a casual observer, he looked exactly as he had when they started out. But Sophie was more than a casual observer. Deeply tanned, he was pale under the tan and the lines around his mouth were deeper.

Well, maybe she could make him feel better.

"That is actually very good news. The best. All this time, I've been terrified that the virus could infect animals as well. If that happened, our vaccine wouldn't work forever and we'd have to inoculate the entire population again. It would be like what happens with the flu, where each year you are inoculated against last year's mutation. However, if animals aren't acting as a reservoir for the virus, we really can hope it can be vanquished forever, like smallpox." She turned to him and smiled for the first time in what felt like forever. "There's hope, Jon. Hope that we can win this thing."

"Hope. Man." He shook his head. "Hard to believe it."

But he smiled too.

The ground lifted even more as they began climbing the mountain in earnest. The Lynx was still silent, but Sophie had the impression that it was straining a little. After a few miles she could see individual trees, barely. A dense morning fog curled around the trees, swirling and dancing in the morning breeze just off the surface of the ground.

Jon slowed the vehicle. "This is a dangerous moment. The light will blind me soon through the night vision goggles, but there isn't enough light to drive by. I'm going to have to go really slow until there's more light."

Sophie nodded.

He slowed even further, pulling the goggles up over his head, placing them in the divider container between their seats. His eyes narrowed, hands tightened. Sophie's eyesight was acclimated but not even she could see well enough to drive. The terrain grew rougher as they climbed. Rocks, fallen tree limbs, thick bushes. Jon was tense, checking their position constantly on the map. Then Jon glanced at the GPS and relaxed. "Okay. We have a series of tiny EMP sources ringing the mountain, releasing when any electronic device crosses a waypoint. It will kill any engine with electronics." He smiled at some memory. "Killed Catherine's little purple eCar stone dead. Mac went down to get her and threw her over his shoulder."

"That sounds like caveman tactics."

He shrugged one broad shoulder. "Worked, though. They're expecting a kid. Some time in October."

Sophie gasped. "Dr. Young—Catherine is pregnant? Isn't that dangerous right now?"

"It was dangerous when she conceived because we had the entire U.S. government looking for us—Mac, top of the list. Doubly dangerous now. Danger hasn't ever stopped people from having kids. Life goes on."

*Life goes on.* Indeed it did, she thought. Children. Well, she'd been talking about rebuilding. You can't rebuild without a next generation.

God, maybe they would already have begun rebuilding by the time Catherine's child was born.

Jon wrenched the wheel again. "From now on, there will not be, there cannot be, any vehicles on the road. They were all killed dead half a mile back. Our vehicles have transponders in them so the sensors know not to emit the pulse. My scanner has been reconfigured to act as a transponder. So right now we're making our way to the road that will lead us straight to Haven."

He tapped his left wrist and glanced at her, ice blue eyes

flashing light. That paleness beneath the tan had disappeared, as had the lines of tension.

"Yeah," he said suddenly, tapping his ear, straightening in his seat. "You've got our bearings, right? I'm heading toward the road. Turn off all the traps, for God's sake. We're friendlies." He grinned. "Roger that. ETA?" He slanted her another glance. "About twenty minutes. Prepare us some food because we're hungry and thirsty and tired. Tell Stella to get her game on. Out."

Food. Good food, apparently. Shower and a bed. Sophie was still mulling that over when with a *crack!* the world exploded. The Lynx smashed its way downhill, rolling over and over. The harness kept her in place, but her head beat hard against the window as the vehicle landed again and again on the passenger side, then continued its roll. It was like being in the spin cycle of a washing machine, almost without gravity, completely out of control. A particularly vicious landing against something hard almost broke her door open. She felt a sharp pain in her wrist and cried out.

It seemed to last forever but suddenly they stopped, crashing up against a huge tree. Sophie banged her head against the window again and everything went black . . .

*Noise. Shaking.* Something was shaking her, but from a distance, as if on a different faraway planet. And screaming.

They were upside down and she was dangling heavily from the harness. Her head was spinning and her wrist hurt.

"Sophie!" Jon shook her again and she realized he'd been shaking her and shouting for the past few minutes. "Talk to me, dammit! Are you okay?"

*Yes. I think.* But the words wouldn't leave her mouth. She turned her head to see Jon draw a big black knife, and before she had time to wonder what he was doing, he cut himself out of the harness, landing on the roof of the vehicle. An instant later, he was at the passenger door, trying to wrench it open, but it had buckled. He ran around the other side, cut her harness from the driver's side, and pulled her out.

"Sophie! Can you hear me?"

She licked dry, parched lips. She hurt all over, particularly her head and her wrist. "Yes." The word came out a dry croak. She coughed and immediately a canteen was at her mouth.

"Drink," Jon ordered.

She did. The water went down like a dream. "Thanks."

"Listen, honey. I have to know if you have any injuries. Are you bleeding anywhere?"

She shook her head.

"Anything hurt?"

She nodded, pointed to her head, held up her wrist. As if from far away she noticed it was oddly shaped, like someone had pitched a tent under her skin, which was rapidly turning a dark blue.

"Fuck. Wrist broken." He shined a light in her eyes, holding her chin so she couldn't look away and avoid the painful light. "And mild concussion." There followed a string of words in several languages, which couldn't have been nice words.

So she was concussed. That was why she was seeing double and couldn't seem to coordinate her movements. And a broken wrist. It didn't hurt, adrenaline was masking the pain.

"You fuckheads!" he screamed. Was he talking to her? But there was only one of her. Pain and awareness crept in, in equal measure. As her wrist began throbbing, she took stock of the situation. Jon was shouting into his wrist comms unit. "You forgot to switch off the mini-EDs, you fucks! What the fuck were you thinking? You fucking nearly killed Sophie!"

His distress was visible, certainly perceptible to her. Without thinking, she placed her hand over his. He was trembling, sweating, eyes so wide the whites were clear all around the pupils. He was hurting, he radiated pain and anxiety.

She clasped his hand more strongly, feeling heat rise, feeling his emotions rise to the surface then calm down. Feeling his distress dissipate like the fog curling up and disappearing under the force of the morning sun.

"Yeah," he said suddenly, voice calmer. He never took his ice blue gaze from hers as he talked. "You'll have the location via the transponder. We probably slid a hundred meters. You'll need the hovercar. Bring medical supplies. Sophie has a concussion and a broken wrist. Bring pain meds too. No, I'm fine. Yes, the case is intact, I checked. Roger, we'll see you in fifteen."

He closed the connection then held her tightly again, eyes closed. "I nearly lost it," he said, sounding surprised. "Fuckheads didn't switch off all our protection devices. Whoever is responsible is going to be very, very sorry when I get back."

Tendrils of distress colored his emotions.

Sophie stood on tiptoe and lay her cheek against his. Heat and solace. It was pure instinct. Jon was hurting. She had to help—because she loved him. It was as simple as that.

"I'm not hurt," she murmured. "The wrist will heal. Considering what's happening in the world, a broken wrist is nothing. Please don't be angry at the person who forgot to switch the system off. He or she is probably overwhelmed and would never have endangered us on purpose." She held him tightly as the trembling died down, until finally his head dropped so he could rest his forehead against hers. Her wrist was throbbing with pain, but it was nothing. Not when she could feel that Jon was okay again.

"If anything had happened to you . . ." he murmured.

"It didn't. I'm fine, we're both fine. We'll be—" *Home.* She wanted to say home, but that was crazy. How could home be a place she'd never seen? "We'll be there soon. We'll rest, relax, grab a bite. Start working. Produce the vaccine, save as many people as we can. Look." She stepped slightly back from Jon, turned him around, watched him take in the view.

It was magnificent. They were halfway up the mountain; the green valley floor was spread out before them, with checkerboard orchards and ranches and small towns in the distance. A section was covered with almonds in full bloom, like clouds with trunks. After the dark night, the colors seemed almost supernaturally bright, life blossoming before their eyes.

The sun finally topped the mountain, brilliant buttery light spilling out over the valley. It was so intense Sophie had to shade her eyes.

"Wow," she whispered, glancing up at him then back at the landscape.

Jon gave a half smile. "Wait until you see it in the fall. Just beautiful."

"It's beautiful now. Stunning." And it was. The shafts of light grew denser, picking out details that must have been miles and miles away. The land glowed in the sunlight, pierced by the vegetation. If you'd had to pick an illustration of the Garden of Eden for Sunday school, you'd look no further.

Her new home. Here. Her new mate. By her side.

Her head hurt and her wrist ached and every muscle was

sore, but at the same time she felt suffused by something dangerous—hope. For a second, she could see the future. The virus, stopped. As much of humanity as possible, saved. All the survivors pulling together to create a new future for the children to come, including Catherine and Mac's child. No room for greed and selfishness, everyone would have to pull together to re-create everything that had been lost. She'd see this beauty every day, see it grow even more lush as she worked side by side with Jon to create a new world.

From up here, the damage seemed much less somehow. Not trivial, but redeemable. Most of the fires had burned out. Three small towns were visible, the closest ones looking as if Godzilla had walked over them. But California was resilient. Earthquakes and fires and floods. They never stopped the rebuilding, over and over again.

They'd do it.

"I feel hopeful," she said, almost to herself.

Jon scratched his chin, rasping against golden stubble. "You know, that's exactly the kind of thing that would have made me really mad before. Hope is for chumps, that's what I thought. Only strength keeps you alive. But I was wrong. You made me see that. Hope keeps us alive. So—"

A wild snarl, inhuman and violent, and something heavy and unstoppable crashed into her. Suddenly the air was full of wild cries, animal howls, and for a second she thought they'd been attacked by bears. She'd been thrown onto her back and she was stunned breathless when a terrifying face filled her vision. Wild eyes, a blood-stained howling mouth with broken teeth, a bib of blood down the front.

Not a bear. An infected.

She was so terrified she couldn't scream. The bloody face, with deep gouges in its cheeks, snapped its jaws a couple of times, so close she could hear the horrible clattering. In a panic of self-defense, Sophie shoved hard at the shoulder with her good hand, taking the infected by surprise. It rolled away, then rolled right back, a second from landing back on top of her before she had a chance to get up with only one hand.

Then the face disappeared, as if a strong wind had blown it away.

It all happened in an instant. She tried to scramble up, but her legs wouldn't hold her and she fell. Before she could hit the ground a strong hand caught her, swung her around him. Jon killed an infected that had been crouching, ready to leap.

That face disappeared, too, the head simply dissipating in a cloud of pink mist.

"Sophie!" Jon held her with one arm, the other holding his gun up as he looked around them. There were four bodies on the ground. She hadn't even realized they'd been attacked by several infected until she saw them lying bonelessly, red spattering the ground. "God! Are you okay?"

*Was she okay?*

Sophie patted herself down fast, checking herself. She'd been so overwhelmed she hadn't even heard the shot that killed her attacker. She could easily have been bitten without realizing it. But she was intact. There wasn't even any blood on her. Somehow Jon had shot in such a way that there'd been no spatter on her.

"How did we not see them on scanners?" Sophie's voice was tight. "How could they get past us?" She'd carried the scanner out with her from the car wreck. She checked it, moving it over the four dead bodies, but the scanner was blank. "God, they must have been freshly infected. They'd turned before their body temperature rose. Are there any more around?" She tapped frantically on the scanner, bringing the temperature threshold down to 97 degrees, where even uninfected would show up. She extended the range of the scan and there were no sources of life within a radius of 500 meters, and after she extended the range even further, they were clear out to a kilometer.

She turned to Jon. "Man, that was close. It's a good thing you were so fast—"

She stopped. Brought a hand to her mouth.

"What, honey?" Jon asked, holstering the gun. He wouldn't have used the stunner for fear of hurting her. Something about her stillness caught his attention. His gaze sharpened. "Honey? What's wrong?"

Sophie lifted her shaking hand and pointed.

He looked down at himself and froze. Right there, on the back of his hand, was a bite mark. Unmistakably human.

He was infected.

Jon's face turned to stone. He handed his gun to her, butt first.

"Here," he said, tapping the bridge of his nose. "Aim here. Take the cortex out. Do it now."

Sophie was white as the scattered snow on the ground. Crazily, when he handed his gun to her, she put her hands behind her back and shook her head.

No? She was saying fucking *no*?

Jon hardened his heart. He had to. Because not half an hour

ago he'd been daydreaming about him and Sophie working hard the rest of their lives to build up Haven, raising their kids in a tight circle of people who were dedicated to creating a community.

Every single objection he'd had to even thinking of settling down was gone. Sophie was his future and he'd embraced it.

Now all that was gone, gone. Due to a bite he hadn't even felt.

He looked down at his hand, at the elliptical oval marks the human mouth left. Whichever monster had bitten him had broken skin, and now he was a heartbeat away from becoming a monster himself.

"Take the gun, goddammit." His voice was harsh, angry.

Ghost Ops soldiers always had a discreet method of suicide on them. His had been a vial of dimethylmercury. He carried it around his neck on a chain. Which was in his bedroom back in Haven, of no use to him whatsoever.

Sophie had to do it. *Now.*

But she was shaking her head.

Now he was really mad. "Fuck this, Sophie. I don't know how long I've got. I'll bet you don't know either. Take me out before I turn."

"No," she pleaded. "Listen to me. I—"

"No, goddammit! You listen to *me!*" He was furious, and the feeling of being angry at Sophie—at lovely, gentle Sophie—was so strange he wondered if he was already turning. "I will not be responsible for your death. You've seen these creatures, Sophie. If you think that somehow I'll turn but recognize you, that you're *you*, and not hurt you—you're wrong. You've seen them—you've seen mothers kill their kids, children kill their grandparents. In I don't know how many minutes, I'm going to turn into a homicidal maniac and will rip you to shreds, and I can't live with the thought. Not for one second." He tapped the bridge of his nose again. "So do it. Right now. Because death is nothing. We all die. At least let me die knowing I won't hurt you."

His voice broke. It was pointless pretending to be mad at her when his heart was pounding with fear. Fear that he'd hurt her.

He'd spent all his adult life training to kill. He was good at it. He had killed often and he knew precisely what to do. Though he wouldn't be aware of tearing Sophie to pieces, he'd do it. He could see it clearly, what he'd do to her. Death was a precious gift in comparison, if it could stop him.

If she shot him now, someone from Haven would be coming soon. They'd see the bite marks, his dead body, and understand completely. And he knew, beyond a shadow of a doubt, that for the rest of her life, Mac and Nick would look after Sophie as if she were their own. She'd be safe. That was all that counted.

"Sophie," he said evenly. "Now. Please."

She took the gun from his hand, watching him out of those beautiful eyes, sad and sober.

Jon braced.

And Sophie threw the gun into the bushes.

Before Jon could run to see if he could find it, she leaped forward and put her hand on his forearm. Even through his clothes he could feel the warmth.

"Jon," she said urgently, "listen to me."

The anger was back. "Fuck that. We don't have time for farewells, Sophie. I might be turning right now."

"I'm a healer," she answered and he frowned.

"You're a what?"

"A healer. I didn't tell you because—because I don't tell people. It's complicated and I can't use it to clear up colds, but I can heal people who are really sick."

He opened his mouth, then closed it.

She gently closed her good hand around his and led him to the foot of a huge pine tree. "Sit." And just like that, he sat. Nervous energy was humming in him, he knew he had to find a way to kill himself fast, but somehow Sophie was overriding his system. He sat and she sat next to him, close enough for him to feel the warmth radiating off her.

She lifted the sleeve of the arm that had been bitten, pulling it up over his elbows, and put both hands on his hand, right above the bite. One hand was already becoming purple and swollen from the broken wrist but she paid no attention to that at all. Where she curled her hands around his forearm there was an enormous sensation of heat. Painless, enveloping.

"I've healed you already." She absorbed the jolt his hand made.

"What?"

Sophie nodded. "Do you remember feeling heat when you landed on me? You'd just made a run for your life and you'd seen the horrors on the street and you were heartsick. And when—when you told me about your parents. It was like a grievous wound, I could tell. I don't know exactly how it works—it's actually scary to me—but you felt better after-ward, didn't you?"

Jon kept his stone face on, though he mind was whirling.

Sophie shook his arm. "Answer me, damn it! You felt better afterward, didn't you?"

He felt like his lips were made of stone. He had trouble formulating the words. "Everyone feels better after talking about something painful. Psychology 101."

She looked him in the eyes. "I am absolutely convinced I can cure this, Jon. I wouldn't be playing with my safety like this if I weren't. I can do this and I will. I am not going to go back to Haven with your dead body. We are going to go back together, we are going to work hard with the others to heal the world, and we are going to get married and have wonderful children who will be brought up to be smart, loving, and kind. That is not a wish, that is the truth. Do you believe me?"

*No, of course not.* The words were there, on his lips, but somehow they wouldn't come out.

She looked smart and strong and very capable. Not crazy at all. The furthest thing from crazy, as a matter of fact.

And—he'd seen this before. Catherine and Elle. Both scientists, both women of reason, with unusual gifts. Catherine could feel emotions—and lately thoughts—through touch. And Elle—Elle could project herself out of her body thousands and thousands of miles away.

He'd have scoffed at even the hint of any of this before last year, but he'd seen it with his own eyes. Catherine had found them in their secret lair, where the entire U.S. military had failed to find them, simply because she'd touched Lucius Ward.

She'd touched *him* and uncovered secrets he'd never told another human being. And Elle—Elle's body had been back at Haven, but she'd been with him and Nick when they broke into Arka's headquarters in San Francisco. There was no doubt about that.

So . . . maybe . . .

Sophie's good hand clutched his more tightly and the heat was like a painless fire. She leaned forward toward him, toward a man who could be turning into a monster right now. "Give me a chance, Jon. Give *us* a chance. Please. I don't want to live without you."

It was nuts. It went against every single instinct he had.

Jon reached to his boot, pulled out his combat knife, placed it in her lap. One good thing—if he turned, he wouldn't know what it was for.

"At the first sign, and I mean the very first sign, that I am turning, you slash me across the throat with that Sophie, and jump away. If we're going to try this, I need your promise."

"I promise," she said, her voice low, gaze unwavering.

*Nail it down.* "Promise what? Say it out loud."

"I promise that if I can't heal you, if you show signs of turning, that I will take the knife, slash you across the throat, and run."

He nodded. "They're coming for you from Haven. They'll find you. And they'll protect you. If I go, I want to know you'll live."

She swallowed heavily. "I know."

Jon couldn't believe he was doing this, but he was. "Okay. What do we do?"

"I touch you. And I heal you."

Jon frowned. "That's it? That's your strategy? You touch me? You're touching me now."

She nodded. "Do you trust me?"

"Well . . . yeah. But—"

"Close your eyes."

He closed them, hoping she was right, terrified she was wrong. Would she be able to slit his throat in time? They had no way to know how the infected turned. No one had observed it. Or at least no one had observed it and lived. Was it a slow gradual process? Was it sudden? If it was like throwing a switch, Sophie'd have no chance. The only way she had any chance at all was if she could see him turning, and decide to put an end to it. To him. He wouldn't block her in any way. In fact, he hoped to be aware enough to tilt his head back and offer his throat.

His life was, in every sense of the words, in her hands.

"So how—" he began, then stopped. Suddenly the heat became even more intense, like a sun blooming in his arm, the heat spreading up through his arm, through his chest. He could feel his heart heating up, the strangest sensation he'd ever had.

At the same time, he could feel a nasty chill inside him, ice prickling in his veins, horrible and painful. With a lurch to his heart, he realized that the sensation of cold was the virus. He was turning.

God, he was turning.

Black cold ice eating him up, pushing away the heat. His body was a battlefield, like a cold dead planet approaching the sun.

Pain wrenched through his muscles, and he felt his heart contract from the cold that gripped it. Something freezing cold, like Satan's hand, was squeezing his heart.

Jon gasped for breath but breathing hurt. His lungs were on fire but encased in ice. He couldn't move his lungs, he couldn't breathe, his heart tried to beat its way through his chest as it fought the cold. The cold swam through his system like black smoke, infiltrating every cell, eagerly seeking out the warm places so it could squeeze them in its cold dead embrace.

It wasn't working. Jon could feel himself start to go under. To his horror, visions of blood and violence started filling his head. The *pleasure* of biting and tearing and maiming. A deep satisfactory bloodlust in a rising tide, like sexual desire. He fought it, he fought it as hard as he could. Sweat broke out all over his body. It felt like he was sweating blood.

"Sophie." He could barely get the words out. "The knife. Now." He clenched his fists, willing them not to move, but he could feel control slipping away, cold and elusive like smoke. Inside his clenched fists it was as if he could feel Sophie's soft neck, how good it would feel when he had his hands around it, squeezing . . . "Sophie!"

He opened his eyes, the lids as heavy as lead. *Fuck.* Sophie wasn't reaching for the knife. Both hands were on his arm and her eyes glowed as if a firebomb had been lit behind them. An eerie light, almost supernatural, the glow so bright he couldn't look away.

His hands opened, closed. Heat was pouring into him from Sophie, heat and light. Light he could feel under his skin. Now her entire face glowed, as if the sun had just risen inside her. She was trembling with the force of the power inside her. For it was a power, no question about it. Something more powerful than her, some outside force. A force she was transmitting to him.

His entire body was a battleground, ice and fire. Ice wanted him to turn on her, tear her, bite her, feel her blood in his mouth. He could taste it, the blood rich and fine, a need so strong he was shaking with it. But fire—fire was love and life, Sophie beside him for all his days.

The trembling grew, both of them were shaking hard, sweat pouring out of them. Jon's jaw had locked, he couldn't speak, could barely breathe. He wanted to kiss her, he wanted to kill her while the fire and ice fought in his blood, bringing the bloody battlefield to his veins and bones.

Sophie tightened her hold on him even more, that glow so bright it blinded him. With a sudden blast, the ice around his heart exploded and heat suffused his body, running through him, filling him like hot honey down to his fingertips. Every inch of him was filled with heat, even the memory of ice gone.

Sophie let go of his arm and he gasped for air. It came. It filled his lungs with sweetness, where before they had been unable to expand. He drew in air like a man cresting a wave, the sensation sweet and full of life.

A swirl of wind, pine needles blowing in his face, shouts.

The hovercar. Haven. Rescue. Nick's worried face bending over him, shaking him.

Jon could barely feel his body, but he knew he missed Sophie's touch. "Sophie," he whispered and Nick frowned and shook his head.

The ice was suddenly back. Not the ice of the infection but the ice of terror. Jon looked down and saw Sophie lying bonelessly on her side, all color and light gone from her face. Motionless. He moved slowly, as if underwater.

"Sophie!" he screamed but nothing came out, just air. He couldn't move. All his muscles were lax, exhausted from the battle. He toppled over, close to Sophie, one hand on her face. She didn't move when he touched her, not even a flicker of her eyelids.

Nick had two fingers to her throat. He said something, something absurd. Jon couldn't hear him, the words were crazy. One word in particular.

Dead.

Jon crawled to cover Sophie's body with his. She'd given him life, he was going to give it right back.

Nick pulled at his arm, but Jon punched him weakly.

"She's dead, Jon. I'm so sorry, but Sophie's dead." Nick's voice was low, sad.

No. He shook his head, the movement slow and weary. She wasn't dead.

She couldn't be. She'd just given him life.

But she wasn't moving. She wasn't moving.

Suddenly, the energy of panic suffused him. She'd somehow exhausted herself healing him, used up all her body's reserves. Stopped her own heart.

He'd start it again for her. Because he wouldn't let her die. Couldn't.

With newfound energy, he rolled Sophie over, not allowing himself to see her head loll listlessly or the utter stillness of her body.

He was suddenly frantic. Every bit of his medic training, which had been extensive, came back to him. This was a wounded comrade who needed his help. This was the woman who'd saved his life, risking her own. This was the woman who held his heart. If she was no longer in the world, then neither was he.

He leaned over her, placing his left hand over her heart, right hand angled over it to strengthen the pressure, and began pumping, pushing her chest muscles, trying to replicate with his hands what her heart had stopped doing.

He leaned in heavily, working hard. Chest compressions had to be at least 5 cm deep, at 100 compressions a minute, to manually make blood flow through her heart. And he wasn't going to stop until her heart pumped on its own.

He would stay here forever, with his Sophie, until she came back to him.

He had no notion of time, none. All he knew was that the

sweat pouring off him was pooling in the small hollow of her neck. All he knew was that his world was reduced to his two hands over Sophie's heart, working, working . . .

"Jon." Nick's voice was low. His hand landed on Jon's shoulder. He shrugged it off angrily. He couldn't miss a beat, not one. Because it might be the pump that jump-started Sophie's heart, that would bring her back to him.

Nick's voice was louder. "Jon, she's gone. I'm sorry, but she's gone."

"No!" he screamed. That wasn't true, she wasn't gone, she was still with him. Jon's hands didn't stop for one second. He was curled over her now, shoulders blocking her from the sun because he didn't want her blinded when she opened those beautiful eyes. Which she was going to do . . . any second now.

Vaguely, he realized that several people were standing over him, in a circle, watching him. He didn't give a fuck. Let them watch. Let them watch him forever because that's how long he'd stay here, letting his hands pump blood through Sophie's heart until her own heart could do it. It was only fair, because she held his heart in her hands. Her still, cold hands.

He wished there were two of him. One would continue applying CPR, the other would hold her hands, make sure she knew—wherever it was she'd gone—that he was with her. The other Jon would kiss those cold, still lips, bring her back like some prince whose princess had been put under a spell by an evil witch.

He was no prince, but she was his princess. She owned him. She'd saved him and she owned him, forever.

His hands continued, tirelessly, while the people around him were murmuring, voices becoming louder. He heard his name, hers. The crackle of a commo communication. Nick's voice.

"Jon." Nick's hand landed on his shoulder again, and stayed there even though he shrugged angrily. "Elle says to reach inside her heart. She says you know how to do that."

*What?* What the *fuck?*

Was she saying to slice open Sophie's chest using his knife as a scalpel and try manual massage, as field surgeons somehow did?

No, she meant something else, but he couldn't figure out what. Reach inside her heart? How could he do that? What the fuck did that mean?

And then—the world slipped sideways, fractured. And his hands reached inside to touch Sophie's heart. At one level, his hands were still on her chest, over her rib cage, working hard. But at another . . . his hands touched her heart, reached in and touched it because her heart belonged to him and only he could do this.

He reached, with his mind not his hands, and touched.

And Sophie coughed.

*God.*

Everyone was shocked into silence. Nick kneeled beside him. Sophie coughed again and drew in a long, choked breath.

Jon's eyes were dripping water, falling now on Sophie's chest and he couldn't wipe his eyes because his hands had to be over her heart, the heart that was now . . .

Beating. On its own.

Nick placed his hands over Jon's and stilled them. They both watched as Sophie's head turned and she coughed again and took in air in long gasps. Jon's hands were trembling under Nick's.

"Sophie?" His voice was a croak, he could barely shape the word.

And her eyes opened, those glorious eyes, dark blue and loving.

"Jon," she whispered and reached for his hand.

# Epilogue

*Haven*
*Five years later*

"And I hereby declare Haven Elementary School # 1 . . . open!"
Mac cut the ribbon and everyone applauded.

Mac, who was President Pro Tem of the Republic of California didn't even try to make this a solemn occasion. He was dirty and sweaty from helping plant fifty maple saplings in a circle around the school and the ribbon was cut with garden shears, still dirty from pruning shrubbery.

Jon emitted a piercing whistle and Sophie rolled her eyes as she plugged her ears. Her husband was a world-class whistler and used his ability often. One of the many, many things about him she'd learned in the past five years.

The essentials, though—they hadn't changed. He was exactly as she thought he was—loyal and brave and incredibly hard-working. As were the other Ghost Ops members. Their unwavering fortitude allowed Haven, and later the entire state of California—now the Republic of California—to survive.

Nobody had worked harder to get the mass inoculations completed than the men of Haven. Sophie, Catherine, and Elle had worked around the clock to prepare vaccine patches as fast as the four labs that eventually came on line could produce them. But it was the men of Haven who had to move out in armored convoys to get them to the survivors throughout the entire state. It meant sending drones to identify each and every survivor and reaching the survivors with the vaccine and food and water, wherever they were.

The first foci of infection, California, became the first state to declare itself virus-free five months after the initial outbreak.

By that time, however, the rest of the United States was still battling the infection, still trying to get the virus under control, and so California broke itself off and became a sovereign state. It had a small population—2,143,402 at the first census. But a lot of very smart and very hardy people had survived, and they were rebuilding almost faster than the eye could see.

Haven had become its capital, and Mac—very much against his wishes—its first president. Pro Tem, he kept saying, though no one listened.

Catherine kept Sophie and Elle in stitches with Mac's complaints about being the most powerful man in California. He hated every second not spent shoring up Haven's defenses, helping oversee establishing a transport system, helping organize rebuilding the physical plant of the Republic of California.

When representatives began pouring into Haven to establish a constitutional government, Mac had to be kicked by Catherine—hard—to go into the room with the 'politicos'.

While he was planting the trees, the rest of California was conducting its very first political election for the presidency. Mac against Sarah Kellerman, a former councilwoman in Sacramento.

Mac campaigned hard for Sarah every chance he got. He extolled her virtues, sang her praises, pushed her forward at every photo op. He all but offered to rub her feet for her.

Jon leaned down and whispered in Sophie's ear. "He's nervous."

"Well, you could have taken his place. It's not like he didn't ask you. Often," Sophie said. It had become a running joke. Mac would have handed the reins of power over to anyone over sixteen who wanted it. Nobody accepted because, though he hated it, he was doing a really good job.

Jon gave an elaborate shudder and woke up Emma, sleeping on his shoulder.

"Daddy?" Their daughter lifted her curly blonde head from her daddy's shoulder and knuckled her eyes. "What's wrong?"

Jon got that panicky look whenever their four-year-old daughter was inconvenienced or uncomfortable in any way. "I'm so sorry, sweetheart. Nothing's wrong. Everything is fine."

Ice blue eyes regarded ice blue eyes. Emma looked so remarkably like her dad.

Jon kissed her forehead and gently pressed her head back into his shoulder. Like all the kids, Emma had stayed up late last night celebrating the new school and was now paying the price. There were a lot of four- and five-year-olds sleeping against their daddies' shoulders.

*Sorry*, Jon mouthed at her and Sophie repressed a smile.

Big tough badass Jon, who melted around Emma.

At the beginning of their marriage, he'd confessed to her

that he had no clue how to be a good husband and father. But for someone so absolutely clueless, he was doing a very good job. He loved her and Emma deeply, and he showed it every day. He was as solid a family man as he was a leader of their community. They would never have made it during those first terrifying and difficult months without Jon flying the helo over perilous terrain, flying mission after mission, ferrying vaccines and medicine and food and water.

"Here's to the new school!" Lora Harris, who taught math, handed each of them a glass of champagne, the first vintage produced from a Haven winery down in the valley.

She clicked glasses with Jon and Sophie and moved off, cheeks glowing. Lora had insisted six months into reconstruction on starting school again. They barely had enough food at that time and were pressed for every single resource available, but she insisted and she was right. That first year there were 147 students of all grades, taught by volunteers, meeting in the mess hall when it was free. They were so eager to learn that each student was more than caught up with their grade level within two months.

Lora then insisted on building a proper school for the kids of Haven and the surrounding communities, and she finally wore everyone down. She was going to be the first principal.

Three universities—at Davis, Berkeley, and Santa Cruz—were going to start lessons in two years, once the campuses were rebuilt.

Sophie took a sip of the champagne. She shouldn't be drinking alcohol, but it was early on and one sip couldn't hurt. It was excellent—tart, dry, rich.

Stella Cummings—now Stella Ward—elbowed her in the ribs. "Not more than one glass in your condition, honey," she whispered. Sophie had no idea how Stella knew, but she was more perceptive than most. Stella leaned against her husband, who could be leaned against forever. Lucius had thrown away the walking sticks three years ago and was their acting head of security. He smiled down at his wife and kissed her gently on the cheek.

Jon clicked glasses with her again. He bent his head down to her so only she could hear his words. "Here's to us, honey. We made it."

Sophie smiled up at him. Thanks to Jon and the other Ghost Ops men, they weren't hunkering in caves, eating squirrel brains, and wearing bearskins. "Yes, we did." She used her glass to indicate the brand-new school. "It's a miracle. Our Emma will attend a real school. And she'll grow up with schools and hospitals and libraries. She'll grow up in civilization, strong and proud."

Jon bent even lower, careful not to wake Emma slumped on his shoulder. He used his nose to shift a lock away from her ear, kissed it, and whispered, "It's all thanks to you."

For a second Sophie couldn't grasp his words. Jon knew that her ear was an erogenous zone. Actually, when he was around, pretty much every part of her body was an erogenous zone. Jon kissing her ear gave her goose bumps, quickened her breathing.

She should have gotten used to this after five years of marriage, but he could still reduce her to a quivering wreck in no time.

She pulled in a breath, shifted, and kissed him. She could taste surprise and champagne. But Jon was good with surprises, he rolled immediately with them. He deepened the kiss and she felt that familiar warmth, shot through with bolts of desire, course through her.

Someone whistled, and, startled, Sophie pulled back, spilling a little champagne down Jon's back.

"Sorry," she whispered and he laughed.

"They weren't whistling at us, love. Look—someone's got news."

One of the Haven councillors, Kristin Moore, was running toward them. She was over sixty-five, but she regularly ran marathons and she reached them in a minute.

She stopped right in front of Mac and gave him an ironic salute. "Sir, I bring tidings of the election!"

Mac froze, and if Sophie didn't know better, she'd have said he looked . . . frightened. But that wasn't possible. Mac didn't do fear.

Nick rolled his eyes. "Cut the crap, Kristin. Come on. Put Mac here out of his misery."

Kristin stuck her hands in the back pockets of her jeans. "What's it worth to you, Mac? Because we've been petitioning the local government here for a bike path for a long time."

Mac's eyes showed the whites all around like a runaway pony's.

"Kristin," Nick growled.

Sophie glanced up at Jon, amused, and found he was looking at her, eyes suddenly intense. He kissed Emma's head, his eyes never leaving hers.

She suddenly realized how moved Jon was—at the inauguration of the school, at the first free election of a new president, at how far they'd come, together.

Something in Jon had changed since that horrible moment when he'd been infected. Something in that warrior carapace had cracked open. He loved Sophie and when Emma arrived, he was overjoyed. He often told her he had no idea he was capable of love that deep. There was an ease about him now that everyone said hadn't been there before. He made friends easily, laughed often.

He was happy.

So was she. Particularly now.

"Okay, everyone, listen up!" From somewhere Kristen produced a bell and rang it. Eventually everyone quieted down. "I have official news," she said and pulled a piece of paper from her jacket. With great ceremony, and very slowly, she extracted a pair of reading glasses, adjusted them carefully on her nose, and held the piece of paper up, seemingly translating it in her head from Assyrian.

"So. The results of the election held this day and yesterday in the great Republic of California—"

"Kristen!" Mac barked and Catherine placed a hand on his arm. It was still amazing to Sophie how such a small woman could control such a large man. But she did. He clamped his mouth shut.

Kristen cricked her neck one way and then the other and widened her stance.

Suddenly, a small ball of dust rose up. Nick and Elle's twin boys, fighting as usual. Nick broke them up, picking them both up by the seat of their pants and holding them apart. They were both scruffy and dirty and still trying to beat each other up though they were a foot apart. Elle sighed and bent to them.

Mac made a noise in the back of his throat. His face was perilously red. Kristen obviously realized that causing a gasket to blow in the head of the current President (Pro Tem) of the Republic of California was not a good idea.

So she said, simply, "Votes cast for Thomas McEnroe—263,404. Votes cast for Sarah Kellerman—323,516.

Ladies and gentlemen, Sarah Kellerman is the new President of the Republic of California. She just called with her acceptance and will be traveling tomorrow to Haven to take up her duties. Sorry you lost, Mac."

Mac whooped with joy, picked Catherine up, and whirled her around. When he put her down, he saw their daughter, Delia, was weeping.

Mac picked her up, frowning. "What's the matter, sweetheart?"

Delia cried as if her heart had broken. "You lost, Daddy! You lost. I'm so *sowwy.*"

Mac looked around with a big grin, then schooled his face to seriousness. "No, darling, you didn't hear Kristen properly. Daddy *won.* Now Daddy doesn't have to waste his time with political assholes like—"

"Mac!" Catherine's voice was like a whip. Mac bit his lips, looking around for help. Someone shuffled and someone coughed.

Mac took in a deep breath and addressed his daughter. "So, since Daddy just won, how about we go celebrate with some ice cream. How does that sound?" He addressed the crowd. "Ice cream for everyone! Treat's on me!"

He turned and led the crowd over to the community center.

Jon looked down at Sophie. "Think Emma might like some of that ice cream? Should I wake her up?"

Sophie looked up at him, at Mac's departing broad back, radiating happiness, at the community of people they'd gathered around them, grateful for every bit of it. Grateful for something else too.

She put a hand on Jon's arm, feeling that familiar warmth.

She'd healed him but he'd healed her too. He'd opened up her heart and filled it to the brim.

"Before we go in, there's something I have to tell you. Maybe it's appropriate on the day the citizens of California voted." She placed his big hand over her belly.

"We're making a new citizen. I think it might be a boy."

Everyone trooping to the community center stopped and turned when they heard Jon's whoop of joy.

# Sensual Books
## by LISA MARIE RICE

### DANGEROUS SECRETS
#### Available in Paperback and eBook

Charity never thought she'd fall in love with a man like Nicholas: rich, witty, and sexy. It's like a dream come true. And then the nightmare begins . . .

### INTO THE CROSSFIRE
#### *A Protectors Novel: Navy SEAL*
#### Available in Paperback and eBook

When evil men come after Nicole, she must turn to the cold-eyed man who makes her heart pound—with fear and excitement.

### HOTTER THAN WILDFIRE
#### *A Protectors Novel: Delta Force*
#### Available in Paperback and eBook

Harry's mission is to help abused women escape violence. When a damaged beauty shows up on his doorstep, Harry realizes that this is the woman of his dreams.

### NIGHTFIRE
#### *A Protectors Novel: Marine Force Recon*
#### Available in Paperback and eBook

When Chloe steps into the path of the Russian Mafia, it's her long-lost brother Harry's colleague Mike who risks everything to protect her, despite his own painful past.

Visit www.HarperCollins.com/LisaMarieRice for more information.